The One Who Told The Desert Stories

Shirley Robinson

This story is lovingly dedicated to Kevin Garman.

Daddy, in my earliest memories, you reside - in the church office or at home, studying the Word of God. You taught me to pursue the Scripture, and I believe it was your example that provided the root of this story within my imagination. I love the Word, and drew this story from it, because of you. Thank you for giving me that gift.

CONTENTS

THE ONE WHO TOLD THE DESERT STORIES

Shirley Robinson

"The name of Amram's wife was Jochebed, the daughter of Levi, who was born to Levi in Egypt; and she bore to Amram: Aaron and Moses and their sister Miriam." (Numbers 26:59)

"Miriam the prophetess, Aaron's sister, took the timbrel in her hand, and all the women went out after her with timbrels and with dancing. Miriam answered them,

"Sing to the Lord, for He is highly exalted;
The horse and his rider He has hurled into the sea."' (Exodus 15:20-21)

CHAPTER ONE

"Let us see, Datya!" Datya turned to the crowd of young, curious girls who had flocked around her. Many of them were still young enough to move about the camp without the longer tunic of womanhood, freeing them to frisk rapidly about her. "What should you all like to see it for? It's an old, rusty trinket." Datya felt it best to make these little ones wait a bit longer, as she hugged her small bundle tightly to her. Hadn't Miriam always told her that anticipation was good for the soul? Still, she tried to keep the smile out of her eyes, to turn a serious look upon these sweet sisters; it wouldn't do to let them believe she was enjoying their desperation. "Settle yourselves, little ones! I will show it to my family first. My abba arranged for my walks with Miriam long ago; the honor of viewing this gift will go first to him!" Datya released her smile as her dear friends scattered to their families. She knew they would not give her long to enjoy her treasure before they swarmed again so she commanded her legs swiftly to her father's tent. How these childhood friends had so quickly learned or realized that she was carrying a gift, she didn't know. Perhaps a neighboring servant had been listening in to her lesson today? It was not unusual for Miriam and Datya to conclude a day's lessons to find a handful of young children hovering around the tent. Mostly, other girls who treated Datya as though she were famed among Israel, would gather, but occasionally little boys who were too young to begin their own studies with one of the Levite tutors would join the crowd. Datya had not seen any of those nosy ones today, but they may have departed before she exited Miriam's tent. Truly, it didn't matter how they learned of the treasure she carried; here in the lively camps of Israel, secrets had little chance of staying hidden.

Though she was thankful for the crowd of friends she still possessed, Datya often felt a thick distance from them. Many parents among the Levite tribe did not approve of a young woman being groomed for leadership, especially if it meant the delay of marriage. Datya's parents had generously stalled that particular covenant for her, and, though nothing was ever said to her, Datya knew that neighboring families often shook their heads at the bizarre decision. For all their grim disapproval, it did not stop fathers and mothers of every tribe from pursuing Miriam in the hopes that she would take on an additional student. At least once a week their lesson was disrupted from the approach of one bold parent or another, "Please, Wisest Woman of Israel, adopt my own daughter into your care; raise her also for the work of a prophet." Miriam always remained steadfast, "I am already teaching the one called to my work; only Yahweh could call another." Custom dictated that the inquisitive families receive their dismissal quietly and respectfully, but Datya knew many families remained bitter over the rejection. She didn't quite understand why Miriam did not raise more than one young woman as a prophetess. Afterall, if one prophetess did so much good for Israel, then surely many would improve the camp's faith immensely? Of course there were other prophetesses from time to time among the Tribes, but none were trained by a great granddaughter of Levi, like Miriam. The Chief Prophetess had lightly explained that God poured out his spirit in his own way, in his own time, on the persons of his choosing. While Datya continued to wonder, she was thankful for the nearly ten years she had spent, largely alone, with her teacher. It was a gift, an inpouring that was so rare among the young women of Israel.

Brushing away the unknown, Datya neared her family's tent. The anticipation of her Father and Mother's pride in her had grown as she strolled home. Other girls her age were married for two and even three years already, depending on how many seasons had passed since they each began their womanly flow. Their offspring often produced bragging rights among her father's generation. Her parents had waited so long, given up Datya's early years of womanhood, all to honor the Lord's calling - that Datya should follow Miriam's path. Father had often said a husband was only around the corner for Datya, but, surely not, until Miriam declared that Datya had completed her tutelage. A chance to display a gift that would produce similar appreciation was all Datya had hoped for; this morning Miriam had stunned her by placing just the thing in her hand. How she had trembled as Miriam's beloved hands had handed it into her own! Though Datya had seen it put to use to aid Miriam's voice many times, she had never used it herself. In all these years, it had never occurred to her that one day, she would take possession of Miriam's most iconic relic!

"Father! Mother! Where are Ziva and Idan? I have something to show you all! It is a precious gift!" As Datya flooded the tent with daylight, she looked about for her little sister Ziva and her toddling brother Idan, but found only her parents. Her mother was prepping the family belongings for the next day's journey, wrapping, tying, and triple-checking their supplies. The camp would begin moving early, even in the midst of the manna gathering, so all must be made ready. When Moses' two short trumpet blasts sounded in the morning, her family would need to set out on another day's journey. Anything left behind would be swallowed up by the families to the west who would follow them. Her father was studying his robes, being sure to note any filth or tears. It must be mended and prepared for his levitical duties. His turn, his honor, had come around again. He always paid the most careful attention to every detail, often setting his wife to work on fixing even the slightest marring. Datya had even seen her father check each individual strand of the tassels that stretched the length of his outer robe. Little was more important to men like her father than flawless *tzittzit*, the all-important tassels that reminded them of their perfect God and his law.

Datya's mother, Lisbet, answered softly, "Ziva sought out Huldah and Manya. Evidently the three plan to walk together from daybreak tomorrow. We'll see her for the evening meal. Idan nodded off to sleep while I was visiting with my sister." Her mother's ever soft voice seemed to float with more joy tonight, as it often did after time spent with her sister. "She promised to return him when he awoke. I imagine one of her daughters will bring him by shortly, but your father and I would love to see what you've brought, Datya." Father, who had been murmuring quietly making notes here and there over his garments, lifted his eyes when his wife spoke. Datya knew he preferred to stay focused in the days before his tabernacle service, but she could not wait the many weeks it would be before his mind concentrated on them once again. Though she should be used to the way things are, for she had grown up this way, her father's ability to forget about them entirely for weeks at a time, was bizzare to Datya. It is not that she felt unloved, and she knew her father carefully monitored their trades and possessions to make sure the family was provided for, it was just, as though he were another man entirely when he was in the service of Yahweh's tabernacle. She began unwrapping the scraps of cloth in her hands as her mother and father stepped before her. As the layers unfolded, the aged scent of Miriam's gift rose beneath her nose; she was sure she fairly glowed with the joy of holding such a vessel of history in her own hands.

"It is for you, Father. To thank you for making a way for me." Datya's smile halted as she saw the confusion on their faces. They did not recognize the beautiful instrument she held. "Miriam gave it into my hands, only this morning. She recounted the earliest miracles that she witnessed and told me that it was time for me to take possession of it and time for me to sing. For Israel." Datya beamed. To be trusted with Miriam's timbrel was the greatest moment of her life, thus far. She waited for her parents to exalt the blessing with her. Datya lowered the almost sacred timbrel. "Are you not pleased with it, Father? With me?" She felt the burn of tears surfacing in her eyes as she lowered them to the dirt beneath her father's feet. *Why are they not rejoicing?* Datya's mind raced to discover the source of her parent's dismay in the strange silence that tied the three of them in stillness.

"Daughter, we are well pleased!" Datya's mother Lisbet began. "We are just," Lisbet was still for a moment before finishing, "sorrowful." Confused, Datya swerved her eyes to her father. Surely, her mother did not understand the value of the gift they'd received to make such a statement. Her father would enlighten Lisbet, and remind her of the great miracle that had brought about Miriam's faithful praise. Wouldn't he?

Cohen was silent and grim for long moments as Datya waited with stalled breath, trying to understand. "Datya, beloved, we are honored with you that Miriam chose you - of all the young girls in camp clamoring for her attention, for her wisdom, for her song! - that good prophetess chose my little girl to honor with this gift! It is a treasure of our people and I trust you will be a new light to Jacob's offspring as Miriam has always been." Cohen's words slowed. Though Datya knew his eyes would not crest with tears, she could see dark turmoil roiling in them. When her father was troubled, his eyes always brewed with the evidence, though he rarely confided such woes to his wife and children.

"What is it, Father? Have I done something wrong?" Datya's heart was breaking. She wanted her Father and Mother to be pleased, but to see their dismay tore at her spirit! When Miriam had given her the very timbrel that she'd used to exalt Yahweh after the Miracle of the Red Sea, she never imagined her parents reacting like this!

"No, darling girl. You have been a blessing to us. We celebrate with you! We thank God for your spirit and talents! We are ready to witness all that you will do and become!" Cohen tenderly reached out for the timbrel. Datya let it pass willingly, hoping it would be a boon to her father's mind. Instead, with quiet grief, he uttered, "Miriam would only give this away, would only part with it, at the time when her life was closing. It is not just a token of remembrance, Datya, it is the passing on of her work, of her calling." Confusion must have lit her face afresh for her father finished simply, "Miriam must believe she is dying." He handed the timbrel back, and enveloped her tightly. The rare embrace, though comforting, was as disconcerting as the blow of words her father had just delivered. As Datya and her mother let quiet tears fall, Cohen turned back to the work of his robes, but Datya had seen his surging grief as well, before he turned away. Though Cohen and Lisbet had not been alive yet for the Song of the Red Sea that Miriam sang over the redeemed children of Israel, they had grown up in the blessed shadow of her ministry. None in Israel had evaded the impact of the ever-faithful Miriam who served the wayward tribes.

Datya took gasping breaths to try to stem her tears. She knew her father would not appreciate the distraction of noisy sobs; he may already be cross with the weight of the news she hadn't meant to deliver. He never liked to enter into his duty season with anything that would tug his thoughts away from his Lord. In truth, she had not known the message, and the gift she was carrying was a tragic one. She had not even suspected, believing, only that she was walking home with the highest honor paid her yet! Only a little while ago, happiness had propelled her towards her small family - to think of such an honorable gift being placed in her humble hands! She'd smiled all the way back from her morning session with Miriam, her beloved teacher! Datya's grief engulfed her joy; the tent, stretched above and about her, became oppressive as though she had entered the fire-pit where her people once slaved over the baking earthen bricks. With a mumbled excuse, she turned to flee. Her mother, who believed in letting her children conquer their own frights and sorrows, reached out in a rare touch of comfort, but Datya's garments were already passing through the doorway. Her call of comfort, "Datya, wait!" also failed to land on Datya as she barreled away to escape the horror of what she'd just heard.

Thinking first to head to the western edges of camp where she had spotted a small cluster of hills that may offer a bit of shade, Datya rushed ahead. As she drew close, she could see several of her friends in the distance, the same ones who had been pestering her for a peek at the timbrel only a little while ago. The bitter truth of this desert journey came to mind, privacy and solitude were ideas never realized. Quickly, Datya darted away. She loved them all like sisters, closer even than that, but she knew she couldn't joyously share her gift while thinking about her father's suspicion. In her mind, Datya heard his words again, "Miriam, must believe she is dying," her heart sinking at the surety that had been on his face. She knew few men wiser than her own father. Cohen believed in honesty as a top tenant of one's life. If he made a statement, the listener could trust that it was true and right. Though Datya wished with all her might that, somehow, the gift of the timbrel meant something else, anything else. Though she couldn't believe where her own thoughts led her she found herself hoping that her father would be proven wrong, this one time.

Perhaps she could head to the widow Ravit's tent. She was so seldom there anymore that Datya felt sure she would be able to dwell silently and alone for a time. Ravit never minded. She was such a young widow that staying with the other families and helping to care for the children meant more to her than keeping a presence in her lonely tent. Ravit was only 3 years older than Datya, but seemed so much wiser after having married and become a widow so early. Perhaps Ravit would be home. Perhaps she would have the wisdom and grace to bring comfort. Her mind was in such turmoil that Datya hardly knew which scenario she wanted. Should she seek comfort? Should she bear the pain of the past hour to a friend? Or should she kneel, alone in the dust, and beg Yahweh to erase this day, and cancel the heartbreaking prophecy that had just been spoken over her beloved teacher?

Ravit's tent was only steps away now and Datya was struggling to keep her tears in check until she passed under the flap. Before she closed the gap, her sister Ziva stepped in front of her. Huldah and Manya were on her heels, as was the usual formation of this trouble-loving threesome. Datya tensed. She knew she should love her cousins, and certainly her own sister. She was taught to be kind to them, but, more often than not, these three inspired only frustration, not friendship. How Datya wished Ravit was her sister and not the moody, wild Ziva! Too long, Ziva, whether out of jealousy or a natural meanness, had haunted Datya's shadow. Truthfully, Datya wasn't the only target, since Ziva was also making a reputation for herself among their closest families as a rebellious, and bitter young woman. This fact alone often brought shame to their parents. Their first daughter, currently unable to wed, brought honor to the family, but not grandchildren. Their second, and last daughter, was winnowing away her potential for a decent betrothal, mostly through the actions of an untamed tongue. *And heart,* Datya's thoughts singled out the true source of Ziva's ill reputation, feeling a pang of sympathy for her parent's sake. The girl had cultivated the bitterness and frustration that was common to many of the grumbling Israelites, rather than the joy of being one of a chosen nation.

"Huldah, Manya, stop for a moment! Look who we found! It is the wonderful, impressive daughter of Cohen! It is Miriam's beloved student, Datya!" Their two cousins snickered as Ziva taunted her, all three dipping low in mock bows. Datya wanted to rush ahead, but how could she ignore Ziva's disrespect? "Ziva! Stop speaking about our father with rudeness in your mouth. He gives you all you need and he will find a place for you as well.

Why should our little cousins think less of him just because you say so?" Datya would have been better off to speak her words to the very dust around them than to speak to Ziva who seemed to not hear her at all. *Typical Ziva! Only her own thoughts make an impact on her ears,* Datya's mind steamed with exasperation. How their mother's face would burn with shame if she were here! She knew also, if their father were observing this behavior, his whip, or the slender cane he used to discipline his children would make an appearance.

Ziva's laugh, far prettier than her spirit, tumbled free again. She was always laughing, and she laughed most when others were uncomfortable. Her mother had named her "Shining" believing that she would bring light and beauty and, yes, fun to the world. Lisbet's name choice had certainly come true. Ziva had the ability to stir others up around her, and she was certainly beautiful. She'd had only 12 birthdays and yet was widely considered one of the most beautiful faces in camp. Certainly among the Levite daughters. Though, with the passing seasons of Ziva's increasing rebellion, she said it less frequently, their mother had often said that Ziva had indeed brought much joy with her birth. "She is my little shining one!" Lisbet would say when the girls were young and playful, "how she brings light where once there was sadness." Their mother's conclusion was the constant reminder that Ziva was a joyful light, after the loss of the three babies who had been born to Cohen and Lisbet between Datya and Ziva. All three had died, leaving an ache in Lisbet who seemed to despair before Ziva arrived. Then, Ziva had been born, and after passing her first year, Lisbet began to hope that she would finally raise two daughters. She could never have predicted the careening emotions Ziva's wild moods would conjure. Huldah and Manya were always willing to follow her lead into any trouble. Many times already they'd been sorely punished because of Ziva's whims. Ziva herself never stayed repentant for long. "Oh will he? Do you think, Sister? And what position will there be? My sister with the golden voice and the sweetly bowed head is already elevated to prophetess." With mockery and vehemence, she spat, "What will I be, do you think? Little more than a wife!" Huldah and Manya mirrored Ziva's own distasteful face as she launched her latest slur. How three daughters of Levi, managed to arrive on the eve of womanhood with such utter disrespect for marriage and family, Datya would never know.

"Ziva! A wife is a gift to the whole community! All of our great men were born by and cared for by a wife! And you well know I am not a prophetess! Miriam has been teaching me to sing and dance and how to be an example, but only God can decide if I will be a prophetess." Datya offered the argument in sincerity, ignoring the harsh way her future had progressed only that morning. Hadn't Cohen looked into her eyes and told her that very soon she would indeed step into the role of prophetess? Trembling with anger over her sister's volatile speech, Datya bit her tongue, keeping her father's words to herself. Nothing good would come from sharing them with her sister when she was clearly on the hunt for something exciting. *Exciting trouble, no doubt,* her fuming thoughts were escalating. Datya knew the warning in her mind well; *Walk away. Don't let her provoke you. Don't respond.* But, as her self-control faltered, the response was coming now, whether Ziva would hear her or not. "Why do you screech at me day in and day out about what will be or what won't be? We should all serve joyfully; it isn't right to squabble so." Looking at the two younger girls she continued, "Do you treat Huldah and Manya this way? Why do they seek your company when you are so sour all the time?"

Datya was fuming, why did she let Ziva work her up so? She should have walked around her the moment she saw her instead of being goaded to anger. Yahweh would be displeased at the way she was lashing out, and she well knew that correcting Ziva was not her place, but her father's. Chancing a glance at their cousins, she saw Huldah and Manya were staring at her darkly. They were used to the bold statements Ziva threw at the other girls of the camp, and sometimes even to the adults, but to hear Datya rebuke her sister in public apparently shocked them. Deciding enough time had been wasted in Ziva's snare, Datya moved to go past them. She needed to pray about Miriam! Standing with these spiteful children was the last thing she intended to do. Certainly, Yahweh would be displeased if her self-control slipped further under her sister's taunting. No matter how wrong the younger girl was, no matter how shamefully she acted, Datya knew that Yahweh expected righteous behavior from her. How could she fail him in this moment, only to beg him for Miriam's life in the next? Miriam would tell her that Yahweh's grace was sufficient for all her failures, for none in Israel managed to live a sinless life, but little was more important to Datya than serving the Holy God as best she could.

Datya looked away and moved around Ziva, hoping she'd let it go, but Ziva snatched at the scarf in her hands. Along with the timbrel, Miriam had given her the finest length of cloth Datya had ever owned. The scarf was a deep, dusty purple, and though it was aged, she could tell it had been woven with immense skill and patience. Ziva tugged it so quickly that the timbrel fell to the ground. With a glare, Datya swiftly rescued the relic from the hard-packed earth, biting her tongue fiercely to hold back her frustration. The scraggly grass that grew here clung to the timbrel as she raised it up, though the blades were long dead from thousands of traveler's feet that had tramped here. "Ziva! Stop! You have no right! Father will whip you if he hears how you behaved. Do you know what this is?"

"Oh sister, don't you know? I don't care what it is and I've been whipped before." Ziva laughed and fairly skipped away, Huldah and Manya rushing to keep pace with both her vicious laughter and her haunting pace.

~ ~ ~

Ravit's tent flap fell closed as quickly as Datya threw it open. She could not see if Ravit was indeed home because her sobs had disrupted her sight. Why was Ziva so unpredictable and wild? What could she hope to gain? Datya was weeping for Miriam, and sobbing at the sorry state of her sisterhood. Ravit must be away. For by now she surely would have wrapped Datya up in her arms with the natural croonings of a mother. Few among Israel moved and breathed with the quiet strength of empathy Ravit possessed. Lisbet had told her that her mourning season had curated the young widow's compassionate wisdom, though Datya remembered how Ravit was always kind and considerate, a true listener, even as a child. Datya worked to slow her breathing; she would never be able to pray for Miriam if she continued weeping so! Her mind kept running to her sister. It seemed her grief for Miriam and her grief for her sister would war to garner the greatest weight in her prayers! She couldn't understand why the burden for Miriam wasn't swiftly drowning out all other concerns. Admittedly, her relationship with Ziva had long been weighing down her heart, and had seeped into her prayers with increasing frequency.

Datya shook her head at the empty tent, Ziva had been so spiteful today, but there were certainly days when she wasn't like that. Ziva and Datya had plenty of tender moments and good memories to laugh over, but Datya could never predict what mood her sister would be in. Because she longed for a friend in her sister, she always tried to forgive Ziva's crudeness and love her on the other side, but both of those feelings were only getting harder as they got older. If she could only make sense of her sister! If only Ziva would settle, and remain kind and loving all the time - their whole family might have peace! Once, when she'd mustered the courage to approach Miriam, asking her to intervene, to take her sister to task, Miriam had responded with hearty laughter. "Dear One," she had managed between her chuckling, "so you have a real life picture of what Yahweh deals with in each of us." Leaving the mysterious statement hanging in the air, Miriam had dismissed her for the day, with no hope or help for Ziva and Datya's troubled relationship. "Agh, God of Abraham! I am dwelling on the changeable sister you gave me and her restless ways instead of crying out for Miriam! Settle my heart, O God!

"O God, your ways are perfect and you lead us well! I do not doubt you, Father! But I plead with you for more time with Miriam. She is the mother of my heart! She shows me what you are really like. I know you know best, but I feel as though I still need her." What could she say to the Almighty? How could she make the One who lit the great column by night see her continued need for her teacher. Her teacher. What would Miriam pray if it were her? Try as she might to discern it, the answer wouldn't come, and Datya knew there was one more request to offer up. With broken breath she finished, "O God, if Miriam is at the end of her days, do not let her linger in suffering!" Datya quieted, as the words she never thought she'd pray left her lips. She knew she needed to tell her God that she trusted him, but she also couldn't speak if it wasn't true. Nothing was more sinful than voicing false words to the God of all life. Datya wanted to honor him with her trust, but losing Miriam felt like the Red Sea was rushing over her, rather than the Pharaoh of old. She had been born many years after those waters had rushed about the ill-fated army of the Egyptians. She had not heard the thunder of the mighty waters returning to their proper places; she had not heard the screams of horses in panic, the clatter of chariots smashing one another as though they were in a great melee. Miriam had described it to her through the eyes of a witness. It was a favorite story, especially when Miriam launched into the holy Song of the Red Sea. Though the ending was both fearsome and triumphant, Datya had always known that God had placed her on the favored side of the victor. Today she felt, instead, like the one who had despaired as the waters stole both breath and life.

"Sister, forgive me!" Datya jumped, a raspy scream tearing from her chest. Ziva's apology was only slightly less startling than her sudden presence in Ravit's tent. "Are these tears my burden? I am ashamed that I was so cruel; please don't be hurt any longer. I don't know why I throw such words at others, especially at you, my only sister!" The one who had looked so haughty and vile only moments ago, dropped to her knees and pressed her forehead against Datya's. Humility cloaked her sister though it had been entirely absent during Ziva's harsh abuse. Datya need not bother to look about for Huldah and Manya to enter behind her sister; she knew that Ziva would never condescend to apologize in the presence of her cohorts.

Datya couldn't speak. Ziva often apologized, and she felt that she was usually sincere, but it seldom came so quickly or so... Emphatically. Datya struggled with whether she should trust Ziva, but what possible ill motive could she have for reuniting with her "only sister?" Ziva pleaded now, "Please, Datya, I'm sorry, forgive me!" Her sister even accompanied the pitiful plea with a few tears that dropped from the girl's chin. Datya supposed that Ziva may be apologizing with the hope that their Father wouldn't indeed find out about her behavior. As much as she acted tough, Father's whip hurt even the bravest body. Ziva knew that Datya would not tell, and she doubted that Huldah and Manya would say a word, so it seemed that avoiding punishment wasn't the reason Ziva was here. Perhaps genuine sorrow, perhaps curiosity? Datya decided to show her the timbrel, but she wouldn't entrust Ziva with the disappointment Father had spoken of or the real reason for her tears. She would seek only the Lord's comfort for that for now, and perhaps Ravit's counsel later on.

Hoping she could soothe and dismiss Ziva quickly, she knew she must offer forgiveness, though she was tempted to nurse the wound a bit longer. "Ziva, calm down. Of course I forgive you. It breaks my heart when we squabble, but I hope you won't act so brazen in public anymore!" Datya saw that Ziva relaxed a bit, as she stood, although she didn't agree to behave from now on. "Come, Ziva, look! Here is a gift from Miriam! It is the very timbrel that she used as she praised the Almighty for our deliverance from Pharaoh of Egypt!" Gently, she unrolled the scarf, which still bore the grime of it's earlier tumble in the dirt, and let the timbrel peek out. Watching her sister's face closely, Datya hoped to see some reverence appear, or a softening of any kind, really, but the girl's face didn't change. She had likely already discerned what the gift was after she glanced at it briefly during their tussle. She may even have overheard the chatter about it which was surely flowing through the camp by this time. She wondered if other elders would come to the same conclusion her father had? Would they spread that rumor too? Or would they remain silent, waiting to see what would happen?

"Miriam gave this to you? Why? I mean, why wouldn't she want to keep it?" Ziva gently reached for the timbrel. She seemed to appreciate the significance of the gift, but quickly gave it back. In fact, Ziva's gaze, which landed on the purple linen Miriam had wrapped the timbrel in, seemed more enchanted with the fabric, than with the instrument. *How like Ziva,* Datya sighed inwardly. Her sister had always been preoccupied with lovely things, and fine fabrics were nearly an idol to her. Her mother often rebuked Ziva for her love of rich garments, frequently reminding the girls that while they were not impoverished by any means, their father would never tolerate vain choices. Cohen and Lisbet had even commanded Ziva to spend an entire week in mourning veil, only a year ago, after Ziva had been particularly preoccupied with the garb of a passing nomadic family. How Ziva had detested the heat and shame of the garment often seen on only widows and the noble nomadic women who passed by high upon camels. Her father had lectured long and hard that Ziva needed humility more than she needed manna. Pulling her eyes away from the scarf, it was clear that Ziva was ready to move on.

"Well, we should head home and help mother, don't you think? The timbrel will have to be packed away for now. Let's walk together." Yanking Datya's arm through the tent, Ziva began fairly marching home, arms locked with her sister. Datya left behind a sigh as they trudged across the nearly lifeless land. She had hoped that Ziva would leave and that she could remain to pray, but it was best not to stir the waters again. Ziva was as unpredictable as ever, but this was better than being enemies, at least.

CHAPTER TWO

Though much of the packing was finished by the time she and Ziva made it home, Datya set about quietly wrapping up odds and ends. Her mother had spent a majority of their time in their current location making robes and tunics for the family. Father had traded not long ago for fine, new lengths of linen and wool. Replacements for their worn out garments were much needed. The remaining items that must be stashed away were the knives, needles and frames that their mother used to craft new clothing for their family. The dish her mother used to burn oil for light in the hours before dawn would likely be the last item tucked away before the first steps of tomorrow's journey.

Though Datya and Ziva had both been thoroughly instructed in the ways of turning linen to robes and, even weaving strips of tanned hides into lovely belts, neither excelled in the art like Lisbet did. Still, Datya tried to help her mother finish up the last few items. She knew her mother wouldn't allow any of them to be worn until the camp settled once more. For the long days of travel would be disastrous for the hems Lisbet labored over. Still the family could look forward to crisp, new tunics soon enough.

A belt had been finished for each family member except for Ziva. Though the stretching and softening of the leather had been completed, and though the braiding had begun, it needed several more hours of work. Ziva was likely to leave the tedious task to others, so Datya settled into it, praying the tedium would numb her mind for a time. Idan who had been returned to the tent in her absence played with the ends of leather trailing off her lap. Her baby brother was the sweetest of young children. He was generally sticky from playing or from suckling, and nearly always sweaty as he toddled about in the baby plumpness that hadn't yet fallen away from him. Lisbet often told Datya and Ziva that the little boy was her "final delight," saying that he'd be the last child to nurse at her breast. Though Datya had entered the ranks of womanhood, she still felt in the dark about so much including how her mother could know that there would be no more babes following Idan. Swelling with thankfulness for the playful smiles and chatter he offered up at her while she worked, she cooed quiet love to her brother. Her mind strayed to Miriam with every twist of the leather, her worries weaving through her thoughts as swiftly as her fingers wove the strands into thick, flat braids. With each satisfying cinch to tighten her work, she tried to send up a prayer of peace, all the while feeling as though it was her heart, not the leather that was being cinched. Datya knew fear had a strange way of manipulating everything from one's heartbeat to the breath in her lungs; this was the worst fear she'd ever tasted. Looking down, she realized the braided portion had grown nearly long enough to encircle her beautiful sister.

Many of the Israelites, especially the women, simply tied unfinished, frayed strips of fabric about them each morning rather than tackling the task of preparing such a fine belt. Some simply lacked a knife sharp enough to cut thin, fine strips in the tough animal hides, others refused to pay for the service, and still more had not bothered to learn the art. Her mother treated such people with compassion, for few of the grandmothers who had fled Egypt had ever developed the necessary skills. The life of slavery had consumed their time and strength in the service of Egyptian whims. With less tenderness, her father had often insisted he would rather "have a fine belt, than a decent tunic," for the hidden undergarment could not be fully seen, whereas a belt was likely the first thing a passing friend or neighbor would notice. Most of the Levite families refused to join in this lazy habit of tying unfinished sashes where a belt should be, while the trend was widespread in the other tribes. Dayta sucked in a tense breath as a painful memory surfaced. Long ago she had pointed out to her father that his statement seemed like a vanity of sorts, the very thing he was always lecturing Ziva about. She hadn't meant to be disrespectful, as she made her honest observation. Nevertheless, Cohen had burned with anger at the perceived insult. She had been whipped severely, though it was one of the few whippings she ever remembered receiving.

The day had advanced to within a breath of the night as her fingers had made the final loops. Idan had stayed close by bringing cheer in his own way, but Datya's thoughts had fluttered near and far, attempting the feat of staying the tears that came if she envisioned Miriam's dear face. Though she had set to her task without complaint she had longed for the heat of the day and the evening to pass so that tomorrow could come. Her one hope was to seek the truth from her teacher. Her mother circulated the small batch of manna that remained in the breakfast basket. As each family member took a wafer with each passing, Datya tried to nourish her body. The manna, which she usually delighted in, lacked it's warm sweetness tonight. From beyond the distant hills, the night chill had begun creeping towards them. Thankfully, with the pattern finished, Datya could release the project into her mother's hands. She watched as Lisbet began applying "the blood of the trees" to the ends. It would be dry by morning and Datya felt proud of the work she and her mother had done so that the family could be well clothed. She had seen her mother use what the elders called "the blood of trees," many times though Lisbet had said the sticky resin was getting difficult to find, here where the vegetation was so different than along Egypt's great river. Still occasionally other nomadic family groups, at least those not interested in violent skirmishes, would pass by and be willing to trade a small cask or two of the precious substance. The bizarre truth of their flight from Egypt danced with unspoken humor whenever they met other travelers; the

Israelites may be free now, but they remained alarmingly close to Egypt, and it's provisions, all these many years later.

On evenings like this when they worked at such crafts, Lisbet often recalled stories of her grandfather Aatami who had been enslaved as a "bonder" in Egypt. Though Lisbet had not been born in those days, she knew the tales of the way her grandfather had spent his days using "the blood of trees," to seal, bind, protect, and preserve all manner of Egyptian goods. She often wondered if her mother had somehow inherited this skill for often women in the camp would bring their nearly finished belts and tools to her for the final sealing. Lisbet had made a small, happy profit from the many years of performing this trade among the traveling tribes. Every year she sent a large portion of it to the tabernacle as an offering. She and Ziva had questioned their mother, why didn't she keep more of it? But her mother always answered, "I have no need for coins and treasure, girls. Yahweh provides us with plenty; He meets every need."

Feeling her cheeks burn with surprise, Datya realized her mother was watching her closely. Lisbet's task was long finished and the tools of their trade cleaned and put away. Datya had sat, encased in thoughtful silence even as the other members of her family washed for bed, and sank to their pallets. Her mother remained, watching her closely, and Datya could hear Idan making sleepy, suckling sounds from within the folds of Lisbet's favored, wool cloak. "Mother, may I make a request?" Datya whispered in the near dark. She knew Lisbet would nod off as soon as Idan had finished his suckling. Lisbet turned her face toward her daughter, her tired eyes landed with tenderness. "May I take my rest in Ravit's tent? I should like to gather the manna with her in the morning, but I will return to help with the cart when the trumpets sound our departure." Lisbet studied her daughter with soft concern. Datya knew her mother could tell she had been upset earlier, when her opposite daughters had trooped into the tent. Lisbet never pried into her daughters' squabbles, but she often tried to soothe them while they were apart. She didn't often make peace happen between the girls, but she always tried to nudge them towards forgiveness and fresh beginnings. Datya had not told her the events of the day after the revelation about Miriam. She knew her mother would have spoken about it with her father. And Datya had no doubt that Cohen would have whipped Ziva. Datya couldn't bear watching her sister take such punishment even if she had earned it. Lisbet seemed as though she wanted to ask her daughter about the day, to solicit her confidence, but the weariness of the evening won out and she simply nodded again to her oldest daughter. Taking the scarf-wrapped timbrel and a woolen blanket she crept quietly past her sleeping sister whose mat of woven river grass she wouldn't be sharing tonight.

Ravit's tent was not a lengthy walk, but the night air of the desert was strikingly cool. The men of the camp often said that a great sea to the northwest brought the cooling night breezes. She had never been able to picture it, and had never seen any sign of it, but the elders all agreed that it was so. She mused that they must be right for a great many of the leather skins used in the Tabernacle came from animals only found in the sea. Datya wrapped the wool around her shoulders and walked silently those few moments. Telling anyone about what her father believed about Miriam - even just speaking it aloud - sounded too difficult, but Datya knew she would need the prayers of her friend to face it if it was true. Still, perhaps she would keep the tragic knowledge to herself for the evening and brace herself to face it tomorrow instead. Her father would be furious if Datya gave in to the temptation to sleep under the stars tonight, for this was the behavior of a slave, not a well-taught Levite daughter. With a longing for their bright, gentle comfort, Datya nearly gave into the temptation to spread her thin blanket here in the open. She knew she would find sleep even with the cool breeze skimming over and around her cloak. Rejecting the risk of being found out, she moved to the opening of Ravit's tent instead.

"Ravit, are you still awake? It is Datya." She stepped into the tent and saw Ravit by the small dish of lit oil. Little more than a small saucer of pottery with a tiny pinched spout, the shallow dish brought only faint illumination. It was enough to see her sweet friend as she finished up her evening's work. She was bundling up her spare robe, tunic, tools, and baskets, but quickly set them aside and brought Datya close for a hug. After whispering that she couldn't share what was on her heart this night, Datya fell asleep on a sliver of Ravit's own woven mat. The pallet, a luxury even amongst the now wealthy tribes, was no more comforting than the ground would be, as Datya's aching heart sought the peace of sleep.

Sunlight didn't often make it into the thickly patched tents of the camp; Datya often wished it would so that rising in the morning would be easier. Instead she came to when Ravit rose, tugging her outer robe back over her head and settling it about her for the day. Datya quickly helped to roll up the bed mat and pack the last of Ravit's possessions, shaking out the endless dust as she went. Miriam had told her that even the slaves in Egypt slept on rough stone floors for the Egyptians commanded cleanliness of even their lowliest citizens. Datya's eyes had widened when Miriam shared that Moses had often slept on cool, polished stone as he traveled with the royal household from palace to palace along the Nile. He'd even slept on the carved couches, surrounded by lush curtains that put the humble tents of her people to shame. Datya and Ravit, who had been working in sleepy silence, turned towards the small entrance gap in Ravit's small tent. Her eldest brother would send someone to help with the tent after manna gathering, so the two slipped through the opening and made their way out to the open ground. Ravit had often questioned whether she should continue to raise her own tent, the one her husband had commissioned for them. It was a rare luxury for a childless widow to have her own dwelling, but Ravit's brother had patiently suggested that she continue to use it as long as she felt safe. He was only a few tents away according to the order of their family line, for Koppel had come from their uncle's family. Thus Ravit had been close to her brothers, and parents, through the tumultuous months of her mourning. Ravit often remarked that Yahweh had shown her a small favor by providing a husband from her own family, for now in her widowhood she was not alone. Datya wondered again how Ravit could utter such a graceful statement, let alone believe it, for Datya felt she would surely lack gratitude of every kind if she experienced a loss like Ravit's. This morning, the young widow was quiet, but smiled and hummed the Song of the Sea as they walked. The tune, a favorite among the children, was nearly always on Ravit's lips. As the notes flowed into the sunlight, Datya was humbled once more by her friend's steadfast faithfulness. While the Israelites largely lacked patience and understanding, Ravit walked in an abundance of both. She was a joy to be around, even though a touch of sorrow remained about her.

Datya knew that Ravit would not press her to explain her sudden appearance last night. Longing to confide in her warred with the wisdom of waiting to share what her parents had revealed with her teacher first. She would collect manna with Ravit, eat what she needed and then find Miriam right away. Ravit would have plenty of family to head out of camp with, and her mother would forgive her if she did not make it back for the first leg of the journey.

It seemed as though every child in camp was rushing through the pathways. Most of the youth, Ziva's age and up, were loading animals in front of their tents. Everywhere she looked she saw servants bundling loads of goods to animals. A few families had carts, like the ones her father had purchased for them, though mostly pack animals and the people themselves would bear the burden of tools, goods, and treasures. She knew most of the pack animals had been secured through trades or purchased from nomads who knew this land better than her people. Miriam had shared with Datya during one of their many walking lessons that although the tribes had fled Egypt with the choicest livestock, and plenty of wares, the herds had failed to produce the amount of offspring their people needed. The shepherds, used to the lush plains of Goshen did their best, but the results of wilderness grazing were pitiful at best, especially for the large animals. Each year only a small portion of the would-be animal mothers welcomed babies into their herds; Datya loved the rare glimpses of the stubborn donkey foals taking the first haphazard steps among near wild herds and the awkward way camel calves tippled for milk under their mother's tall stomachs. She especially loved the plump calves of the mother oxen, as they trundled along with the marching stock. Of course, she'd heard the shepherds who dwelt among the sheep remark that the smaller beasts seemed unaffected by the less than desirable vegetation, at least reproductive-wise. The dry land seemed to swirl upwards and fill the air around them from all the comings and goings, though the activity could only be an hour or so old. A majority of the mothers, of course, were already shuffling back to their tents with their allotted bread from heaven. Ravit and Datya shared a smile. They didn't yet possess that mysterious ability to rise before dawn for the benefit of others, that the mothers of the camp seemed to mystically develop. Still, even with all the Israelite mothers' arms full, plenty of manna remained for the stragglers. Stragglers like "Israel's youngest widow," and "Miriam's apprentice," epithets she had frequently heard tossed about in the whispers that circulated on harried mornings like these.

Datya bent to collect a palmful. It never ceased to amaze her the sweet, delicate taste that melted as quickly as it landed on her tongue. She had plenty of moments where she longed to try the flavorful treats of the Nile that Miriam and the elders had spoken of. Or sample the fruits and grains that belonged to stationary people. But the longing for something different, didn't change the appreciation that she was tasting a miracle. So many puzzling questions surfaced as she sampled the blessing. She chiefly wanted to know, how was it that not a single desert critter, nor crawling creature, nor flying insect ever molested the miniature loaves? It was as though the creation God had allotted for this place knew well that the bread was supplied for the Israelites and company, and for them alone. Datya marveled at Yahweh's strange but wonderful provision. She hadn't dared to ask such a silly question of Miriam in many years, not since she was new to her service, but the longing to know remained all the same.

Ravit seemed to be eating light, while Datya was eating a wide radius around her. Looking askance to her friend, she felt concern rise. Her friend's normally bright and joyful countenance seemed dim and downcast, though the sun was lavishing great beams of light on the awakening camp. Aware that she was being studied, Ravit looked down, "Do not be mindful of me Datya, I have no right to cast sorrow on the day." Sweet and humble as she was, Datya's heart went out to her friend who had already known too much sorrow. Though she had awoken with her own troubles, seeing her friend's head dipping low under an invisible weight stirred her heart; the cause was unknown to her, but her friend needed her care.

"Nonsense, Ravit, you are my dear friend," with an emphatic nudge of her elbow to Ravit's, she added, "Please, share your heart with me." Datya had gathered enough bread to walk a ways and fill her stomach all at once. She sensed Ravit needed distance from the camp's bustle this morning as much as she craved it. As the two moved further from the clatter of the packing camp, Datya urged again, "Ravit, what is it? Are you afraid?" The long days of desert treks and the unknown lying before them had the ability to tease the nerves of even the bravest of the tribes. Datya's mother had once shared that the widows often struggled with the greatest portion of fear. Some, that by day, they'd be left behind, and others, by night, couldn't rest well through the strange sounds of the lonely, desert wind and the haunting calls of the night creatures. Though marauding groups hadn't been seen by the Israelites in their lifetime, she knew Ravit had heard plenty of the alarming ambush stories. Afterall, who didn't approach one of the craggy, tumble-down mountains or pass by a mysterious clutch of caves without feeling a bit nervous about what might be hidden in the shadows?

Ravit seemed to struggle with what to say. Patience was an easy thing to return to her friend, who offered the virtue in surplus to all she knew. It was true too that Ravit believed in the goodness of Yahweh too much to give in to complaining. The usual grumbles of dissatisfied Hebrews couldn't explain Ravit's struggle. Finally her lips parted to release a fearful whisper, "I slept little last night. I dreamed of Koppel." As Ravit inhaled sharply and deeply, Datya wondered if she would cry. Ravit had rarely wept since Koppel was buried 3 camps ago. Many amongst the Levites and Gaddites, the tribe that was so close to them, the families were nearly intertwined, felt she would surely mourn more openly in time. Datya was unsure; nearly 10 moons had passed since Koppel had died in his sleep. Without tears, but with a shaking voice, Ravit continued, "I dreamed of the night before Koppel died. I dreamed that Yahweh whispered to my beloved, 'Koppel come away to me, others will follow after'." Ravit paused, her face looked stricken.

"Ravit, we have talked of his name many times. You have always said he was named "follow after," because the Lord would someday let you follow Koppel to Heaven. Why do you look sick with worry?" Datya was startled by her grieving friend. In the past, Ravit had taken joy and comfort in what she believed was a quiet promise. Her husband's name "Follow After," had always been a precious promise that her friend repeated on the hard, lonely days. How could the very name that had once comforted Ravit now be the cause of such woeful trembling?

"I will share with you Datya, because I know you will keep this dream in your heart and pray with me, but I mustn't let others hear these words. Yahweh will reveal it in time; I do not know, yet, why He chose to show me this dream." Ravit walked several more paces holding closely to Datya's arm. They were already far from earshot and their breakfast long finished, when Ravit continued: "In my dream, the night before Koppel died, he heard God whispering the call to him. 'Koppel come away to me, and others will follow,' and that night Koppel died. His spirit was gathered up to the heavens. In the dream, when Koppel heard the whisper, I did not hear it, even though I was lying by his side, wrapped tightly in his comforting mantle. After that, Yahweh showed me faces of others in the camp, and as I saw their faces, I heard His whisper to them. First, I saw our beloved midwife, Noya. Yahweh whispered to her, 'Noya come away to me and others will follow.' Datya, you remember, she breathed her last, not even one full moon after Koppel was gone. Second, I saw your mother's own father, Yaco. We have always said he was named 'following after,' because he led so many with quiet encouragement in Egypt! But in my dream, Datya, Yahweh whispered the same to him, and I was filled with fear. Yaco did indeed meet the end of his life in the last camp, but even to him Yahweh whispered, '...others will follow.' I wish I had woken up! I wish I had not seen any more faces! I cry out to Yahweh to take the memory of the dream from me!" Datya was anxious for her friend's sake. Ravit was known as calm, and wise, and patient; she had often seemed unshakeable, as sturdy as the aged, wiry trees that sprawled, low to the ground, everywhere they journeyed. To see her filled with dread made Datya's own heart awaken with panic.

"Ravit, be calm, it was just a dream - a remembrance of loved ones lost. Do not fear so." Datya whispered and urged her dearest friend to settle. Ravit's face darkened as the tumultuous vision surfaced, fresh and fearsome in her mind. Datya watched as her friend's trembling fingers tugged at the frayed tassel tied to her belt. Most often Ravit kept the precious momento tucked deeper in the folds of her garments, but today it was freed from it's snug place, a sure sign that Ravit was rattled to her core. The tassel which had been cut from her husband's outer mantle before he was wrapped in it for burial comforted Ravit far more than words. Though it was common knowledge among the nearby women that Ravit had sliced the tassel off, Datya did not know if the men knew. She doubted men would take kindly to the thought of the nearly sacred *tzittzit* being removed from a man's garment. Truthfully, Ravit needed the solace it brought, Koppel didn't.

"There is more Datya, the dream showed me three more faces, with three more whispers." Frantic darts of her dark eyes coupled with the quake in her voice disturbed Datya's senses. But Ravit wasn't finished with the revelation, "Three faces of ones who are great in Israel, and still so alive! They are working in the camp at this very minute! A vision of their deaths could not be a remembrance for they are still amongst us!" Ravit did begin to cry now. Not hard or loud, for it wasn't her way, but the tears fled toward her jaw none-the-less. Not even her beloved husband's tassel could stem the worry that overflowed the disturbed widow.

Datya barely wanted her friend to continue. She had already had so much worry and fear on behalf of Miriam that she couldn't bear the thought of others she loved leaving this world as well. Suddenly, great fear rose up to nearly choke her words. She stared at Ravit, praying that this moment was a dream itself, that they would both awake and the alarm would vanish. Datya shook her head slowly, almost unwilling to let Ravit finish the dream. "Ravit, you cannot trust this vision! Don't even speak it!" Though Datya knew the taste of fear she was not one given to panic. Still, the horror of yesterday's revelation combined with the deadly vision her friend had been given rose to a throbbing fear within her. She had never turned her back on her friend before but a relentless urge to silence her friend by turning to flee overwhelmed her.

Ravit took her hand. The touch, meant in love, burned "I have never been untruthful with you Datya; I would not share it with you, except that Yahweh is pressing on my heart that I must." Datya shuddered now, with dreadful certainty about what Ravit would reveal. "After Koppel had heard the whisper and been taken up, and Noya and Yaco had heard their own call. I saw three more faces, with each one I heard the same whisper. First - I am sorry my dearest! - Miriam's face was before me and Yahweh whispered, 'Miriam come away to me and others will follow." After her true and good face faded, Aaron's was in my sight, and I heard that holy but now dreaded whisper! Finally, - it is too much to bear! - Moses' own face came into view. Yahweh whispered to Moses, the same that my beloved Koppel had heard! Then I saw the whole of the camp stretching wide and many raised their heads as Yahweh spoke loudly. 'Children of my Covenant! My servant Moses will meet me on the mountain, and you will follow him no longer.' I woke then Datya, while you and the camp still slept and I prayed that the dream would fade from my mind! Why would Abba give this vision to me?" Ravit finished with all the dread in her voice that Datya felt. Her friend clutched tightly to her arm, wanting to share one another's strength, and began uttering quiet, fervent prayers to Yahweh. Silence was all that issued from Datya as she reeled from her friend's dispiriting prophecy. Ravit's prayers convicted her, but none would rise from her own lips.

Datya felt she would not be able to control her tears enough to return to the busiest parts of camp, but Ravit turned her that way. "I am sorry, sweet Datya, I know Yahweh is right in all things, but I would keep this burden from you if I could." Ravit's voice was tender, seeking to soothe and comfort her, but shock and fear called loudly within, "flee!". Through yesterday's strange turn and this morning's daunting word, turmoil had seeded itself in her innermost; her spirit was wracked with fury and fright.

Desperate, Datya began pleading in her heart for the peace of Heaven! How could she join the procession of the camp with this horrible revelation hanging over her? How could she seek Miriam for her beloved walks under the shadow of such a cloud? The grief did not break off of her, though she beseeched Yahweh. Finally, even in the dryscape with the painful storm stirring, Yahweh seemed to hold her close. Peace flowed in and around the grief, though it did not dispel it, as she reached for Ravit's arm again. "You have always been a dreamer, Ravit. Many times the young mothers in the camp named their children because of the beautiful visions you had following their births. And think how often you dreamed about our Ancestors' stories from the time before Egypt just when our people needed to hear those testimonies once again. I do not know why Yahweh has now sent you such a grave vision. I pray it is a sign to our leaders, and yet I pray that it will not hold true!" Datya stuttered to a pause, holding back the false assurance she most wanted to declare - the dream surely meant something else, entirely! She must seek Miriam! "Ravit, you must forgive me, I can walk with you no longer. Miriam may already be nearing the front of the procession." It would be far from this spot for Miriam's honored position allowed her to walk with the forward most leaders rather than journeying in the middle of the caravans with the majority of the Levites. "I must catch up with her and be a servant to her!" After accepting the briefest touch, as Ravit kissed her cheek in parting, Datya darted away.

CHAPTER THREE

Frustration descended upon Datya as she left her friend behind. Only when the camp came back into view did she realize just how far she and Ravit had wandered, in the direction opposite from her teacher, no less! Though the heat of the day was yet a long way off, Datya felt the burning touch of the sun rushing over her forearms. It's heat spoke a violent whisper, "Make haste!" Hurried steps did nothing to distract her mind which rallied to her teacher's side far ahead of her body. Miriam had always been one of a few among Israel who had no complaints about the great fiery light that scorched earth and creature alike. It showed in the way she dressed, always choosing tunics with sleeves cropped far above the elbow, and often wearing her mantle wrapped about her only when she was participating in official work. Why, Miriam had even told her that in Egypt she and the other slave women often wore tunics with only a single sleeve that had stopped at the knee rather than lower on the legs, much as the children of the camp did now. Datya couldn't picture Miriam in such attire, though she had no doubt Miriam would welcome it, if Yahweh permitted it. The prophetess loved the sun too much to stay wrapped in fabric meant "to be worn by the sheep alone!" as she would so often say. Although Datya knew she was certainly grateful for the embellished wool of her cloak when the sun lowered.

Once, as a little girl, she had overheard Miriam talking to a servant about the bizarre sun worship of Egypt. She had told how the Egyptian princesses and noble daughters would dance at the edge of the Nile, completely bare! How Datya had shuddered as she listened to the unholy account. First the girls had danced in the heat of the sun's waves until their skin felt crisp and feverish. Then they would plunge into the reedy waters. Miriam had spied them once as a young girl herself and never forgot the sight of the steam hissing up from the water's surface as the pagan women sank in the cool waters. Of course, Miriam hadn't known that Datya was so near, listening to the tale. It had been conveyed to the servant, an older woman who had also left Egypt after Yahweh's Great Displays. Unlike Miriam, the servant hadn't even a drop of Jacob's blood and felt no kinship to the God who had caused such a stir for mighty Pharaoh's people. The tale of the Egyptian princesses' sun dance was meant to illustrate the foolishness of serving anything other than Yahweh. The story had been shared so long ago, when Datya was new to Miriam's service, she couldn't recall whether it made any helpful impression on the old serving woman. Datya wondered how many other servants and foreigners had heard a similar lectionary portrayal from Miriam.

Many packed and parting tents were disappearing behind Datya as she swiftly made her way. Her feet were moving as quickly as she dared, her tunic nearly whipping with sound at the speed, but Miriam's tent was not yet in view. *So many people! Surely this nation is everything Yahweh promised to Abraham and more, at least in numbers!* She didn't dare add the thought that perhaps it was big enough, although in the next breath her shame burnt hotter than the sun for the fussy direction of her thoughts. Thankfulness, worship, rejoicing - these should be her exclamations over the swelling nation about her. Surely it was a miracle in itself that the God of Abraham had cultivated such a strong group from a ragged string of slaves. That Yahweh had been able to produce anything at all from the exhausted refugees was a source of wonderment.

Few, if any of the elders of the Exodus remained now, but Datya could recall knowing a handful when she had been young. Her father had taken her to visit several, instructing her to listen and not to speak for the words each elder would share were more valuable than a child's. A handful of other Levite parents would often be invited to the small circle, and many of the other children were cousins Datya knew well. On such days, one elder would share about the evil ways the Egyptians preyed upon her people; men were beaten unto weakness and then great feats of strength were demanded of them. Women were sent to work-rooms and hot fires, either laboring over the Egyptian's beloved luxurious linen or preparing meals for their masters. Other elders would tell the tale of the Red Sea, and look for awed faces among her cousins, though there would be none since the story had already been told to each of them day in and day out. Miriam often fumed that Israelite parents had done their children a disservice by allowing the wonder to fade. Understanding Yahweh's power flowed from understanding the true setting of his miracles. Hadn't Miriam told her as much many times over? A few elders would tell of faraway people, other nations and other gods and the strange customs that gripped the pagan worlds. The elders who enjoyed frightening the little ones would end with a tale of child sacrifice, or some other horrific injustice. Datya's father always frowned at the elders who felt the pagan legends had any instructive value for Israel's youngest generation. A small smile lit as she remembered the tender way her father would kneel as they left the meeting. With his eyes capturing hers, his huge palms nearly covering the sides of her face, his voice became a command for her to remember, "This is what makes us different, Datya. Not the blood of your ancestors, but the customs Yahweh has given us. A better way is what sets us apart." Always nodding her head, Datya had come to understand that he meant the evils that most of mankind endured had no part in the nation chosen by Yahweh.

Though it did little to assuage the anxiety coursing through her, Datya finally saw the animals and carts she knew to be those of Miriam's neighbors. Miriam would not be far now, and then all her fears would surely be snuffed out.

"Young girl! Why are you rushing so much?" Miriam's beloved voice teased Datya as she drew close, weaving in and out of the vast hordes of rushing Israelites. The older woman held her arms aloft as though she were overjoyed to see her student's approach; this was one thing Datya treasured in her mentor, no matter how many days and years they spent together, Miriam always seemed as thrilled by Datya's presence as she had been the first day. Miriam's thorough kindness and love towards her seemed so unlike the accounts of the tutors she'd heard the young boys speak of. While her male peers often endured endless hours of recitation and repetition, Datya had learned their history through largely pleasant days of storytelling, singing, questioning, and praying. Though she had hurried, to be of service, the place where Miriam's revered tent had stood for so many weeks was barren now except for the packed impressions in the earth where her belongings had settled. Miriam never had any shortage of willing hands to do the work of putting her tent to cart and hauling away her household, unlike some of the other widows. Many young men were sent by their families to offer Miriam aid at such times with the hope that they would be noticed and blessed by the prophetess. Her beloved mentor spoke again and with much more cheer than Datya felt. "I know why you are distressed, Datya. Your mother's own concern for you brought her to my tent early this morning. She told me what your father said upon seeing the timbrel." Always, Miriam's voice had flowed over Datya bearing the wisdom and grace of a lifetime, but her words this morning only served to heighten Datya's alarm. "Let us walk a little ways together, hmm? There will be time enough for you to gather your answers." Fear threatened the breath intended to move her muscles along the path; if her father's prophecy had been false, wouldn't Miriam offer assurance right away?

Datya had never before walked arm and arm with Miriam. Out of respect, and perhaps child-like awe, she always stayed a step to her side, wanting to be close enough to hear her, but without being presumptive. She was more than a little shocked when Miriam thrust her arm through hers and leaned into her for the first steps of the journey. Miriam had held Datya close on occasion. In moments of sorrow or when celebrating achievements, but they had been special, tender times, never an everyday occurrence! For the first time, Datya, being so near to her teacher, felt the weakening in Miriam's arms, the slight tremble as she held on. Her heartbeat stuttered at the confirmation that Miriam's newly offered closeness was more than intimate friendship. She was holding on because she had too. Datya had wanted to arrive at Miriam's side to hear her teacher fully denounce Father's grievous assumption. Instead Miriam's behavior lent credence; once again, alarm reigned. Winding their way to the far forward edges of the procession, linked closely together as two sisters, should have been the height of joy for Datya. All who saw them would know how dearly valued she was in Miriam's sight, and the whispers would begin that a lovely, deep friendship had blossomed where once tutelage had been. Warm delight should have overcome her from head to toe with the thought, but she felt a bewildered cold despite the great beams of sunshine that lit the way before them. Knowing that many frowns would be turned on her if she dared to throw herself at Miriam's feet, Datya resisted the urge. But, with all her heart, she wanted to fall to her knees and plead with Miriam to be forthright with her! To tell her what was happening and why, but the meaning of Miriam's words were all too clear. They would walk in silence, the prophetess most likely praying silently, until she was ready to speak to Datya's heartache.

Many walks in the past had included the old tales which introduced Datya to Yahweh's character. It was through such walks that Datya had grown. Miriam had used the ancient art of storytelling to cultivate the faith of her student. Other days had included Miriam's observations of the travelers around them. Miriam would keep her voice low, to spare disgraced persons from further shame, but she would remind Datya to always flee temptation. Though her people had been called to holiness, sin still wove it's deadly fingers through the camp. Miriam had often told Datya that she would not escape the trap of sin, but that she must seek the holy God on the other side of all her failures, rather than remaining in the lifeless trap. Datya shuddered at the memory; such chilling lessons were the walks she dreaded. Her favorite walks of all, of course, were the ones where Miriam's voice would lift above the thousands of footfalls to declare the goodness of God. How she treasured striding along in the holy, healing melodies of Israel's great Prophetess.

But today, Miriam had commanded silence. There would be no story. No song. Nor even dire warnings to guard her heart. Datya could do nothing but wait. She would try to pray; she would try to be patient. Feeling strong in neither category, she focused simply on the dusty earth shifting beneath her feet. The dirt, long stripped of any meaningful life, was the only ground she'd ever known. A lesson lurked within its colors, a rusty mixture of burnt reds, dusty tans, darker browns where the shadows fell, and the cream color that reminded her of newly woven linen. In its own way, the colorful shades of the ground, reminded Datya of the horde of people who had become a traveling kingdom. They too, teemed with an ever-changing variety of hues, each one an image-bearer of the One True God, whether they acknowledged it or not. She had walked thousands of miles, in her young life, but the land remained the same. Sometimes it stirred feelings of wonder, reminding her of the Creator God and his promises to her people. Today it simply mirrored the dry, aching fear riddling her soul. Would the remainder of the day serve to restore her like the rare rains replenished the earth, or would it bring her down to the very dust in despair?

Much to her mentor's amusement, the desert journeys occasionally held humor. When an animal would stubbornly hold up its driver, when a child would tumble in such an animal's leavings, when the wives and widows would spare their breath to tell stories. But mostly, the wilderness wanderings were somber, often quiet as the people coped with the heat and the unknown. Datya often felt, as did many others, that falling into a bit of a daze was unavoidable. So many steps forward leading into so many more steps forward had a way of fatiguing one's mind. For Datya, many miles would often pass before she would walk awake again, and stumble out of cobwebbed thoughts. Today promised to be one of those days.

A smile teased but could not break through as she thought of how easily she could look Miriam in the face now. When her father had first brought her to Miriam for a day's learning and service, Datya had looked up at the wise prophetess with a touch of fear. She'd been so little, with only seven years of this wandering life! All of those, of course, had been spent near the family tent, in this vast wilderness, but Miriam had seen other lands! She had seen the lush Nile, and although she rarely spoke of life in Egypt, Datya knew that the words of someone who had seen so much were as valuable as gems. To her, Miriam's wealth of knowledge surpassed the value of a king's possessions. Not long ago, Miriam and Datya had spent the morning together singing praises as they celebrated ten full years together! For ten years, Miriam had been pouring heart and soul into Datya, training her in the Way of the Almighty!

In those early days, Datya's instruction was kept to a minimum, perhaps an hour or so in the morning. The rest of the day had been spent helping Miriam with tasks of all kinds. Sometimes Datya would be sent as a messenger around the camp, sometimes she would help Miriam with her household, sometimes Miriam would simply sing the history of the people to her. Datya had been so young; it took her many years to realize that Miriam sang them so often so that Datya would memorize them. Nearly every ballad was solid like stone within her now, for she could sing them all start to finish in a moment's notice. Miriam had told her recently, that she had spent many hours praying for Datya's mind to strengthen to the task of holding so many melodies. With an exuberant embrace, Miriam had rejoiced that Yahweh had answered those prayers! In more recent years, the lessons of the morning had grown to cover most of the day, and Datya often sang the stories back to Miriam as a sort of test. Lectures and songs were only the tool of her calling, Miriam always said. Learning to be ever in prayer was the heart of her mission, the source. This skill had been the hardest to cultivate for Datya. Constant communication with a Being one could not see had become a hurdle for her. Once, when she was very little she had even set out on her own to approach the Pillar of Cloud at the front of the camp. After Miriam's lesson on the Pillar being Yahweh's guiding light to their People, Datya had felt that prayer would be easier for her if she could get closeby, perhaps even touch it's shadow. Miriam had caught up to her, and swept her back towards the tent, long before she had the chance. With her typical delighted chuckle, Miriam had rebuked her saying that Datya would have to learn to pray, and to trust, just as everyone else did. There were no shortcuts. She couldn't withhold the sigh at the silly memory and the long-ago lesson. How would she ever improve her dependence on Yahweh if she lost Miriam's guidance?

While encamped in a sheltered little valley before this most recent camp, Miriam had surprised her with a challenge that stunned Datya at first. She had arrived early, while many others were still pursuing morning manna. Miriam had greeted her and had her sit on a cushion just inside the tent. "Datya, listen carefully. This will be the last time you hear my voice this week. I will not be speaking with you for the rest of the week, but you will learn much. Each day you must come and sit at this post. We will partake of our manna then fast together until evening." The tell-tale twinkle had blossomed in Miriam's eyes, even as she took a serious tone with her student. "I will be listening to you this week. You must dwell on our time together, and recite lessons to me that you have learned." Suddenly thrusting her volume upwards, she had startled Datya with the intensity of her behest. "Dig deep, Datya! I am looking to see what your very spirit has absorbed from these years of testimonies and teachings! I will speak with the Lord, and you will listen and hear, but I will teach you no more this week." She had been too stunned to ask questions. After the shock of the assignment wore off, Datya's stomach had churned with nervous rebellion. Miriam was dear to her and their discussions had always been a balance of academia and friendship, and, yes, even mothering, so there was no true reason for the queasiness. It was just so - unexpected. It had felt like something new, a great test. Datya remembered feeling that she would be more equipped to suddenly take over the shepherding of the lambs, a task she had never been taught, than to pass through this unnerving evaluation. More than that, she felt she always bungled challenges set before her. While Miriam held confidence as thorough as the sunshine, Datya's confidence was as unproductive as the slight wisps of clouds that occasionally graced the desert sky. As surely as they failed to cast shade on the weary travelers, her heart had sunk, doubting that she would be able to honor Miriam.

That day she had said little and the hours had passed slowly. Miriam seemed neither bothered by the silence nor amused by her discomfort. She had simply waited for Datya to share what she would. How she had tried! But mostly she was only able to recall recent lectures and to recount a few of Miriam's most memorable testimonies. Eventually she trailed off with how she often repeated each day's lessons to her father, noting to Miriam that Cohen always seemed interested in her days, but rarely commented. More than a little embarrassed by her struggle, Datya finally threw a question at the awkward silence. "Miriam, I know you will not be speaking with me, but would you speak to the Lord for me? Would you pray for me today?"

Pleasure had passed over the deep lines of Miriam's countenance. The prophetess had stood, placed her hands softly on the sides of Datya's face and prayed over her then, as she had so many times before. "Almighty Lord, here is your young child. Remove the scales from her eyes Lord and show her the knowledge you promise. Help her spirit to understand! Let the truth settle in her that she is not merely training to receive my spirit and my knowledge, but yours! I ask your anointing for this dear child, for this new prophetess. Draw her into your calling and into your light." Miriam spoke her prayer with firmness. Clearly, she didn't doubt that Yahweh would hear it and honor it, but what Datya loved most about that moment was the small smile, the bespoke pride in her pupil that settled on Miriam's face. Datya had not been able to hold back the tears that were gathering. Miriam had prayed for her day in and day out for years, but she had never yet told Datya that she would indeed become a prophetess, until this humbling prayer! Datya had known something was changing but she couldn't yet discern what was going to become of her. With the prayer's end, Miriam began to tidy her tent for the evening. This was Miriam's task every day, as she sent Datya home, and she realized, even though the meal hour was long off, that their day was concluded.

Datya had walked home slowly that evening, reliving the day in her mind. Had Miriam been offering her clues of knowledge that she had missed? Her teacher was not a trickster, nor selfish or false, so she had known that the week's agenda must truly be a directive of the Lord. Datya had felt so ill-equipped to the test until she remembered yet another of Miriam's lessons. This memory floated from a time when Datya had been studying with the great prophetess of Israel for only a week's time. She had been preparing for the walk home to her family's tent when Miriam called out to her a final time. "Datya, spend your walks as heavenly currency. Dwell on our lessons, yes, but dwell even more on all the words of the Almighty! They must be as constant in you as breath!" She'd turned away with those words to seek out and minister to other women in the camp for the evening. Miriam had spoken these same words to Datya hundreds of times in the years that followed, though their first utterance was a memory she would never forget. That day, Datya had walked home in thoughtful silence.

Just as they were doing now.

~ ~ ~

Often when they were in one another's company Miriam would struggle, as she was now, to keep her face serious, like that of a teacher or mother! But more often than not, the challenge was intense for Datya's quiet, serious ways often amused her. Datya's discomfort or confusion, or fear, or wonder always played across her face forcing Miriam to hold back chuckles most of the day for her student's sake. Oh, she was truly thankful that Datya had been called to receive her mantle someday. She was a lovely, gentle spirit, but every now and then she wished the girl had a bit more room for humor in her day. A pinch of the laughter and zest her sister, who had confidence even the Egyptians would admire, showed for life would be plenty to spice up their long days of desert lessons. How Lisbet and Cohen produced such utterly different daughters was beyond even Miriam's wisdom. Datya's calling was clear as day, while Ziva's purpose among the tribes remained quite veiled to all, including Miriam. Of course, their baby brother's personality, with just two years to his sweaty little dimpled life was anyone's guess. Thinking back to the arrival of the little cherub Miriam grinned once more. He brought joy to his parents who had so long mourned the many sons and daughters lost to them. Cohen was a noble man, thankful for his daughters, but he had been reborn when his son arrived, alive and full of the fury and fuss of a newborn. All the elders had offered up prayers of thanks to Yahweh for sparing the young couple the pain of burying another baby. Often she had wondered if her student's nervous demeanor stemmed from watching the frequent grief her parents had endured through Datya's childhood. She would never say as much to Cohen and Lisbet, but the thought lingered none-the-less. Miriam peeked again at Datya. The girl's uncertainty with her teacher even after these delightful years together was one of her biggest struggles. Miriam knew too, that too many of the tribes still struggled with doubts that became the only floods in this dry place!

Too many times Miriam stepped from her tent morning and evening to hear the conversations buzzing around with the wonderings of "What?" and "Why?" Yahweh's hand was obvious and yet, because the timing displeased the Israelites, they cultivated doubts where nothing else would grow. *Faithless tribes!* Often a flare of impatience in her mind was matched with a swift check in her spirit. *Forgive me, Almighty One! They are Your beloved, I know. I have no right to fume at the state of their hearts! Show me how to minister to them; teach me even more, Father, while I am still here. I ask, as ever, Lord, that you heal my impatience and my temper. Forgive me!*

Softening, Miriam let the smile rise and break through; Datya's sweet, studious patience was so unlike her bold ways, and yet, God had told her clearly that Datya would rise to hold this post among Jacob's descendants. "Datya, did you know that I too have a mentor, a teacher, that I meet with every day?" Datya looked startled to hear the question and relieved that the period of walking in silence was ending, "But you have no need? You never struggle with what to do or what to say. You know all there is to know!" Miriam was in high spirits today, so she let the chuckle slip through as well, though she knew it would be a costly withdrawal of the breath in her lungs. "Dear One, only Yahweh knows all, and you must never ascribe his attributes to me or anyone else. I do not know all, but God does. I am not good, but God is. I am not love, but God is. I can not heal, but God can. I bring no miracles to this camp, I simply stand by while He does. Even the great stories I sing are His, and the great wonders I tell are the works of Him alone! You must always remember this Datya, for He is the One I meet with every day. Even with this old, ragged body, I must learn new lessons at His feet." Miriam watched Datya closely. She saw understanding pass over her youthful face even as a wince at the reference to her advanced years puckered her brows. Caring for this young charge was a challenge; so often she wanted to mother, nurture, and protect Datya. But Yahweh had not called her to be Datya's mother. She was here to train Datya, and sometimes that meant withholding a hug in times of discouragement, or bearing painful witness to a truth she would rather shelter the young girl from.

Miriam well remembered how young and innocent Datya was in the earliest days of her service. It had been so easy to love and dote on the well behaved little girl entrusted to her care, but Yahweh had swiftly spoken to her that this girl was not entrusted to Miriam as a playmate but as a student. Still, Miriam also knew that God had given Datya a gentle way that provided a sweet companionship for Miriam.

Her thoughts strayed to the future now, wondering what kind of student Datya would all too soon acquire. Israel would always need wise and courageous prophetesses. Miriam and Datya were only the first of many Yahweh would raise up. Indeed, Yahweh had begun to whisper to her that in the future many would be needed to carry out this work. All too soon, great distances would spread the Israelites out like honeybees scattered to the far corners of a vast field. It was right that it was so, and yet, Miriam knew the divied up Promised Land would breed a new series of challenges for the prophets and leaders. This too would be a discussion Miriam must take up with Datya during the coming days. Time was short now, and Miriam still had much to transfer to Datya.

How she would grow and change in these days! It was

difficult for Miriam to know that she would not get to see Datya launch into the ministry they had both poured so many years into, but it was enough to know that Miriam had fulfilled this last great task for her beloved King. Many days had been spent carefully detailing the People's history to this young one, and many more hours had been spent helping her to master the many songs and legends. Datya had always lit up whenever a bit of knowledge from the time before the enslavement was shared. She loved hearing about the time Abraham willingly laid Isaac upon the altar, only to lift him down from it once more with mighty shouts of praise! She was equally fond of learning about Jacob's wives and the antics of the boys born into his household who later founded the families she had grown up with. Perhaps, the story she loved best though was hearing how Joseph asked for his bones to leave Egypt when the Israelites left their temporary home. Datya had always come alive when Miriam shared the details of Joseph's request, once responding, "He prophesied over them, Miriam! None knew that they were going back to the land God had promised them, except Joseph! He made them promise so they wouldn't forget that God had a home for them! How clever, how wise he was!" Like Datya, Miriam too loved the now ancient story. Joseph was kin to them, of course, but he was also kindred for he had spoken prophetically over the same stubborn people that Miriam now cared for. Wryly, she often added that Joseph had worked with a bit of advantage, as the favored son of Jacob. Her student loved to innocently remind her that Miriam was quite favored among Israel herself, more than many women!

"Do you know what I dwell on now, Child?" Miriam's voice relieved the silence once more. "I think on your own student, your own ministry, and the days to come when Yahweh will use you to shore up the hearts of His people!" Miriam tugged at Datya's pace as she spoke. The pace of the camp was never grueling. With this many people trudging through the desert tugging their households on their shoulders, it couldn't be. Still it taxed

Miriam more than ever before, the walk to the front alone sapping her strength. She could instruct Datya or she could walk; the breath in her lungs would not support both.

Datya stumbled with her still unasked question. Miriam had pointed her focus to Datya's own future. She had never done that before, and once again she was overcome with one single thought. *I'm not ready.* Still if Yahweh's voice was calling Miriam home, who could hold him back? None could, not even her revered teacher who often seemed to be a vessel of God's miracles. She could hold back her questions no longer. "Miriam, the loss Father spoke of - you must tell me it isn't true. Surely, it is not that time. The camp needs you; I need you!" Her throat was thick with more than the dust that filled the air around her, yet the Prophetess would not appreciate her spilling tears with so many people passing by. She paused, battling her own emotions, to contain the oncoming grief.

"Datya, I always told you that looking at all of life with those serious eyes was what would hold you back. Look ahead, girl! Look at all the camp may experience under the example of worship and prayer you will set! Look to the growth and favor you will experience as you minister to Israel. And what of me, Datya? Look to the Promised Land I will enter; even more golden and precious than the one we seek now!" Miriam, ever jovial, sprinkled in another portion of laughter, "The news is bitter for you I know, but it ushers in much joy!" Knowing Datya would struggle to accept such words simply because they had been uttered, Miriam rushed a prayer from her lips: *Help her, Father.* The elder caught the younger's eye before continuing, "You know, don't you Datya, that God's Kingdom works that way? What seems the seed of sorrow is often truly a harvest of joy." Slowly now, so that her student's mind would trap the words forever, Miriam clarified. "Only our God has that wonderful, merciful kind of power! Of all the pagan caravans that pass us by none know of or serve a god so alive and astounding!"

Perhaps a metaphor of a seed of sorrow and a crop of joy had been a poor choice for the young woman had never lived in one place long enough to tend even the swiftest growing crop. Certainly not the strong flax that both the Israelite and Egyptian women preferred. Nevertheless, it was what had come to mind, and Datya was clever! If she would open her heart to hear Miriam's words, despite her despair, she would learn much, even in this brief closing time. What would one call the season of life that begins a countdown? When one knows they are dying, but still sees much work awaiting their hands? Her people loved words, adored them and spent them heavily each day, but even their healthy minds lacked a word for this ending season of life - a season that could be lived, but never taught. Oh, many prophets and people had experienced it before her, but none had ever contributed anymore understanding. As always, Miriam herself would learn by listening to the Spirit of Yahweh, whose faithful presence was truly the best teacher. She prayed quietly now that her dear Datya would learn this truth, in haste, for she would have desperate need for his wisdom in the coming years. Miriam had meant to assure Datya, but the younger woman seemed more shaken than ever by the nearness of death. She sighed, this girl would soar despite the fear of loss, because her heart wholly belonged to Yahweh. Miriam would help her see that, if nothing else, before Yahweh took her home. Miriam had heard little from her God on the subject but somehow she knew, that moment would come before a new moon arrived. This she would keep to herself since Datya would surely panic. For the new moon was scarcely eight days away.

CHAPTER FOUR

Weaving between half shelters, and large clusters of families, Datya searched the exhausted parties for her own family's tent. Many of the marching families would put up only a wall or two of their tent each night, some of the smaller families may even climb atop their possessions on their unhitched carts and sleep under the stars. Datya's family always set up the tent with each stop. It was a true luxury at the end of a long day of travel, and Datya had always been thankful that her father insisted on it. "There is no reason to live like the herds," Cohen would tell the family, even as he labored with the help of a few hirelings to raise the tent in the near dark. Tonight they will have raised the tent without his help, for he was with the procession of the Levite men in service to the east of them. 'Carrying the loads, supplies and furnishings for the Tabernacle was an honor," this, she had heard from her father more times than she could count. Where others would complain of the weight of their packs, Cohen looked at the one assigned to him as a blessing though Moses had eventually secured enough carts and oxen to bear the brunt of the burden. Each and every item was carefully supervised and monitored through the day. She remembered how her father had told her that as the Israelietes were falling asleep each night, there were tireless Levites still working to dust, clean, and check each Tabernacle treasure. Every night. Datya had thought it strange that each item was cleaned at the nightly resting places. Why not wait until the people were settling for a time, and clean them as they were being placed back into the whole Tabernacle? Eventually she understood that her father saw his work as an offering to Yahweh. He was not able to fulfill a priestly work, for Aaron had not been his father, but he was able to work diligently servicing the Tabernacle's altars and ornaments. This he did with all his heart. Long had her father's commitment inspired the depth of her own.

Great distances were disrupted by the thickly packed crowds of people, but Datya finally saw a fully erect tent. The families she was passing by were Levite families whose sons were her father's cousins. She was close now, and the tent rising a ways before her looked more familiar with every step. The day's journey with Miriam had been long and tiring, but not because of the steps they had taken. Though they had gone far, the day had drained her because Miriam had all but confirmed her father's awful suspicion, and Ravit's terrible dream. How Datya would give anything to erase the day and trade its conversations for the simplicity of her everyday lessons. Miriam's voice had always been a treasure to her as it spoke life and wisdom, even wonder, but today that same voice brandished a dark sword at her, cutting her hopes down to be trampled beneath their feet. Passing into her family's tent, she offered her mother a brief, appropriate kiss and then sank to the woven mat already pulled out for her. She knew her mother would be dismayed that Datya did not wipe away the dust from her face and feet, but Datya's heart was too heavy to produce such an effort tonight. Tugging her wool cloak over her Datya pressed her eyes tightly together. Ziva, who had shared the other half of her mat since she was weaned, quietly landed beside her. Though their backs were separated only by the thin layers of their woolen blankets, Datya felt far from her sister. She had no doubt that Ziva had never known agony, at least not this bitter choking kind. No sympathy, nor sisterly embrace, would pass between them this night. Guilt added to her burdens before sleep claimed her. Her family was not even given the chance to meet her need, for she had offered them only her silence. Burning with shame for her harsh feelings, she spilt silent tears on the arm beneath her head. *Father, I need your racham. Send me your mercy, Lord.* Sleep, a mercy in its own way, claimed her quickly, quieting her mind for the night.

Datya was startled awake by the sound of Miriam's voice. She had loved and respected that voice for so long that it quickly commanded her attention, even from a dead sleep. Dawn was only moments away. She quietly stood, untangling her tunic from her sister's limbs. Though the pallet had always supported two in the past, she and Ziva were no longer little. Perhaps it was time to weave a new mat and leave this one to Ziva. It pained her to realize, yet again, that their sisterly bond was much like the lower edges of the mat where the dried and carefully woven plants were starting to pull away from each other from age and heavy use. Datya had seen before a sisterly bond that had only grown closer with passing years, her aunt and her mother displayed such an affectionate friendship, but the pattern hadn't seemed to pass on to Ziva and Datya.

Rarely did she awake early enough to see the flaming arms of the sun spreading across the dry hills. As curious as she was about God's glorious dawn, she wanted to know, even more, why Miriam was with her family this morning. In all her years as Miriam's apprentice, Miriam had never sought her out in the morning. Instead, she had always promptly attended Miriam's tent after gathering the manna she'd need for the day. Even as a little girl, Datya's mother and father had patiently taught her the general direction to take to find her teacher's tent, alerting her to the little clues, like spotting Miriam's husband's kin, to know when she was close. Of course, Miriam's tent was easy to identify. Her husband, who died long before Datya was born, had been the son of an embroiderer. Miriam had inherited several lovely pieces of stitching from the older woman. Always generous, Miriam had given several away, but had stitched a particularly skilled section to her tent's opening. Datya always felt rather noble passing through the decorated slit in Miriam's front wall.

Thankfully her sister woke on her heels and began shaking out the mat for the day even as Datya slipped into a fresh tunic her mother had thoughtfully laid out for her. It was her only spare, and would normally be saved for an evening marking the end of one of their journeys. Lisbet's concern must run very deep indeed for her to go through the trouble of finding the clean linen dress among their densely packed carts. Datya's eyes misted with gratefulness for her mother. Often the woman was quiet, dutiful and industrious, but she communicated little. It was hard to feel loved even while knowing she and her siblings were well cared for. Today, Lisbet had offered this small kindness as an unspoken, "I love you, Daughter," and the warmth of the rare morning greeting spoke more than volumes of words ever could. Datya heard their voices conclude, 'I thank you for sparing her for the week. Many changes are coming for her; for your family. I know you are all dedicated to the tasks of the Lord, but my prayers are with you nonetheless.' Miriam looked up to her student as she stood waiting; surely her pensive approach allowed all to see that Datya's tension remained. The questions and uncertainty spilling across her face must have been comical to Miriam for she raised her face to Datya with her usual delighted mirth pressing up the corners of her mouth and eyes. *Is she never downcast? Her joy returns so quickly!* With a flustered feeling all too familiar, Datya stood before her teacher aching to hear the explanation for her presence here this morning.

In the next moment, Miriam sent her to retrieve her bedding and whatever she would need. Ziva, who was typically, blessedly quiet in the mornings, handed the mat over with care. She seemed puzzled too, as she whispered goodbye. With her parents' permission Datya would be attending Miriam day and night for the next week! Never before had Miriam requested this of her family. It felt glorious to be invited into Miriam's life even more, and yet Datya realized it was an act much like the transfer of the precious timbrel. It was the next stage of her training, yes, but it was also the last. Grief rose as Datya's mind finished unraveling this little piece of the puzzle. She fell into place beside her mentor. An overwhelming thought caused her unease to rise like leavened bread left overnight; she would soon advance and leave her learning years behind her. The trouble was, she wasn't at all sure she wanted to grow past this stage, especially if it meant being separated forever from Miriam.

"You are doing it again, Datya," Miriam's voice broke into her mind as they entered Miriam's tent. Though the elder's tent was not far, certainly compared to yesterday's march, they had needed to pass by nearly all of the other Levite families in their section. Datya had spent every footstep ruminating on the mixture of fear and gratitude for the coming week. This tent, larger and more finely worked than her own, was one of the few in camp that would be completely set up with each evening stop. She often had 2 or 3 of the other widows stay with her on the journey nights - women who were older and alone, and had few relatives to aid them. But as she looked around she saw no additional bedding and realized that this time Miriam had reserved the honor just for her. Undoubtedly, Miriam had negotiated with other families to make a different provision for such widows this time around. Wondering why Miriam had not asked her mother for her service yesterday, Datya felt warmed by more than just the sunrise at the gift of Miriam's sole attention. Despite the swiftly approaching heartache, Datya knew she would always treasure the gift of this time spent with her guide.

"Doing what?" Datya mused, for she was still rolling over all of her unsettled thoughts. As expected, Miriam's chuckle, hoarser than it once was, filled the air following Datya's response.

"You are staring at life through those serious eyes again! And here I thought you would enjoy a week spent with your teacher!" Miriam's early teasing revealed much. The prophetess will be ever-joyous until the very last moment. She realized what she should have known all along that Miriam would not embrace grief before it's time; it was not her way. Even more so,

Datya felt Yahweh reveal to her that holding onto sorrow with a stranglehold did not honor Him either. The conviction was clear; the act itself seemed a mountain before her. And yet, if Miriam would not spend their time together in grief, then neither would she. It may be the only gift of thanks she would be able to offer her beloved guide.

Though her smile would surely not match her mentor's bright but weathered face, she turned it to her as sincerely as she could, "I think I will give your method a try, Miriam. That is, if you'll help me." Datya began checking Miriam's bundles and packs. "I suggest I make sure all of your packs are tight and ready to go, while you rest and tell me a story. Perhaps, one I've yet to hear?" Asking for a story was Datya's way of asking for more time. She knew Miriam would need to pour much into her this week, but first she wanted a few moments reminiscent of their beginning. When she had been so little, Miriam had often patted her hand to remind her that their partnership was a good thing and she had nothing to be nervous about. Though Datya had already busily approached the bundles of goods to make sure everything had survived the trip, she had no doubt that Miriam would have reached for her hand, offered that familiar pat and begun to soothe her with that ever-loving voice.

~ ~ ~

Miriam returned an affectionate smile to her sweet pupil. Loving, tender, Datya, worried as she was, was unwilling to cast sorrow over the day. Miriam knew well the young girl's pep didn't flow from the heart. Seventeen years the girl had grown in this hard-packed wild, how could Miriam fault her for being so serious and often downhearted? Miriam would indeed tell her a story, a living legend, rather, and perhaps Datya's smile would stretch a little wider today. "A story? Shall I? Hmm... I think, Datya, that your curiosity has been too long in check. You have seen the many strong carts of my brother's caravan? The protective way he watches his aides as they steady the load? Don't play timid with me, girl, I know you've heard the tittering around camp: 'What does the old man do with all the stones?' Well?" Miriam teased Datya all the more for her parents would never stand for even a root of nosiness stewing in their daughter's character, yet Miriam could see the curiosity tucked away in Datya's dark eyes. Having been raised to be a studious, quiet Levite daughter, it would be rather shameful to admit the overwhelming desire to know the secret Miriam dangled before her now.

Hands stilling, Datya confessed, "Yes, I've seen the caravan, Miriam. Once, my father told me he had seen how Moses rose before the Pillar of Fire had faded for the night and began checking each cart. He told me that Moses had several young men carefully hauling three of the large stones to the cart at the back of the line. I remember he said Moses seemed not to breathe as he watched the load, until it was secured." Datya bracketed the quiet admission with her usual reverence. While Miriam battled herself time and again to consistently honor the man who had done so much for Israel, Datya had no trouble viewing him as a great and godly gift to the tribes. And, of course, he was, but for Miriam, Moses was also her impatient, irritable little brother! A check rose in her spirit even as she thought of the judgement she passed over him for all too often the truth had been pointed out to her in a heated moment - she and Moses were mirror images. Two great leaders, full of fire and steeped in pride. Yes, they both battled the same demons, and walked with the same concentrated faith. All in Israel knew as much!

Datya had finished checking each and every parcel and roll that Miriam had unpacked after yesterday's long journey, so Miriam looped their arms together for the second time in as many days, nudging her toward the dwelling's opening. "Come dear one, Aaron's *nechadim* will be along to fetch all this; let's go and find our fill of manna." Miriam gestured at her weathered canvas home, knowing well that her brother's grandsons would indeed take good care of it all. She knew too that if they weren't prompt about it, the boys would face the wrath of her stern oldest brother. Though he too was younger than Miriam, his wisdom and care for her often made him a harbor in a storm for Miriam, especially since her gentle husband had left this world so long ago. The tittering tribes often whispered that Aaron had received a thrice dose of maturity, his own, his sister's and his brother's, for Miriam and Moses struggled more with controlling their tempers than with any other vice.

"Tell me Datya, what whispers have you heard about old Moses' caravan? What do the tribesman say and all the anxious wives? And Moses himself? What does he say?" More than once Miriam had walked behind the wives of her clansmen to hear their chatter about Moses' great 'heap of stones.' She knew the rumors and the flustered way her baby brother tried to keep the secret tied down like the edge of a desert tent when the whipping winds were at their worst. She had never truly agreed with his fierce desire to keep the hoard a secret, but she had done so at his request, often dispelling the rumors without offering a clue in return. They never stayed quelled for long, of course; nearly forty years of mystery and misdirection meant that bored minds couldn't be held back from their gossip. Truly, what people had ever loved an intrigue more than the descendants of Jacob? It was hard to pass complete judgement on these friends and relatives. They had gone from being busy day and night in a great city, to walking and wandering for days on end with only snakes and birds of prey for company. Many had found occupations that could be performed even without the permanence of a home and city, but too many more families lacked the ambition to practice at any skill other than tale-telling.

This time, when Datya answered, Miriam picked up on the nervous hitch in her voice: "They say he wears the oxen out for a pile of worthless stones. They say he plans to build a temple for himself, a hero's palace. My abba says no, that the stones are too flat for such a purpose. Still others suggest he was truly mad to defy Pharoah as he did, and in his madness took worthless stones - that all this time he has thought they were great plunder." Datya's young voice quavered as she spilled these long-quieted suspicions. "None of the rumors have ever seemed right, Miriam, but we cannot help but wonder when he is so tempestuously protective of them. Once Abba's brother Jovon, saw Moses strike at a boy who dared to peefk under the canvas!" Datya seemed as truly bothered by the secrecy as Miriam was amused by it, but she continued with the truth that all of Israel surely felt, "Great, I know he is Miriam, for he talks with Yahweh face-to-face. You and your brothers are champions of Israel! But he is not always kind, not always understood, not always," her student struggled, and quickly sputtered, "easy to follow." She shrunk a bit, not in fear, but with the effort of speaking aloud something she had kept muted for so long. Datya was only willing to tug out such personal musings for one among all the Israelites, and certainly her teacher expected nothing less than her full honesty.

Miriam's compassion quickly stirred for the girl; it was time to offer up the story for her young friend. "Datya, you are right that my brother is not easy to follow at all times. Let me tell you why. He is difficult to follow because he is not the one the Israelites should be looking to. Yahweh appointed him simply because the rest of our fickle hearts would never make it to the Promised Land without Moses' favor and care." Thinking of her own father, Miriam bristled, remembering the generations of nearly faithless Hebrew men who could have done the work Moses was doing now, but in their pagan-distilled confusion and fear had failed to undertake. Pausing to face Datya, Miriam spoke purposefully, "He is however a broken man like the rest of us, and therefore subject to things like temper, despair, and yes, even odd and unexplainable habits. However, the secret really isn't so eccentric once you know the truth. Would you like to know, Datya? You are preparing for a great role; it is not wrong for you to partake in this knowledge now." Miriam knew what the answer would be. She also knew that Datya would try to mask her eagerness for the tale. Once again, Miriam worked to withhold the chuckle that bubbled up so easily. How her student's demeanor tickled her!

"Yes, please, Miriam! I would be honored to hear it from you!" Datya settled herself onto the rough rock of a nearby outcropping, and offered Miriam a handful of the manna she'd been gathering as they walked along. The sweet heavenly bread was always better with a story. Miriam remembered the first time Datya had declared as much to her as a little girl. She had just finished explaining the order that the Israelites marched in, and why they did so, along with trying to help the young girl understand why Joseph's descendants were called by two names, neither of them Joseph. Datya's face had changed since the day her young face had marbled with confusion regarding Ephraim and Mannaseh, but it was still marked with innocent curiosity, another quality Miriam adored in her.

"Moses' carts," she began. "They are certainly more than just a pile of stones, and yet what value could they have? The answer, Datya, takes us all the way back to the former land, the Land of Captivity. Yes, Egypt is where the stones were hastily packed for this great exodus, but it is also where Moses received this task. You know, young one, of Moses' irregular beginnings, of the edict of death that through my brave mother and a rivertime bath for a princess turned into an adoption ceremony. You also know that our humble, erratic leader was then raised as a prince of the very land that aimed to snuff our culture out. Little more could you know than that since Moses does not speak of such times and our people are often bitter at the great differences of his upbringing that set him apart. They care not for the wisdom he built within those mudbrick walls, or the strength and courage instilled in him as he dwelt among peculiar, oppressive gods and ceremonies. I witnessed these things as I served the whims of his faithless Egyptian mother. I watched as she grew less fond of him as he aged, noting the way the enhancement fell off of her. He left boyhood behind and adopted the arrogant ways of the royal family. How could he not when they were his guides in life? And yet she began to pull away, having very little to do with him for his last years of royal life. Her promiscuity and excessence were her only cares, even her own flesh and blood children were often ignored or abused at her hands. Moses bore the worst of her vile ways. He lived between two nations, unwelcome to stay with one, and surely not welcome to return to the other. Think Datya, educated in the courts of one of the richest nations on earth, wise beyond many elders, and yet lonely and lost, knowing precious little of the One who had sent him there so many years ago."

With a grateful grin, Miriam sighed as Datya began to fan her gently with a dried palm that had fallen long ago. "Yet, I believe that even then, our Father was calling to him. The princess' lack of love was steadily mirroring her father's feelings for he had never welcomed the Israelite prince. I feel sure Moses would have been sent far away, perhaps even ritually sacrificed, yet in his anger he acted first. An Egyption was struck down, as you know, and my furious brother fled. His haste and temper cast him into his own desert wilderness." Miriam caught Datya's eyes once more for the girl would need to grasp the reality Moses had endured. "You must understand, much changed in him. Lonely shepherd hours whittled away the arrogance of a prince and kindled the humility of only the greatest leaders."

Miriam paused as she thought about her first sister-in-law, the dark and clever beauty Moses had married in those days of exiled rest. She had resisted Zipporah at first, although Moses had declared her bravery and exotic beauty as outstanding among women. Still, she and Zipporah had forged a kinship, and grown close in the brief time that the shepherdess with the lustrous dark skin lived with them. She had even shared Miriam's tent for a time, after Moses made it clear he had little time for the woman he'd missed so much. Miriam buried the irksome memory deeply, knowing that Datya waited for the promised explanation. She must try to put away, for now, thoughts of her lost sister. All of Israel had thought it was the love match of a century. Moses' joy at crossing the Red Sea and seeing his enemy fail for the last time had been drowned in his loneliness for his wife. Yet, his father-in-law had delivered her so soon after that mighty miracle. Miriam and all the Israelites had rejoiced, believing that Moses' temper and erratic ways would settle once and for all, that he would be happy, and lead them to the Promised Land in peace. How wrong she'd been. Perhaps it was his obsession with the stones, or perhaps it was the great burden of the needy Israelites, he was never able to rekindle the fire that he'd had with the wife of his youth. All too soon it was too late. Zipporah had lived, forgotten, in his shadow, the other women often calling her "the widow with the living husband," and then she was gone. Some say it was a seasoning sickness, that her people couldn't handle this forsaken land, though it was not so very far, nor different, from Zipporah's homeland. Others, Miriam included, said the grief of abandonment had quenched her life.

Datya broke into her reminiscence with a gentle touch on her shoulder, "Are you alright Miriam? Your face is flushed. How sorrowful you look!"

Miriam brightened for Datya's sake, it had all been so long ago anyways. "Let's find out about those stones, shall we? Moses spent many years in the land of his first wife, Zipporah. In time, Yahweh spoke to Moses, called him out of the nearly solitary life, told him to rescue millions, told him that this was why he'd been raised in a family not his own, educated to the highest degree, groomed with the fire of princes in his soul. So Moses departed his second adopted family's land for a vision that seemed as impossible as bringing life back to the Egyptian felled by his own hands. You know dear, the great lore of the many arguments held in Pharaoh's hall as Moses and Aaron fulfilled the words of I Am. Moses was torn apart those many weeks waiting for God's hand to finally move. In the evenings, Aaron returned to his family, a hero, but Moses returned an outcast. Many times the elders of our people raged at him, demanded that he leave for good, even discussed, from the sickness of their abused and corrupted hearts, stoning him. No one could see Yahweh's hand on Moses, and so few even knew the Great One who had sent him back to us." Bitterness stole into her voice remembering the way forgetfulness had spread like a plague among her people. Once, the sons of Jacob had thrived in Egypt with Yahweh's name ever on their lips. But, in the time before the great Exodus, his name and even his memory were largely abandoned. Only a few, faithful elders, and young fiery leaders like she and Aaron still cried out for the God of Abraham to come and rescue them. "One evening, in great despair Moses came to me; he had said Aaron would hear no more complaints from him." Miriam's words grew even softer, realizing that she had never before shared the private conversation of that long ago night.

God's great spirit was urging her to continue, but the tale was old, so long kept in her heart's inner chambers, it was hard to chisel it free again. She knew well her steadfast student's trustworthy heart, but it was difficult to share Moses' anguish none-the-less. "That night, Moses wept as my children and husband slept behind a low mud wall in our home. I thought he grieved for his enslaved people; I thought seeing the horror of their bondage all those weeks had finally broken his gruff exterior. Then he spoke, and I was equally shaken, 'Miriam, I had always known our people were losing themselves in this swirling city of gods and kings. I had always known that their light and heritage were at risk, but now I see that their fire for Yahweh is all but out. Embers of the promises spoken to Abraham, Isaac, and Jacob long ago are all that are left. Why have they turned from him so quickly?' Though I would have argued that four hundred years was enough time for any people to forget a covenant, I was left in tears as he continued, 'Miriam, when I Am found me in the land of my wife, I knew next to nothing of Him. I knew only what you told me in stolen moments in Pharaoh's palace. Since those days, on the long journey back to Egypt, Yahweh himself has had to reveal all to me. I had thought to find elders, priests like our own father, whom you've told me about, who could share the true nature, the history of this covenant God with me. Where are such men, Miriam? For the ones I have found, host not only Pharoah's idols, but idols of all the other slaves and tribes in their possession. And this is the people Yahweh seeks to rescue?' He could say no more, Datya, he was broken by what he saw, what he heard, by the faithless nation who had let go of their God." Miriam struggled with the thought of sharing the tragic revelation with Datya, whose naive life had never known days of slavery, and as of yet, had never known the Promised Land either.

"Is it true, Miriam? Can the Tribes really have been so lost? Your father was a priest, was he not? Surely he remained pure and called the Israelites to holiness?" Datya's voice proved she was shaken by the thought of her ancestors embracing the endless variety of gods that paraded through the cities of the Nile. Miriam had shared before that Egyptian nobles believed the Great River itself drew in gods from all the nations; they were welcome as long as they submitted to Pharoah above all. Israel's elders like to say that Pharoah's rage was so explosive, in the end, because the Israelite God had never bowed to his will.

"Yes, Datya, the man who sired my brothers and I was a priest, and I dearly loved him as a little girl. Looking back, I see how like Aaron and Moses he truly was. Like Moses, he was volatile in temper and emotions that could swell and shrink like a great sea. Yet, I saw Aaron in him too; a quiet leadership whose example compelled those around him, sometimes to their spiritual rot. I wish that I could tell you of his zeal for Yaweh. At times, I know he was sensitive to the Spirit, and embraced righteousness. But, Moses' words were sadly true, even of our own father. He never brought other gods into our home, but he never denounced them either. The practices of the Egyptians were not vulgar to him. He raised our family not so very different from that of an Egyption family. He was only one of many elders, many so-called priests of our heritage, and most were even further from God. Not all hearts were lost in the mire of the Nile gods. Devotion to Yahweh still existed amongst the Israelites. Those voices were mere whispers, lights that sputtered only a small illumination in vast and evil darkness, largely drowned out in the culture of a wicked city." Pausing to gather breath and dust off her garments, Miriam gestured to Datya that they must begin walking. They had both heard the silver trumpets signal departure several moments ago.

Clans stretched in every direction had already begun moving ahead towards the great Column of Cloud. Such a vast people, carts and herds, children and invalids moved precious little in the span of a day. They were in no danger of being left behind, but it would be best to remain fairly close to the carts hauling her tent and their supplies. The need to continue both the journey and the story promised to her student meant that her pace would be slight and she would need to keep watch for more places to rest. Datya would care well for her through this week. Miriam was thankful to be walking with such a sweet, compassionate young woman, but she was keenly aware of the Lord's final directives to her. Datya must be given the Story of Moses' Stones, and many others, before Miriam took her last breath of wilderness air. A great majority of the lessons they had shared over the years had been delivered in the same manner, spoken through the dust and hum of the mighty caravan. Though it was an exhaustive classroom, both women had grown in their own way from both the journeys and the lectures.

Steering around the leavings of one of thousands of oxen, Miriam continued, pacing her words with a slow steady meter, "I had thought, after that night, that Moses would be despondent, too broken-hearted to be much use to Israel. Overcoming his dark moods had always been a mighty exertion for him. I did not see him for three days. Aaron told me that Moses was fasting, that he would speak with no one. Many puzzled as he sat in public prayer wrapped in mourning cloth and masked with the ashes that marked his grief. I joined Moses in fasting and prayer, though I could hardly sit idle for my family depended on me. The morning following his commitment, Moses found me early. I had heard from Aaron the night before that this day, he and Moses would be approaching Pharoah for a fifth time. As he drew near, I realized he was joyful, exuberant almost. I was shocked, because his despair over Israel's decay had been so intense. He took hold of my shoulders saying, 'He has revealed purpose to me! I am given a gift, Sister!' I truly thought him mad in that moment, but I was more than a little relieved. My curiosity was satisfied quickly as he continued, 'I Am has told me to write it all down! I am to make a record for the Tribes! All the way back to Jacob, back further to Abraham, and yes, even to the Creation of the world!' Datya, I know you are not used to the thought of me being speechless, but trust me, in that moment I could find no words!" Miriam chuckled heartily with the memory, finally needing long moments of deep, thirsty breathing to recover from the merry recollection.

Datya's curiosity resurfaced with mingled excitement and confusion, "The stones, they somehow record all of that? How can that be?" Her face betrayed her mind's effort to sort out the mystery. Miriam couldn't blame her. When Moses had first shared his extraordinary plan, she had been stunned and confused as well. She'd asked the same questions as Datya. "It is hard to grasp Datya, but I will tell you what I know. Only a few of us remain who are aged enough to remember the great homes and statues of Egypt. More amazing than the grand columns and city architecture, were the engravings and carvings. You could find them on door frames, bricks, foundation stones, any smooth surface. The carvings were information, the Egyptian's way of telling who or what or why, or even when." Miriam wished she could show Datya the stones that had been finished so far, for it would be easier to explain it to her then.

"Yes, Miriam, I have heard my uncles talk of the images. They say anything that can be uttered can also be marked down in these carvings or paintings. So, you mean to say, that Moses' stones are for the markings? But for what purpose? Why record all of history if he keeps it to himself? Why record it at all in an Egyptian system none of us can understand?" Datya was flustered by the burgeoning unanswered questions, and Miriam was delighted by the girl's swift thinking.

Dropping another comforting pat upon her hand, Miriam steered towards the outer edges of the strolling camp. They would need to get outside of this great moving people to take any sort of dust free rest. She could see a small patch of dried, low growth; it would be just the spot to finish the story of Moses' Secret Stones. Miriam silently praised their God for saving this patch of turf for their rest. It hadn't been trampled or scavenged by the hungry beasts that had been driven by it. Her breath had held out for the first hours of the day, but how she longed for a deep rest. Prayer stirred within her, the unspoken words, the tie between her soul and Heaven. *Beloved Yahweh, hold me fast in these last days. Be the strength that moves these aged feet through this vast land. I know your perfect rest is coming; uphold me for these final moments with Datya.* Miriam's prayer for mercy, for *racham*, went up unknown to Datya, but she wouldn't be surprised if the quiet girl by her side was praying also. Without a touch of the Lord's mercy she felt sure her body would give out before she could deliver Datya's final lessons.

With her student's compassionate assistance, she lowered gently to the sun-scorched grass. She smiled at Datya as they both felt the tremors beneath them. Though the pace was always slight, the shuffling tribes and the many cultures that had fled with them shook the very earth with their parade. "Moses does not inscribe the stones with the Egyptian method of carving. Yes, he knows how to understand all their images and designs, but he knows that none among Israel have the desire to learn such. Moses revealed to me that Yahweh spoke that our very own Hebraic words would be carved into the stones! All of our history, all of Yahweh's words, will be recorded in the very way we speak! Though you have never seen them, some of these words exist already, on the stones Yahweh inscribe the law onto." Miriam's mirth flew free, bubbling from her lips once again; Datya's wonder was comical and delightful. "When Yahweh instructed the rest of us to gather the gold and jewels of our masters, He instructed Moses to seize the oxen and stones dedicated to Pharoah's prized projects. They have journeyed with us ever since - stones called out of Egypt! Moses has been charged with forging a carved collection of our words, by ascribing an image to each sound we say. Yahweh's words will go down on them forever, just like the Tablets of Ten He gave us so early in this journey!" Finishing, she could see the awakening awe on her dear one's face - the reaction, once again, worth the laughter that Miriam loved so much. Truly she lived amongst a serious people, but her love of joy came from I Am. And no custom would cause her to stifle it.

CHAPTER FIVE

Hustling past a dozen or so tents of the Levite elders, who like Miriam, were permitted to set up their homes each night, even in the midst of travels, Datya rushed to find her family. Her father, Cohen, would not be there, of course. Datya wondered if his burdens had been light these last two days. Or were they cumbersome? Did he think of his family as he watched over Yahweh's treasures? Or were they the last thing on his mind? It was strange to see her father so committed to caring for the family for long months, only to see him equally, and separately, devoted to the tabernacle during his rotation. Often, they saw him only once or twice in the many weeks he served in the care of Yahweh's home. He almost seemed to be a different man altogether. With a wispy giggle that didn't match the weight of her heart, she recalled the time that Father had been called to his post just after Idan had started taking steps. As the weeks passed, Idan had burst into toddlerhood with constant joy and adventure. On the day Cohen returned to his family, father and son had hardly recognized each other. Idan, whose infant memory had nearly forgotten his father, and Cohen, because his son had changed so much. The tiny person bearing his son's name had left babyhood behind; Cohen had been unprepared and blindsided by the change. Of course, many of Datya's closest companions were Levite daughters as well, and she knew they felt the same about their fathers. The girls of other tribes would likely not be able to imagine such a life. Though perhaps their fathers had other responsibilities that she knew nothing about? The truth was, she had never sought to understand the other clans and their ways, beyond what Miriam shared in the histories. Abandoning her thoughts to the footpath, Datya increased the pace of her steps. She had a task to do; it was time to set day-dreaming aside.

After Miriam had concluded the story of the Great Stones, Datya had attempted to flood her with questions. More often than not, Miriam would gladly speak to the concerns of her student, but on this day she had sent Datya quickly away. "Check on your family, Datya," she had said. "They spared you willingly for this week, but you will trek through the people once a day to see that your mother is not in need." A smile rose unbidden as she passed more and more resting sojourners. Miriam's concern for her mother was just one of many acts of compassion she would model through the next week. Many thought that Miriam had arrogance in excessance. They assumed with the great privileges and freedoms that Miriam enjoyed, she must also be riddled with pride. In sage-like grace, she had always let others think what they would, often telling Datya that the Creator's voice was more valuable than all the noise and chatter of the many Israelites. Of course, Datya knew that many felt this way about Miriam simply because she had once dared to argue, publicly with Moses. Just the thought of such boldness cinched her breath! Argue with Moses! She herself had seen Miriam bristle with frustration towards her brother, steaming every now and then over their differences of opinion. But never, never had she heard Miriam speak to him with anything but respect, and the adoration of an older sister. Her teacher had long refused to share the details of the long-ago event with her, saying that Datya must learn how to serve their heavenly Father in this role, and that memory held no instructional value. Truly, she believed there was more to the story than that, but she would not argue with the prophetess. Perhaps this week would usher in the moment when Miriam finally revealed the story.

Shifting amidst the gathered families, Datya turned in every direction. She had not wanted to leave Miriam alone for long, even though Aaron's *nechadim* had already put her tent in place for the night. *Where is Mother? I have searched through most of the Levites already!* It was so unlike her mother to let the family fall out of their normal place between her father's older and younger brothers and their wives and children. Turning eastward, Datya headed closer to the Gadite tents. As suspicion lightened, she realized she would have to retrace her steps and painfully passby Miriam's tent to find her mother. Her mother's sister had been married into the sons of Gad; with the Levite tents searched to no avail, she decided to check there. With only two children and no husband to care for this week, Lisbet may be bedding down with her sister's family. Her mother's frugality had likely selected that option to save the coin that would need to be spent on hired men to erect the tent each night. She must find her quickly, and return to Miriam! Something in her spirit urged her not to waste a moment of this precious week with the elder who had taught her so much.

Though her feet already flew at a pace likely to draw attention, she hastened her steps. Drawing closer to the Gadites who always traveled directly ahead of the Levites, she thought she had seen her little brother, the sweet, curly head bouncing along as he ran through the reclining families. "Idan!" Datya called to him as she came close enough for him to see her. With eyes that didn't share the fatigue of the rest of the Tribes, Idan threw himself into Datya's arms giggling. He was holding a small piece of wood that looked as though it had been on the desert floor longer than the Israelites. He must have seen it as a great treasure for he shoved it so close to Datya's face that her eyes crossed each other's paths. Joining her giggles to his, Datya kissed the sweaty little one and bid him show her where Mother was.

She had often wished that Mother and Father had older boys, boys that could carry the weight of the family when Father was gone, but she wouldn't trade the sweet one tugging her along now for anything. Long ago, she too had run wildly about through the exhausted caravaners. Her father had told her that she had been the swiftest of the children, often eluding her mother when it was time to rest for the evening. The stories of Uncle Joshua swooping her up above his head to return her to her parents were her favorites. In those days, Joshua who wasn't truly an uncle at all, had visited their family often in the evenings. He and Cohen would spend long hours discussing the Law and the Tribes, much longer than Datya could keep her eyes open. When Ziva had come along, Joshua had split his evening visits between them, spinning first one girl and then the other wildly about, and winning dozens of peals of laughter in the process. A frown surfaced as she and Idan trotted along. Uncle Joshua's visits had been far apart in recent years. Whether he was kept too busy by Moses' work - she now knew to be the work of the Great Stones - or whether it was his own family that kept him occupied she didn't know. Of course, when she had been little Uncle Joshua had not had his grandchildren yet. Doting on the daughters of his good friend made all the sense in the world, but now he had a handful of little ones from each of his sons. The next generation of his name-bearers were an acceptable reason for his absences in their home, and of course she understood his delighted pride. Datya released the happy memories to dwell on another time as she realized that Idan had finally brought them to their family.

Lisbet greeted her daughter much more serenely than Idan had. Her mother's eyes couldn't hide the honor she felt at Miriam's insistence that Datya report to her once a day. It was another peg in the long tally of thoughtful actions Miriam had offered the family. Datya had overheard Miriam discussing her concern for Lisbet once, many years ago, when she'd first come under her tutelage. She had all but said that she would always honor and care for Lisbet since she was essentially adopting her eldest daughter from her. While Datya had never felt the loss of connection with her own mother, she knew that outwardly, her devotion did appear to be staked with the prophetess, rather than Lisbet. Miriam had said that Datya's mother was a rare jewel among the Israelites because she held nothing back from Yahweh. Not her husband. Not her children. Nor her finances nor her goods. "Are you well, Mother? Did you manage the journey with the children?" She took the cloth her mother offered and began wiping down Idan. He needed the flow of a gentle river to cleanse his little body, but a damp scrap would have to do.

"All is well, Daughter. Ziva was mindful today, and since your Father traded for the additional ox cart, I have so much less to carry. Idan's little body resting upon the bundles is a sweet sight to follow on these lengthy walks." Lisbet offered a tired, dusty smile at her daughter. Her own face bore the telltale evidence of being one of thousands of followers. Be it beast or friend, there was always someone in front of each and every one of them, save Aaron and Moses and those who led the way at the far eastern edge of the procession. Long ago Moses had given careful instructions to the people so they could move while preserving the distance between them, not so much to threaten their safety, and yet not so close that heat and flies stirred up sickness among them. The tribes always started out orderly, but the day never met its end with a tidily intact caravan. "Bless Miriam for her kindness in sending you! But you must tell her, 'Worry, not.' My sister's family welcomes us willingly. We will be safe and aided while you and your father are away." Lisbet was not one to hug her children, or hold on to them longer than necessary, but with her quiet assurance, tonight, she pulled Datya close and whispered her love. Datya was more than a little stunned, but sweetly squeezed her in return. Then she remembered. Of course, she hadn't really forgotten the ill news that Miriam was leaving her behind. For a fraction of time, in the rush to find her family, she had successfully buried the gut-wrenching knowledge, but no, not forgotten. Now, her mother's embrace reminded her that Datya's heart would break, and soon. Honoring the commitment she had made in her heart to not let sorrow have its day before its due, Datya said goodnight to the one who had borne her and nursed her and turned to make her way back to the one who had sealed her to holy work.

Gossip had never had much lure for Datya. She knew others relied on the habit, nearly as much as they relied on manna for sustenance. "Rotted tongues," as Miriam referred to the sin, had no appeal for her. She had seen too many injured spirits, needlessly sacrificed to the idol of gossip. She had seen the cursed speech weave it's fingers around the camp time and time again, reaching towards her family only rarely, but finding its target with Miriam often. As she so often said, Miriam had a "thickened skin covering her heart," often brushing aside rumors as one would swat the flies bred by the herds. Many times Miriam had gently but firmly suggested that she develop a thick skin herself, for one day the rumors would come as they did for all who lead. Datya's fervent hope was that by keeping her head down, focused on each day's task and nothing more, quietly going about her work would be enough to spare her the malicious words. Moses and Miriam rarely worked in the unseen manner that Datya favored and both were frequent targets of the people whose imaginations and tongues were far from honorable. Of course, perhaps it was impossible to hope to work discreetly with so many thousands of needs around them. Poor Moses. Even though she was young she had discerned that Moses had been dredged this way and that through the despicable muddied words her people flung so carelessly. Why her people seem plagued by the habit was beyond her grasp. Still for the wisened leader's sake, Datya almost wished she had the courage to share the story Miriam had told her of Moses' Great Stones. She wouldn't spill a word of it, of course, for Miriam had trusted her, but the desire to reveal it began to pulse within her.

Such a bizarre story! Jacob's people had always relied on Yahweh's voice, through prophets, through fathers, through priests, and even through prophetesses. The Creator faithfully created and called voices from among his Chosen nation to carry out his words and edicts. Those voices led the people; they spoke for Heaven. Why would Yaweh suddenly decide to use cold, hard stone to make His words known? Perhaps he too worried about the idol of gossip, perhaps Yahweh saw how the voices of the ones he called, often spoke for themselves when they should be speaking for him. When she returned to the tent, she would be burgeoning with all the questions. Would Miriam be willing to share more?

Though she was very near the tent now, Datya hesitated. Miriam had often chuckled at Datya's love of solitude. She would say, "Our Abba called this vast people out of Egypt, along with many co-laborers, and you think to find a spot to be alone? This wasteland would sooner sprout lush gardens as far as the eye could see!" Her statement bore testament to the fruitless land she called home, as much as it did to the foolishness of Datya's hopes. She hadn't meant to be unkind, but it dulled her joy nonetheless. Even at night, the Israelite camps did not know silence. Between the natural night noises of mankind and the shifting, grunting, wild noises of the herds, no one among Israel had known true solitude in many years. Datya wondered now, if Moses felt the same struggle towards silence. He had gone from a life among sheep and caves, to a life of ceaseless noise and demand. Could Moses' private character be, in part, the reason Yahweh often called Moses deeper into the wilderness with only Joshua, his equally reserved aid? Now that she thought about it, the long disappearances did seem like merciful provision. How would the Great Stones ever be finished with continuous din and chatter?

Inaudibly stepping into the dwelling that meant so much to her, Datya let her eyes adjust to the dimness. It was disconcerting to be walking in the brightness of the desert afternoon one moment, and then to have little light to see by in the next. Of course shame would flood her if she dared complain about the thick leather walls that served as their homes. They may keep the light out causing one's eyes to strain, but they also blessedly repelled some of the heat as well. Finally spotting Miriam, leaning against some packs in a reclined sleep, a smile rose and lingered over her teacher. She was pleased with how at home she felt in Miriam's tent. Pleased even more so that Miriam had rested for all the time it had required to check on her family. Before she had set out, Miriam had pulled out a sack of dried fruit that she had been given after the Tribes had passed a large nomadic family. With a mischievous grin transforming her face, she had whispered in childlike anticipation "This is just the right occasion to celebrate with something rare!" Datya was honored, of course, and subsequently blown away by the delicious chewy treats. She had never before tasted the strange fruits and she knew she would always remember the pleasure. A few more morsels while she waited for Miriam to rise would be a secondary delight. Perhaps she could convince her own father to make such a trade at the next opportunity; his demeanor often prohibited luxuries, but if Datya told him of the wonderful taste perhaps he could be convinced? Then again, Datya knew little of how he lived and ate while carrying the temple furnishings. It may be that her father had already sampled some exotic treat. She knew that Moses and Aaron fiercely saw to the provision of the Levite men, often gathering large offerings from the roaming tribes, to support them. It was within the realm of possibility that her father had received many abundant goods while apart from his wife and children.

Working her teeth, deliberately, through the hides of the gem-like sweets, Datya's mind wandered to Moses. She had spared only awestruck thoughts for the leader as a child. Now, with increasing frequency and curiosity, she wove through a maze of questions, hoping to understand the man who had blazed a bold path on behalf of slaves who had once rejected him. What caused him to be so steady among a people so faithless? Who knew the secrets to his moods, more changeable than the wilderness wind that whipped the sides of the tent even now? Truly, she never expected to know the answers to these mysteries or the dozen other puzzles Moses represented, but she couldn't shake the thought that understanding Israel's mightiest man would help her be a better leader.

Though her curiosity was certainly far from sinister, it was also unlikely to be quenched. She had been a party to only a small portion of conversations with the man, those more than likely an act of benevolence deposited upon her as Miriam's disciple. She knew that he had adopted many sons of the tribes to be a part of his household over the last several years. Often the boys saw their natural families only once or twice a year. Those who served in Moses' private camp were a cloistered unit, set apart and unlike their neighbors, though borne of women from every tribe. All knew that the boys seemed to transform into sturdy, wise, and righteous young men fairly overnight. It was beginning to dawn on Datya. Moses' great calling, the edict to form the Hebraic words on stone, was so vast, so important, that many must be trained to the work. Some of the camps snickered, saying the boys were merely servants, ordered about because of Moses' pride, like the Egyptian eunuchs who served in the palaces. Datya's father had always believed that untrue, frowning at such injudicious comments. The young men who were chosen quickly became intelligent, respectful, hard working apprentices. Their integrity shone brightly despite the discrete nature of their labor. Surely they would not commit to the work so wholeheartedly if the edict did not call to them as well.

There must be a wondrous lure as each young man saw the Hebraic words set in stone for the first time. All this time a league of Israel's descendants had been learning this puzzling new art, while her people largely knew nothing about it! Deliberation kindled; Why did Moses strap the great secret down so tightly? Surely the camp would be better off knowing what work their sons were sent to, rather than being left in the dark. Her people puzzled her once more. So many families were desperate for the honor of having their son selected as an apprentice to Moses, but Moses still believed that if his purpose was made known the Israelites would reject it. Datya wandered now what her own father would think of the great plan. Would he support the Israelite's having their own written words? Or would he be furious that Moses, once again, seemed to be pedaling his Egyptian influence amongst the Tribes? One thing was certain, the Israelites detested the princely roots that still dangled from their leader, though Datya believed, like Miriam, that he had been transformed through his own wilderness.

"Well, dear one, your face is more pensive than when you left," an adored timbre broke into her thoughts. "Your mother was not well?" Miriam didn't fool her for even one moment. She knew that Lisbet was able to care for herself and her children just as she always did. Her mother was ever steady and self-sufficient. She never complained, and other than normal travel fatigue, she never seemed to give out from the weight of her family. She was sure of her place, unlike worrisome Datya and carefree Ziva.

"Mother is well and Idan and Ziva behaved for the day's walk. We have no need to worry over them." She batted away Miriam's gentle teasing with her riposte. A pause breathed fresh air on her hope that Miriam would be free with her knowledge as evening stirred. "Miriam. I don't understand many things about Moses' Great Stones. Why does he take on so many stewards? Why does his household stay so shut off from the people? Surely if he let his work be known, the people would rally and all this gossip would be a thing of the past." Datya stopped to breathe. She had meant to sound more composed in her curiosity. Instead, like the fabled Rock that had flowed with *ma-yim*, water for her thirsty people, it had all surged from her at once.

The laughter of one who had lived a lifetime filled the air. "Perhaps, Datya, perhaps. Moses' ways are peculiar, indeed, and many are the tribesmen who find fault with him. But none, Datya, have authority over him barring Yahweh himself. We cannot force Moses to reveal his work. Those of us who have tried to appeal to him have paid for the mistake dearly." Miriam's face took on a rare pained quality, a long ago memory flitting agonizingly across her leathery skin. The older woman's hand trembled as she brought it close to her cheek as though she would cradle her face in her palms, yet the fingers fell away, just as quickly, sinking into the folds of her tunic.

Shadowed dread hovered within the tent, darkening what light made it through the small, fluttering opening. Datya hardly knew if the woman was experiencing physical pain, perhaps from the overexertion of the day, or mental anguish? A memory, but of what? Would she share more? Her own voice hoarse with confusion, shattered the uncomfortable pause, "What is it, Miriam? What troubles you?"

Long moments of silence and stillness answered her. Datya wished she could recall the question, and cancel the tormenting memory her teacher was clearly enduring. With great sorrow, the prophetess turned to her student, "Another story needs telling before you will understand why the Israelites are too afraid to press Moses for answers. Still, they are not too afraid to cause him endless headaches through their complaints and tale-telling."

<div style="text-align:center">~~~</div>

Even to her own ears, Miriam realized her voice was slow in coming, croaky with age and dust when it finally left her throat. *Where to begin? How does one explain the behavior of Israel's greatest man?* "Moses had no chance of becoming a model Israelite. He grew up in luxury, and yet shunned by the family who bore his care. When the opportunity to embrace a new life came, it was with an entirely different culture, one my own mother and father would not have chosen for my baby brother. Many years later, after enduring his private grief and turmoil,

Moses was finally ushered back into the fold of the Israelites. The reception was cold, and Moses' speeches were often met with the offer to stone him." With a shudder, Miriam recalled the many dark nights her family had housed Moses, protecting him from the volatility of slaves, left too long under their burdens. "He found himself in a place he loathed, speaking for a people he felt little connection to, to a king he would rather never see again. He had ever been a private man, for he grew up with no trustworthy companion, but in those days he turned inward to himself even more."

Miriam's heart broke once again for her brother. It was almost comical to her how she could feel both furious at and protective of him all at once. "His loneliness meant ample time to be in the Lord's presence where his righteousness grew into the great filament between our nation and our Creator. Many, including Aaron and myself, hoped that when he reunited with his wife, Zipporah, he would be soothed and truly make a new start with the people he had come from. We had never met Zipporah." Thoughts rushed back to her, visions of the woman, so beautiful even long after her youthful years were spent, while her husband still shepherded. "She was not a daughter of Israel, but we knew Moses adored her. She had been sent to stay in her father's house while Moses verbally sparred for our freedom. Still, we all pinned our hopes on her influence. Finally, the Red Sea parted for us and buried our enemies. For the people, freedom was no longer far in the distance; it was a day's journey away. Within days, there she was, Moses' beautiful shepherdess wife had arrived. He was overjoyed for several days." Miriam recalled the moment Moses had swept his wife into his arms. Many men among the elders had frowned at the public embrace, but Miriam and Aaron had grinned like children. They had been so sure that Zipporah was the answer to Moses' ongoing torment. Half-hearted snickers had matched the general assumption that Moses and Zipporah would not be seen for days, but would remain in Moses' tent. Alone and terribly happy. *Of course, my young Datya doesn't need to hear that detail. If only it had been so!*

"I know not how to describe the great failure we witnessed next. Aaron believes the interruptions of squabbling families caused the couple to fight. I believe that Moses' commitment to the stones, to prayer left no room in his heart for Zipporah. His sons, who knew their mother's people far better than their father's, were distant. One could tell they struggled, that this new life was not one they chose. We all began to realize that Moses, wonderful rescuer that he was, would never fit the mold of the Israelite elders. He was something altogether new and different for us." How he had given the elders grief, bewildering them over and over with his judgements, his temper, and his headstrong ways! "We had compassion in abundance for one another, even for Zipporah, who was so foreign to us, but we had little grace for Moses." Sighing, she wondered for the hundredth time, *would grace have made a difference for Moses and Zipporah? Who could have ministered to the man who walks with God?* Age hadn't dimmed Moses' vibrant strength, but it had made him impenetrable, heart and soul, even for the wife whose love had sustained him from afar. Of course, age alone couldn't be blamed for the mysteries of Moses after the Red Sea, but no one could discern what really caused Moses' great pulling away.

"Within weeks, Moses came to me quietly, asking for a place among my household for Zipporah. He had already negotiated engagements for both of his sons, whose tents were placed very close to his own. I argued fiercely that her place was with her husband; I was furious that he would dishonor her so! Moses continually promised that it was for only a time, until he had accomplished the work of Yahweh. Then he would reclaim his family and she would be honored by him and among all Israel, as the wife of Moses." A lowering of her voice foreshadowed her regret. "Perhaps, I should not speak of it even now, though I know it is my own pride for I long to forget my shame. Still I think you must know all the history, even of Moses and Miriam. Many times I have struggled with the urge to lash out at Moses for his foolhardy ways; that day was black for me, but I managed, summoning great restraint, to bury deep my anger at our anointed guide." Miriam recalled how her muscles had shook with fury at what Moses suggested. Only the God of Heaven had been able to prevent her from letting her temper loose that day. And what a temper it would have been. Though her hands had long been dedicated to ministering to others, that day she had itched to turn them into rods of chastisement. To hit the man who stood so close to God would have surely been the end of her life, but the temptation to strike at him had nearly overcome her. It pained her to share the rest of the account, but Datya needed to know how thoroughly she deserved, had indeed earned, the painful discipline Yahweh had meted out.

"I welcomed Zipporah into my family. You know that all my own sweet babes, save one daughter, long married by that point, did not live to see this wandering life. I had been widowed too, only months before our Great Exodus. I was glad to have a new sister to share my tent. Even her sons' infrequent visits were a delight to my home." Moses had initiated tutoring for Gershom and Eliezer on their very first day in camp. A highly revered selection of Levite elders had been tasked with teaching Moses' sons everything from the history of the Hebrews to their modern customs.

She could still see sweet and fiery Zipporah in her mind as she thought about her long lost sister-in-law. "When she had arrived in camp, all could see that she was exotic, a touch wild, but beautiful, even beyond the Egyptian women." The shepherdess had been tall and upright, she didn't look to the ground like the women Miriam and Datya knew. Even after they had been freed from slavery, few of the Israelites walked so proudly, so lively and bold as Zipporah. Though a small portion of her kind had been found among the variety in Egypt during Miriam's lifetime, Miriam knew that Zipporah was different, even from them. All the Israelites knew. Something within her they could not see had made her Moses' equal, though she was a woman. "Oh, Datya, she was so unlike the Israelite women, and yet wise, strong, and kind. When Moses pulled away from her, her spirit seemed to dissolve. I have rarely witnessed such devastation before. My beautiful new sister began to fade, losing herself every bit as much as she was losing Moses. Zipporah had been in my tent for little over a year when Moses sent a messenger. Her sons, so often given to the work of study, were to be fully dedicated, and ceremonially consecrated, to Moses' holy work. "It is an honor," his message said, but Zipporah understood the meaning; she was only the woman who bore them now. Nothing more. She demanded an audience with him and began railing at the sky that he had the nerve to divorce her like this, from himself, from her own flesh and blood."

Zipporah didn't begrudge the opportunity for her two sons, but she was unnerved by the suddenness and the coldness of Moses' announcement. Had he come to her and discussed it, given her time to prepare, treated her with compassion, the arguments may have faded away. "The law gave him the right to conscript their sons, and Zipporah's fight fell on deaf walls. Few among the Israelites know what really conspired in those days, but even fewer felt Moses was right. Rarely did the Tribes agree on anything, and certainly not in the defense of a foreigner, but Zipporah had meant hope for us, and we all longed to defend her. Still I said little to Moses for he would not hear it. Aaron tried to bring Moses to a place of sense, but Aaron too failed to get through to our hardened brother. Yahweh pressed on me, on many of us, that Moses was our leader, and we were to humbly follow him." It had been only one of many hard seasons of conviction for her. Moses' private battles seemed to bring out Miriam's private demons. "How hard that was, Datya! I love my brother, he has been through great suffering, but for a time I wanted to berate him into the very dust! If Yahweh had let me unleash it, I feel certain that my tongue would have lashed

Moses with devastating fire as the sun does to this land each dawn."

Datya looked nearly frightened by the strength of her tutor's words. Had Miriam not been feeling the rush of that long ago anger, she probably would have chuckled at the astounded look on Datya's sweet face. Datya whispered, "I had no idea Miriam. My father and mother never speak of Moses' first wife. I never realized it was such a dark tale. What happened to her? I mean, I know that she died many years ago, but did they ever reconcile?" Miriam could tell by her soft tone that Datya only half wanted to hear how the story played out, but Miriam never began a tale without finishing it. The history, half-known, would be a stumbling block for Datya. All-known it would compliment her crown of wisdom.

Though her legs were weak from many years of walking under burden, and though the days were quickly using up the last of her strength, Miriam's feet were tempted to pace. Datya had learned much at her knee in this very tent, though nearly always on a different, new patch of earth. For all the pleasant memories, it was likely they would both agree that the best lessons had been taught in the sunlight. With her feet propelling her onward, it was always a bit easier to let the stories, even the tragic ones, pass through her lips. Both the awful trembling of her weakened body, and the deepening evening precluded any chance walking out the remainder of the tale. With a sigh, Miriam prepared to reveal the end of Zipporah's tragic days amongst the Tribes. "After many weeks, Aaron spoke to me that Moses was finally seeing relief in his workload. The hierarchy which still governs the camp, the judges for each tribe and family, had finally begun to work. These wise men had shifted the weight of this great people off of Moses. He would be our leader still, but he would be freed to work on the Great Stones, and free, hopefully to reclaim his wife. We were so convinced that he would come for her that we shared with her the news; her sorrow and longing had turned her into a shadow of her former self." Miriam thought of that day, how Zipporah had not been cheered, even though the news was happy. Perhaps Zipporah had known, or perhaps she had just given up hope. "More months passed, but Moses never retrieved Zipporah. One morning she could not rise from her pallet, so we nursed her as best we could. The next morning she could not lift her arms or open her eyes. As far as we could tell, there were no other symptoms. She didn't seem to be in pain; she made no complaints. Even our best herbalists were puzzled. She was gone forever within days. In all, she traveled with us for less than two years before she died." Here Miriam felt tears quicken. Years of witnessing hardship and horror had left her with what the elders called a "thick hide," but Zipporah's memory would always bring weeping. She had known Zipporah so briefly, and yet she had felt a true sistership with her. The days when Zipporah's grief hadn't clouded her personality had often found the two laughing, singing, and sharing one another's cultures.

"Upon learning of her death, Moses' grief was genuine; he seemed more broken than any man in camp could be after losing his mate. The camp didn't move for many weeks, and even the work of the stones ceased. Despite his grief, his regret, the people judged him harshly. All these many years, Datya, one thing has held constant, there is no grace for the man they call Moses." With a squeeze in her conscience, Miriam quietly confessed that she too had never borne much mercy for her brother. Her own distraught mind began to lash out with the many reasons Moses wasn't worthy of mercy: he was erratic, moody, temperamental, unreachable, and, the most heartless, he had brought it on himself. Quieting the turmoil, Miriam's head shook as though to clear away the judgement. She knew better. Yahweh had shown her in her very own life. Mercy had nothing to do with what a person had earned; it had everything to do with the God whose love would outlive them all.

Did Datya hear the tragedy and believe the story over? Would she accept it when Miriam revealed her own sin? Or would the girl's loyalty surge in fierce denial? She pushed on. A teacher's greatest struggle was revealing her weakness to her student, but it must be done, for Datya's benefit. "Datya, this is the part of the story that you have only heard murmurs of. This is the part where I confess great sin, and where you can learn great lessons." Miriam reached out, letting her palm mold gently to Datya's cheek. She hoped the young girl never endured the punishment she had, never knew the pain of skin that betrayed her. "After Zipporah's loss, I managed to offer compassion to Moses. I was angry at him, for her life's early close, seemed very much his fault, but I was also genuinely saddened by his heart-ache." She remembered well how he had wept, how he had slept outside, with no blankets, no comfort, how he had shredded his clothes, how he had taken no food the first two weeks.

"Seeing his raw, broken spirit, I wanted badly to question him. Why had he set Zipporah aside if she was so dearly loved? Even then I felt the Spirit of God urge me to hold back, and so I did. I sometimes felt as though I had the greatest control of my tongue in all of Israel, a prideful thought that had come from years of practice with two bull-headed brothers. Finally, Moses purified himself once again. He spent a week in the Tent of the Presence, and then ordered the camp broken down. We were to begin moving, and would not make full camp again for a whole moon." She thought back to that grueling journey. Moses rarely kept the camp in such a temporary status for so long. Often their journeys were little more than a week before they found enough tufts of dried brush to feed the herds. The pace of grief, the month-long trek had taken its toll on many; it had certainly not endeared him to the people.

"Datya, you have heard whispers, I am sure, of the time when 'the Great Prophetess was cast out'?" The question was raised more to direct Datya to prepare for what was coming than in need of an answer. The answer would be affirmative, for it was a favorite legend among the gossiping masses.

Datya nodded, the concern still rode high in her heavy eyes, "I have heard it, though my mother and father have often refused to tell me why you were sent out from the camp. They always say, 'it is Miriam's story to tell, if she will.' Lack of patience made Datya's voice sting as her frustration turned towards the people. "Little truthful insight can be overheard from the tale-telling of the huddled wives. It seems such a foreign thought, Miriam! How could one as wise and devoted as you be cast out?" A stricken countenance stared at Miriam, waiting for the tale to be set right. No doubt hoping that it was all a mistake, the hope that her teacher was truly innocent colored Datya's young face. The same threatened to drain Miriam for Datya's hopes would be met with a dismal confession. Relief and disappointment gripped her; this was the moment when her student would finally see her humanity. It was vital that she revealed it, stepped down from Datya's treasured pedestal, but how the grief of her foolishness tore at her!

Wanting both to come clean with the forbidden memory while also tucking it forever away, Miriam safeguarded Datya's hand within hers. "It may be hard for you to hear, Dear One, and it will be harder still for me to pour out." A familiar, but long-dormant, burn began to creep across her arms and face as though the leprosy were attacking her affresh. Perhaps the pain would have been bearable if it had laid atop her skin with its sting. Perhaps she could have comforted herself with the thought that it would pass, but the pain had seemed to come from the inside, from deep within. Her skin had warped with the disease but the agony was bone deep. Though she had known Moses would intercede for her, she hadn't known if Yahweh would heal her. Her one thought between the pain and fear was "Will Yahweh have mercy?" She had never since felt terror as she had the day Yahweh had punished her skin.

"You see, Child, my self-control failed me. I became much like the gossipers you so often hear. Moses' wife had been lost to us for only a few moons when an unnerving report reached my ears. I doubted it fiercely, but knowing my brother and his unpredictable ways, I set out to seek him. I had to hear a denial from his own lips. A slave woman had passed along the shocking story: Moses was to remarry." Miriam battled now for her courage. The tale was old, and certainly not so secret as the Great Stones, but it fought, nevertheless, to stay buried. Perhaps her anger would sound silly to Datya. Afterall Moses' 'new wife,' was certainly not new to Datya; she had known the woman all her life. To be fair, Moses' wife was kind and well-liked. She was humble, if a little bold, and, yes, beautiful among women. However, her traits, whether good or bad, had been the last thing on Miriam's mind when she had heard the news over thirty years ago. "Gossip began to spread that Moses had contacted a man in the camp to pursue his daughter. The man was of the land of Cush, but had come out of Egypt as a slave. He had enslaved his family to one of our kin to ensure the protection and provision of Yahweh. A foreign slave's offspring for the wife of Moses! How dismayed I was Datya. The girl was barely a woman, but she was to rise above all women in camp. You see, Datya, I could not fathom why Moses had chosen the daughter of a slave, rather than a daughter of Israel! Oh, the girl's father had eventually bought his freedom, and he had been circumcised. He celebrated the feasts with us. In truth, he had become as much an Israelite as you and I, but I couldn't accept it. For all my excuses, Datya, the truth is that I felt outraged for Zipporah's sake. And I told Moses so." Miriam shuddered. She would rather wrangle the desert snakes so enamored by the Egyptians than to reveal the horror of her own behavior on that day.

As deeply as she could, she took in the air around her. Yahweh's hand was guiding her, and his Promised Land was so near.

She could feel it's distant hope. Calmed by his strength alone, she released the story. "The day was late when I found Moses. He was gathered with elders on a far edge of the camp. There, men from every tribe gathered in circles dotted across the packed earth. I know not what discussions took place that day. I do know my punishment, horrific as it was, was less than it should have been. For I marched up to Moses and hurled every word of accusation and fury I could think of. I am blessed that my brother's patience for me far outweighs his patience for the rest of our people. Surely the elders would have seen me punished in that very moment. Moses however led me away, all the while I nearly screamed at him. How could he seek a new wife when he had caused the death of so wonderful a one? I felt I could not stop my words, though I knew them to be unfair. When Moses reached my tent he spoke with surprising gentleness, 'You will meet Aaron and I at the Tent of the Presence tomorrow at dawn.' I was enraged by the dismissal but also relieved. I was beginning to feel the humiliation of the day. I felt Aaron would likely see it my way and could perhaps persuade Moses to pursue a different marriage or postpone the idea altogether."

Miriam's face burnt with the memory of the shame she had endured all that long night. What had ever possessed her to speak against Yahweh's anointed leader? "I am sure you have heard bits and pieces of what happened next, Datya, but it was rather more understated than the theatrics you hear in the stories. Aaron and I met Moses in the outer chamber of the Tent. You know of course that we do not go into the core of the tent where Moses communes with our Savior. Moses' words were simple, 'Miriam, you sinned against me, and against Yahweh. I have prayed for you, begged Yahweh to have mercy on you, but I do not know what will become of you. As for my new wife, Yahweh told me clearly to take one, to not remain alone. The young woman you have taken issue with will be joined to me. That she is a Cushite should not trouble you.' With those words he swept us from the tent and the three of us immediately heard the Lord's words. His voice was so close Datya, as though it layed like a garment, moulded to my form. I heard the words both around me, and within me. They were angry words, yes, but laced also with sorrow and compassion. I received my discipline in the same breath that seemed to hold me in love. I knew in that moment, my life would be spared, but I knew also that I would be forever marked. I was told I would contract leprosy and be cast out from the community." The answering gasp filled the space between them. Datya's face leapt from quiet listener to tormented companion, and she seemed as though she herself wanted to argue. Thankfully she held her tongue and looked once more to Miriam. The blend of fear, confusion, and even anger pulled the lines of her face in a way Miriam had never seen on her before. Datya's heart leapt to her eyes in defense of Miriam. Instead, it chastised her further. If she had refused the temptation to assert her authority against Moses' she would be spared this moment. Spared the knowledge that it was her own mistake that opened Datya's eyes, casting some of the girl's precious innocence away like so much dust in one's sandal.

"I have never before or since experienced pain like the feeling of Yahweh's hand spreading leprosy across my skin. Fear, humiliation, disgust, regret, and agony burst to life within my soul. Moses and Aaron looked at me with compassion but stepped quickly away. I knew in my own heart that Aaron would experience his own punishment for speaking against Moses, for he had done so as well, although less publicly. For the moment, all I could dwell on was my own despair. Here, Datya, you will recognize much of the story. My repentance was swift and sincere, and in my week spent in the wilds beyond the camp, I learned much about the condition of my heart. You see, child, I had thought at one point how skilled I was in self-control. How often I held my tongue! But the truth is, I was not self-controlled in my thoughts. Mentally I often rebelled against Moses, and yes, even against Yahweh. Merciful Yahweh! He had to teach me such a painful lesson or else my ministry would have failed on that day. Yet through leprosy and later healing, the Lord once again anointed me for this task and removed my sin! How great and awesome is he!" Miriam chuckled. Her worrisome student hadn't quite erupted into joy like she had, but that would come in time. Datya would have to learn the wonder and mystery of God's judgement and mercy for herself. Though, with her whole being, Miriam hoped it would not be an abysmal lesson the likes of which she had endured.

CHAPTER SIX

Many visitors had trooped by Datya and Miriam through the morning hours, and consequently, little was taught during this, the second morning of the journey. Even Ravit had wandered by to counsel with Miriam, though Datya had suspected her friend was also attempting to check on her. In the hours that had passed since, her thoughts had been hard to capture, floating at will through the memories Miriam had revealed. It was so staggering to think of what the prophetess went through, when she certainly had been, well somewhat had been righteously provoked! And yet, Miriam seemed overjoyed by the end of the story, as though Yahweh had given her a gift. She supposed lessons were gifts, but surely Miriam could have absorbed such an understanding with less harsh means. Did Miriam know that Datya remained confused, conflicted even, about their mysterious God? Didn't that mark her as unfit for the role Miriam was vacating?

Kicking at the crumbling rocks before her, she struggled with the urge to question Miriam. Her teacher looked tired, to the point that Datya wished she had the authority to tell the caravans to halt for the night. She suspected that her questions wouldn't be met with satisfactory answers anyway. Most likely a "Yahweh will teach you that himself, dear girl, for I cannot," would be the simple reply. A hint of humor took its place at the corners of her mouth, and she wondered if Miriam knew that she was just a little bit maddening to her student. In the next breath, Datya's silent prayers were answered. Messengers were making their way back through the tribes. The animals, wagons, and people were stopping for the remainder of the day. *Bless your name, Yahweh! You are the God of rest and I thank you!* Miriam's earliest teachings had entreated her to fill as many moments of the day with gratitude and praise as she possibly could. Together, they had looked for such opportunities through the years, and shared a smile now, jointly appreciating the relief.

Datya quickly settled Miriam on the edge of a walking neighbor's nearby wagon and went to search for Miriam's own cart. Since she could do little to aid the carts progression or protection, it rarely traveled closeby. Blessedly this time, the cart was not far off; now to find Aaron's *nechadim,* for she could not very well build the tent by herself. The search was short lived as three familiar faces appeared from the cloud of dust that hovered all around them. The High Priest's grandsons set to work and the tent rose in less than half an hour. The boys carried in satchels and pallets, foodstuffs and Miriam's private water barrel. With a parting shalom they wished their great aunt 'goodnight,' and once again Datya prepared to spend the evening in Miriam's tent.

The prophetess had been resting on a pallet near the tent's opening while Datya had bustled around preparing a light nourishment from Miriam's stash. Though Miriam remained humble, Datya was reminded of her teacher's great status amongst the tribes. Though a widow, with no living sons, she was revered and well-honored by the majority of their kinsmen. Many were the passing caravans whose trades graced the stores of Miriam's household. Datya was thankful for the treats, dry as they were, for they would not have been found in her own tent.

"Well, we must tether our lessons to the evening, now that we are journeying again." Miriam's announcement came as a surprise for Datya had assumed her teacher would seek sleep, not stories. Worn as she was, Miriam's ever-present twinkle caused the aged storyteller to come alive with a sapient beauty.

Datya could not resist returning the grin. How thankful she was to have a joyful tutor! She knew many of the boys in camp, who studied the law, did so under the eyes of men who lacked joy entirely.

"Evening lessons it is then, Miriam! And what am I to learn tonight?" Datya hoped it would be the songs! The verses about Yahweh's majesty, worship, and creation were among her favorites. She could even get out the timbrel! How she would love to hear Miriam sing the Song of the Red Sea this evening!

"That will be up to you this evening, Datya," Miriam spoke quietly. As much as the woman treasured joy and humor, nothing could hide the exhaustion that was wrapping around her.

Puzzled, Datya fished for clarity. "What do you mean, Miriam?" Had she heard her teacher correctly?

"I mean, child, that you have questions that must be delved into before you begin your tenure as Israel's prophetess. We must devote our lessons to this. You must cease thinking there is still much to learn. The history is already within you. Why, you can call up facts and dates and names at a moment's notice. The songs have become melodies anchored within you as well; how well you will lead the people in praise!" With maternal love beaming in her face as much as her in eulogy, Miriam built her up even further. "Your foundation of prayer is deeper already than many of God's people who are older than you, and prayer will come more easily to you in the coming days. You know all you need to know, Datya. This week will settle your spirit, settle your questions, and speak to those bothersome mysteries a bit. Do you understand?"

All Datya could do was nod, but she knew that Miriam expected a question from her. The one she most wanted to ask was, *Are you sure, Miriam? Are you sure about me?* Of course, that would be an insult in light of Miriam's praise. What could she say? Where should she start? Aiming for boldness, but suspecting her voice was far from it, Datya launched the lesson. "Miriam, Moses has had two foreign wives, yet Israelite children are taught that we are set apart, that we are chosen among all the nations. Many are the ethnicities that travel amongst us. Though some are still slaves, many others are circumcised and participate in all of our customs with us, though they are not Hebrew. What am I missing, Miriam? Are we set apart, chosen? Or are we not?" Datya grappled with hope that this would not be one of those times when Miriam's answer only deepened the mystery rather than delivering clarity. Her teacher's swift laughter unnerved her once again.

"Marvelous! Datya, you have chosen your lesson well, for it is my favorite to tell! Do you remember the story of Abraham and Sarah? Though they manipulated Yahweh's plan, he still honored his promise to them. Their son Isaac, and grandson Jacob, produced a great nation, a chosen nation. The Israelites still pulse with the blood of our patriarchs, and yet, it is not that blood that makes us chosen. It is not that you look like me, and our names are similar and our fathers and grandfathers are of one family." At this, Miriam accentuated her averment with a rapid shake of her head. "We are chosen simply because Yahweh's great love and mercy falls over this people. And yet, it falls elsewhere too. Forget not, Abraham's son Ishmael by the Egyptian slave Hagar. For to that ancient son, a hope and a future was also promised. Though his generations of offspring abandoned Yahweh, our Lord's heart aches for them as much as it did for us when we are enslaved. You see Datya, all are created by Yahweh and he would freely offer mercy to all who will simply call on his name!"

Miriam's voice deepened as the history of their people began to surge to memory. "The Nile Datya, is a strange place. It is filled with life and abundance but overseeing it all is evil and darkness. Snakes wrapped around the bodies of men are worshipped. Cows and frogs that have no power are given a place of honor. Craven images of men and women are called gods and goddess though they are nothing more than rock and clay. Many are the peoples of Egypt. The cities of the Nile are not only home to Egyptians but to many others as well: Cushites, Jebusites, Perrizites, Midianites. The people groups of the Nile are too numerous to name! In Egyptian society, they were welcome there because they were profitable, many were slaves, as we were, but none were raised to full citizenship which is an honor for Egyptians alone. You see, Datya, Yahweh's community is built differently. He is not building his kingdom nation based on parentage - though so many believe and claim so - he is building it with families, tribes, and men and women who will serve him, who will honor his law. He is building it with the ones who reject all other gods, who reject evil and choose good."

"The people along the Nile, Egyptians and strangers, saw all the works of the mighty hand of our God as the plagues rained down. Some believed, and some didn't, but those who bowed to Yahweh and fully rejected the Egyptian gods were welcome to flee Pharoah's rule with us. Those who chose to join our exodus, and who now obey the law - from circumcision to sacrifice - are spiritually joined to our Tribes. Datya, always remember this, Yahweh does not use bloodlines to build his kingdom. He uses adoption."

Tears spilled from her eyes; how had Datya missed this? Looking back at her people's history, to all she knew of her God, of course he was moved by the plights of all people! She had always known he was unlike earthly parents, but she had never before seen the merciful, wonderful truth, that his will was to adopt all people into his house. Not as slaves, but as chosen, loved children. Datya could well understand why this was Miriam's favorite story. It flowed upstream from the narrative so often believed, even among Hebrews. And somehow Datya felt even more loved than ever before. It melted her inner being to know that God chose her for her work, to be a part of his kingdom, simply because he created her and not because she was a daughter of Israel.

Surely they would sing now! This type of joy always begets praise! How worthy their God was! Miriam allowed a handful of songs before sending Datya to once again check on her mother and siblings. The evening quail would be available any moment, and Datya and Miriam would need that nourishment.

~ ~ ~

Miriam could see Datya returning in the distance. Many people were already making their way to the outskirts of camp to gather the evening's meat. Thankfully Aaron's *nechadim* always gathered and cleaned Miriam's portion for her. She had seen one of the boys on his way by just moments ago and had instructed him to gather enough for Datya this week as well. By the way the girl was smiling as she approached, Miriam could tell she was still feeling light-hearted. What a boon that was to Miriam's heart! To know that her charge truly understood the heart of Yahweh toward people, and rejoiced in it! Too many of the Hebrew elders left the truth of Yahweh's adoptive heart out of their lessons all together. Miriam had seen enough evidence to know that God knitted beautiful stories together when Israelites loved others as well as Yahweh loved them. Hadn't Moses led the way by marrying the Cushite girl? In every way, she seemed every bit Hebrew as the people around her, though her lovely dark skin harkened to a different heritage. What a treasure she was to Moses who had the courage to follow Yahweh rather than exalt bloodlines. Miriam had once been a fool to forget how the Lord cared for all of his creation; she was thankful that Datya had grasped the truth so quickly and so deeply. She had barely been able to convince the young girl to stash away that old timbrel and go to check on her family. "How was sweet Lisbet this evening, child?" Miriam stirred the little, pitiful fire under her baking stone. It would be just enough heat to sear the birds the boys had just returned with.

Datya smiled, a lovely tired smile, "Mother is well. She walked and talked with her sisters and her nieces all day. She is quite content and I don't think she misses me too much." A return smile was sufficient for Miriam knew that Datya was beginning to understand that her life with her family was changing. Most girls left the home, long before her age, for a marriage and a tent of their own, but Datya would very soon be leaving her home for Yahweh's work. Oh, she would marry of course. Probably fairly soon, but her life was coursing towards a track that was unfamiliar to her, or to most of the young Hebrew girls. Datya's mother, Lisbet, seemed to have made peace with her daughter's bold path. Her quiet acceptance was a rare trait among the People, for many loved to issue their opinions from morning until night. Those who were ignored or went on unheard usually just increased their volume.

Her pupil must have been having similar thoughts for she serenely offered up another question: "Miriam, what is it that makes the Israelites grumble so? Why are we a complaining people?"

"Ah, dear one, what a mystery that is, hmm?" An ache, long planted in her heart, tightened once again. How she hated to douse Datya's innocence and vibrancy. All too often the instruction of the day meant revealing the sin of their people. Once again, she must prepare to open her student's eyes. *Bah! Miriam, old fool, you are not the girl's mother. Teach your pupil well!* "I will answer your question with a return question, and we will strike a bargain! How does that sound?"

Once more, her humor broke free at the stunned expression of her student's face. How she thrilled at springing the unpredictable at people. "Alright then, Miriam. A bargain?" Battling her urge for laughter, for the cost it would surely require, Miriam sat forward a bit. The light was so low now, even with the tent gaping open, that seeing one another was becoming a challenge.

"Just this: the bargain shall be that I give you a question rather than the answer. You will devote your mind to the answer as you prepare for sleep. You will pray. You will rest. And in the morning, we shall dig for the answers you seek. Do you agree to this?" Sweet Datya whispered a quiet, confused yes before moving to prep their pallets. The girl still battled the strength intimidation had on her; if only she would grasp what Yahweh whispers day and night that these two women are equal in his sight.

CHAPTER SEVEN

One thought warmed Datya as she strolled past the thinning tents. Sabbath would begin at sundown this eve, and how thankful she was for it! The Sabbath was a treasure to her. It was the quietest she ever heard her people get. Oh, the animals still rustled and lowed, and the children certainly made their share of noise, but as the work stopped and the chatter shifted to whispers, the din in the desert became peaceful rather than harried. Tomorrow would be blessed by Yahweh: a gift to Datya and Miriam, and to all the people. The Prophetess had told her, long ago, that the Egyptians had no traditional rest day. While nobility and royalty certainly had their share of respites, the people whom they stood upon had nothing of the sort. Men and women along the Nile, in the vast cities, worked day and night the whole week through, year after year. She had shuddered when Miriam told her that the men and women died much younger in those days, often when their children were still growing. Many were the enslaved orphans. The voice of the Prophetess was clear in her memory, "Never forget the Sabbath is a gift, Datya. Only a living, loving God would command a law of such kindness." Upon hearing this lesson, she had come to think of all the nations of the world as slaves to their gods, as the Israelites had been slaves to Egypt. It was this teaching that had opened her eyes. The laws and gods that other kingdoms served confined them, whereas Yahweh's law restored life to his people. Datya had loved the Lord a little deeper that day, and many approaching Sabbaths since then had recalled the tender memory.

Miriam had agreed to lengthen her morning rest, staying

behind on her pallet while Datya gathered the manna. A double portion for each would not take her long, but she would enjoy the solitude. Most of the mothers and children who were already out gathering stayed as close to their camp as possible, but she preferred to go to the far edges. She sought and gathered her manna without being elbow to elbow with the bustling mothers and their broods. How wise and thoughtful their God was! Manna never appeared on a tent, or in the common footpath, or near the leavings of animals, or near the herds themselves. Always, it was found in an uncorrupted spot: out of the way, or on low bushes, even on rocks. And what a wonder! It always came away from the earth clean. Datya had never placed a piece in her mouth and ended up with dirt on her tongue. She shifted the large basket she had brought. Seldom had she needed to gather such a large amount, for she often gathered just her own supply on her way to Miriam's tent for their daily lessons, eating as she walked. When she was little she had helped her mother gather enough for their family, although Idan of course, had not yet been born, and Ziva was too little to require much in those days. Today, she would gather her portion as well as Miriam's for this day and for the next, since heaven's provision did not fall on the Sabbath.

The manna amazed Datya. It was the food of her whole life. Many were the Israelites who grumbled at the lack of variety, but she felt truly blessed that of all the people on the earth she was one of the few who would have a taste of this gauzy bread from Heaven! She had never heard of a single other god who provided actual nourishment for their people! Many were the nomadic families that had passed by them in Datya's years; they always wanted to share their god and their ways. None had ever testified of a god who could turn dust to gnats or fill the sky with enough birds to feed a nation. At this very moment, Datya was sampling a miracle, the other Israelites were as well, and yet they were angry about it. Each time she dwelt on it, her spirit ended up in a tangle of fury and frustration; Miriam had often said, 'Perhaps this is where your ministry will take you. Tackling the heart of the people, opening their eyes once again to the miracle.' Datya thought it unlikely. *What could I do to make them see? If they ignore the miracle now, they will continue to, no matter what I say.* The basket, made by Miriam's own hand long-ago with the type of reeds that grew far from here on the shore of the Nile, crested with fresh manna. Angling to return to the tent, she looked up to see Ravit approaching.

"Dear Friend! I had hoped to see you today!" Datya was overjoyed to see Ravit. She was, refreshingly, unlike the other wives. Like Lisbet, she was calm, serene, submitted to God, so different from the women who let their heart sway them about like trees in the wind. Datya felt the Spirit of Yahweh's calm rebuke. Too often she thought in terms of 'all of the Israelites grumble,' or 'they are all hard-hearted,' and 'why won't any of them listen?' The truth is, there were many who had hearts that honored Yawheh both in speech and behavior. Datya was thankful for two such examples in her own life, but she knew there were many more. *Forgive me Lord! I know you love this nation; help me to serve them in love and protect my heart from bitterness!*

"Datya, have you been well? I have just come from Miriam's tent. She told me I would find you far beyond the other gatherers." Turning a bashful look to her friend, Datya was unable to tamp down a smile at her words. So her secret enjoyment wasn't much of a secret, then? Well Ravit and Miriam had pegged her accurately, might as well join in the laughter and acknowledge it.

Quickly, a sobering thought invaded. She would rather stay in the joyful moment, but Datya had to know: "Have you had any more dreams, Ravit?"

"One, my friend, only one." She didn't seem overly grim, and Datya breathed a bit easier. While Ravit's dream couldn't be blamed for the loss that was coming, it would always remain connected in Datya's mind. How hard those words had been to hear! And harder still it would be, when they came to pass. Ravit, the folds of her own tunic loaded with manna, began "I have dreamed every night since we last talked. I dream that the Pillar of Cloud approached a great mountain. Moses begins to walk up it and then the cloud dims until it disappears." Datya gasped, the Pillar of Cloud, the very Spirit of God that led them, had never disappeared. It had always been there every day, transforming to fire at night. Sometimes they traveled close to it, and other times it was in the distance, but it had always been there. Neither she nor Ravit had ever awoken to a day without the cloud's immense presence. What could the strange dream mean?

"Ravit, the cloud has never dimmed! Nor has it disappeared. Yahweh has always been with us!" Ravit smiled, though Datya was clearly disturbed by the dream. *Has Ravit gone mad? How can she be so calm about this?*

"Peace, Datya, peace. Though that is all that happens in the dream, I have hope to share. I cannot explain it, but such peace, hope, and joy overflows me as the cloud disappears. I know! You want to deny the thought, but each time the dream arrives, God's peace always flows into me. It is surely Heaven-sent hope. I do not know what it means or when it will happen, but I know that Yahweh is bringing great and good change for his people!" Ravit's face was fairly glowing, though Datya's remained unsure. "Oh, that peace, Datya! If you could but feel it! Only a living God can stir it up within a weak and doubting human heart like mine!" Datya stared at her friend; no doubt, if her hands had not been supporting the lump of manna, she would have thrust them upwards in praise!

Datya nearly dropped the basket of manna to the ground. Never had she seen Ravit open up in such a way. Her mind went to the story of the passing through of the Red Sea and the peace that Miriam described as they began to ascend the far shore. Was this what she had felt then? Still, how on earth could the removal of the Pillar of Cloud cause anything but fear and trembling? Only last night, Miriam had said that the mysteries that plagued her would begin to settle. Yet, here she was, in the middle of the wilderness, standing with a dreamer, more perplexed than ever.

With a parting kiss to her wind-dried cheek, Ravit had turned back towards camp. She was staying with a young mother, whose Levite husband was currently in tabernacle service, like Datya's father. The girl had three young ones and was thankful for any willing help. Another day, Datya would have wanted more time with her friend, but on this day, she felt eager to return to the Prophetess. Every moment with Miriam now seemed like gold, though deep within, she still clung to a hope that all the predictions of the week were wrong. She prayed that her father had misunderstood the gift of the timbrel. She hoped with all her might that Ravit's dream had an entirely different meaning. Miriam's own conviction that her death was around the next bend, was harder to wish away. Still, Datya couldn't let go of the hope; a conviction settled upon her that she would not be able to breathe if she did.

Miriam's tent was in view now as she hurried, though she could see that a handful of women had gathered in the opening. Miriam was always popular the day before a Sabbath. Though the priests handled confession of sins and sacrifices, the women had their own customs to look to when their hearts needed to return to God. Some had taken to false, outward declarations of piousness, but many had realized that they could discuss temptations and wrongful thoughts with Miriam. She was trustworthy. Though she could not offer an absolving sacrifice for them, she helped them surrender it all to Yahweh and encouraged them to try again. The women gathering for this purpose was another rebuke to Datya, that not all the hearts of Israel were riddled with pride and bitterness. She slowed her steps, she could be generous with her time with Miriam. These women needed her too.

"You're very much in the way, Datya." Closing her eyes, she silently prayed for grace, as Ziva's voice cut at her. Praying she would pass quickly, Datya stepped to the side and mumbled an apology. Ziva stopped, standing nearly toe to toe with her sister. "You've heard the rumors, haven't you?" Her gut clenched. Ziva could not know that Miriam was nearing death, could she? If the knowledge had become known, surely her sister had enough compassion not to goad her about Miriam's last days. "The whole camp is hot with anger! Moses sent word that the journey is canceled, though the people had been told to prepare for two weeks of walking! Only two days in, and the old man says 'halt!' The men are saying we have not made enough progress. Where does he think the herds will eat?" Datya's glare was enough to silence her sister for the moment, but she too was puzzled, though she would refrain from her sister's tendency to spout off about such things.

"Moses obeys Yahweh, Ziva. Every morning, Yahweh himself tells Moses what will be and what won't be for the day. If you argue with Moses, you argue with Yahweh!" They had been over this before. Dozens of times in the last year alone. When her sister had been little, she had paid little or no attention to the man they call Moses. Somewhere along the way she had gotten old enough to choose. She could choose whether she wanted to be a faithful follower or a doubting complainer. Maddeningly, Ziva had chosen the latter, completely ignoring the lessons of men and women who had made the same foolish choice and paid dearly for it. "Oh Datya, ever the prophetess! How loyal you are. Well, I suppose you'll be returning home soon now that our own tent will be unpacked. Maybe then, you will see that Moses is senseless!" Ziva swayed off with her usual bold step. Datya was glad to see her go. A week with Miriam should mean a week without troublemakers, and yet Miriam had already warned her that busybodies would be an ever-present aspect of her ministry. There weren't enough sighs in her lungs to handle that exasperating thought, so she pushed through the crowd toward her place at her teacher's knee instead.

Upon her return, Miriam began speaking gently, but dismissively to the wives gathered about her. Taking the hint, they departed with gratitude and final calls of *shalom*. Datya fought tears as she realized that many of them would not see Miriam alive again. They did not know it, and Miriam gave no hint of suffering or sorrow in their presence. "I suppose, young one, that you have heard the rumors as you bowed for our bread?" Miriam broke into Datya's thoughts with one of her favorite mantras 'Datya, look at the gatherers. Not one among Israel can receive the manna from Heaven without first bowing to the ground to retrieve it. They are out in the open, in public, bowing before Yahweh alone. Only this posture leads to the bread of life!' How often she had spoken so to Datya!

Apparently, the rumor of the day had reached her as well. "Moses himself brought the news to me only moments after you set out. I was surprised that he did not send a messenger, and yet I suspect he wanted to see his pecking old sister once more." Miriam's wrinkled grin was the opposite of Datya's downcast face. How could they approach lessons or companionship in any way when the divide between how they felt at Miriam's coming end was so vast? "Now, now, my girl. My ministry has been one in the wilderness, but the wilderness is ending soon. I wouldn't belong in the refined cities of the Promised Land. You must remember, I go to a better promise than any in the coming land!" Miriam must have been moved with compassion for her, for once again, she found herself wrapped tightly in the arms of her mentor.

"Datya, we will talk of it for a few moments, but we will not give up the day unto sorrow. We had a bargain last night, right? That we would work out the answer together to your question. First, we will acknowledge the sadness you feel, and then we will ask Yahweh to remove it from your life until the proper time."

Datya's eyes were wide, fear and sorrow were warring for first place in her mind. How she wanted her teacher to declare the prophesied death to be false! With every word that already-small hope was diminishing. Miriam's peaceful, sweet, aged face was pouring out the abrasive truth. Her life would close in days. *Days! How can I bear this, Yahweh!*

"Datya, on the day I claimed you from your family I spoke an adoptive blessing over you. I asked your family to give you up wholly, for the work of the Kingdom of God. With humility, they handed you into my care. Now, we are beginning our third day together. You are a daughter of my household now, and will continue to be so through our seventh day together." Miriam's hand was firm on her shoulder, "Datya, after that day, you will no longer be my apprentice; you will be the Chief Prophetess. I will be gone. You will mourn, yes, but you will also begin to serve Israel. I know not God's timing, but I know not many days will pass before you must lead them with praise and worship into the Promised Land. Oh Joshua, will lead them in physically. He will spout assignments, direct armies, broker peace, and place the people where they belong, but you, Dearest, will guide their hearts, their very faith, into the Promised Land."

Datya shook now with the horror wrenching through her. How could Miriam deliver such news without a single tear? Her voice was calm and clear, she seemed strong in this moment, and yet she claimed she was going to die? Datya could make no sense of it, and yet she had no choice. Her teacher stood before her with compassion but also a command. It was time to abandon sorrow and prepare her heart for service in whatever way Yahweh asked of her this day. As Miriam pulled back from her, and stood silently waiting, she realized what Miriam was telling her to do. Slowly, her knees went to the floor, followed by her palms, her head hung as her tears impacted the hard packed earth beneath her face. Could she even get a prayer past the choking breaths in her body?

"Oh God of Heaven, I cannot face this work for the pain that engulfs me. Deliver me from sorrow as you delivered my forefathers from Egypt. I submit to your plan and plead for your forgiveness. My heart convinced me that I knew better than you what was right; how wrong, how foolish I am! Forgive me and be a balm to me, oh God!" Datya realized that she had dropped fully to the earth as her prayer closed. Exhaustion enveloped her head to toe, and the dust of the earth clung to her clothes and skin. She felt Miriam's robe graze her side as the older woman's arm came down to cradle her head. Miriam had never told her, not once, what this surrender to Yahweh would feel like. She had never warned her that, in order to become a prophetess, Datya would have to lay upon an altar, and sacrifice her deepest desires to their King. What a hard thing had passed through her! Her heart had barely been able to push through, her lips had fought her to say the words; but the surrender had come. Datya felt, for the first time, that not only had Miriam adopted her, to provide an inheritance - and a work - for her, but that Yahweh himself had adopted her. She had always known him, but now she felt fully his. Finally, she raised her head; she knew now she could share Miriam's joyful outlook, if not in the death to come, then at least in the divine promises before them.

~ ~ ~

How Miriam wanted to shout and sing Yahweh's praises! What a merciful and loving God he was. He had let her witness as Datya came into his presence and let go of her whole being into his care. Years ago, Yahweh had called this little girl, out of a little family among the Levites, to be the next prophetess. So many wonderful days spent learning and growing together, and now God had allowed her to see Datya become a young woman whose heart was lashed tightly to his work and his will! Sentiment aside, Miriam drew Datya upward and towards the cushions near the tent opening. The basket of manna between them, it was time for the day's lesson to commence. "Datya, do you remember the question you posed last evening? You were wondering about the heart of the people. Why is it so easy and natural for them to complain? I suspect you are also bothered by the way the miracle of manna seems to miss their attention." Datya's nod and guilty grin were enough for Miriam to continue.

Miriam thought once again of her people both beloved by Yahweh and bewitched by gods of the Nile. Her pupil was sure to steam once she realized the rot that still dwelt in the hearts of her clansmen. "The story you are looking for begins, once again, with Moses."

Datya immediately answered with deference, "Miriam, how could that be? Of all the Israelites, he seems to be the only one who completely honors the Lord. He doesn't grumble. He doesn't complain. He never disrespects Yahweh's plans or decisions!" Miriam chuckled. Datya doubted, but a tale from history would clear the waters for her dear little student. First, she reclined against the sacks that housed treasures she would never need again, and prayed. *Yahweh, give my body strength to share this wisdom. Give me breath to tell the tale she needs to hear.*

"Long ago, Moses was not the man you know now, Datya. He was riddled with guilt for surviving what the other boys of his generation did not, and for the life, devoid of labor, that he was blessed to live. He was being choked from within by a serpent of anger that hung over his life. All knew that it was only a matter of time before the serpent struck. When it did, Moses sinned and became a murderer. He fled to his own wilderness. You see, Datya, this is not the first time Moses' has spent forty years in the wild places." Miriam paused and breathed deep.

Thoughts of the day Moses fled as a criminal haunted her. She remembered well, the worry that she would never see Moses again. Their father had long since joined the dust of the earth, but their mother was overcome with grief. She had always believed that Moses had been spared, when so many other baby boys had not, for a great purpose. Never had she imagined her son becoming a fugitive cut off from two nations, the one that had birthed him and the one that had sustained him since.

"Moses walks through the wilderness with the Israelites now, but it is not necessary for him, like it is for us. He endured the Refiner's process long ago. Moses entered the grasslands of the Midianites as a murderer. Surely such a badge is worse than being called a complainer, is it not, Datya?" Datya's face was more than a little lost, but she dutifully nodded. "Yet, the Refiner's process was the same for both sins. Forty years, Datya. Those of us in Egypt heard nothing from him in that time. We knew not if he lived or died. If he murdered again, or if he repented before Yahweh. When Moses did return, he was a changed man. He was no longer a murderer. He was no longer riddled with anger. He was no longer a man lost, a man without an identity. He was Moses, called by God, chosen to lead. I Am had spoken to him from the leaping flames of a burning bush and Moses' former identity had vanished - and been replaced - in an instant." Miriam's smile grew thinking of how her baby brother turned the heads of even the elders as he returned to face-off with Pharoah. "He walked righteously and communed with the Holy God. What a difference! What had made such a transformation in the man, Datya? What had caused such a turn around?" Again, Miriam's thoughts turned toward their mother and father. When Moses returned both were gone; they did not live to see their son as a man called to the very work of freedom. How their faithful mother would have rejoiced! Still, Miriam and Aaron had been blessed to see the transformation. Moses had become someone entirely new, and yet, he was still their Moses, their set-apart brother.

With a shake, she cleared away the memories, and looked at Datya to continue: "Think, dear one, think. How did the transformation come about? Man alone can not change his own course so thoroughly, so we know Moses himself did not bring it about. Time alone certainly ages us, but can it bring such wisdom, such holiness? No, I think not. What then?"

Datya was as puzzled as she had ever seen her. With a bit of courage the girl spoke up, "It was Yahweh, right? Yahweh changed Moses?"

With a clap and burst of laughter Miriam nodded. "Yes, Datya, Yahweh did. Yahweh took the man who couldn't lead himself to right living and transformed him into the man who would lead many thousands to righteousness. But that process took forty years! Do you know why? It's not simply because Moses was hard-headed, though, goodness knows, he is! It wasn't either that he was so utterly sin-riddled, for Moses had his good points, even then. Here is the clue you've been looking for, Datya: Moses had to endure forty years in his own wilderness because Yahweh had to remove Egypt from him. The first step had been removing Moses from Egypt, the next step was cleansing Egypt from his spirit."

It was obvious that her student needed more clarity, so she dug even further in the history. "Many years before Aaron or Moses took their first breath, the father of our people, Jacob moved his sons to Goshen, a fertile little land under the power of the Egyptians. Not even our great devoted ancestor could prevent the creeping of the gods that began. By the time my father and mother were born, the Egyptian gods had reached long, evil fingers into every custom and tradition of our people. Why! My own father attempted to divorce my mother! Surely such a thing would never have been considered except that idols had become a thorough, deep influencer in the lives of the Israelites. Moses was not immune to this, in fact, his spirit was at risk more deeply than all the Hebrews for he grew, and teethed, and learned, and became a man amongst the courts of those whose hearts fully embraced those dark gods." Miriam looked across to Datya whose fear played across her face. Discussing foreign gods was the last thing either of them wanted to do, but it was the very thing at the heart of Israel's great delay. "Datya, what you haven't realized yet is that, although the Hebrews left Egypt, Egypt has not left us. Because traces of Egypt and the false gods of the Nile still remain in us, we earned a 40 year sojourn in the Refiner's wilderness." Miriam laced her voice with firmness; Datya must understand the great fault that cracked the hearts of their people.

"It was only when Moses saw the flaming bush which spoke with the voice of Yahweh that he was able to bow low, shun the Egyptian gods once and for all, and become alive again - through the One True God. Had he been unwilling to let that fire burn up what was left of Egypt in his heart, he never would have left the wilderness. Your people are the very same, Datya. They cannot let go of sins like complaining and gossiping because inwardly they have traveled all these years dragging the bondage of Egypt behind them. Pharaoh was buried long ago in the tumbling waters and churning mud of the Red Sea, but the evils of his homeland evaded that flood for now." Pausing, Miriam could see her student's questions springing to life; her lovely, dark eyes displayed much. "The truth is, Datya, that although Yahweh will very soon bring the Israelites out of the wilderness and into the Promised Land, many will take the wilderness with them in their hearts, just as many still lug around the curses and charms of Egypt. You see, child, we stay in the wilderness because idolatry remains in us. Life is only found in Yahweh: the Promised Land is just another patch of dirt, if we continue to worship the gods of Egypt or worse, the god of self." This last utterance was critical for the formation of any young prophet, but Miriam's breath struggled to release it. Her days of long sermons and lengthy messages were behind her.

Datya had no argument. Once again she was struck by how she had missed this tragic truth. Her people, whom she dearly loved, couldn't be free of something as small as the tongue because of the debris of gods that filled their lives. "I see that you are right, Miriam. What I do not understand is how did Moses ultimately get free of the evil false gods? He must have been more riddled with it than even these people around me."

Datya's puzzle was a fair question. One she had tried to answer before on the rare occasion that one of the Hebrew women would realize their own idolatry and come to her for counsel. "The answer you seek, Datya, is that Moses believed. When God spoke to him in the Midianite wilderness, he had a choice. He could choose to marvel at the sight, but believe both in Yahweh and in the gods of mankind, which would have left him unchanged and lost forever. Or he could choose to bow before the One True God and denounce the false deities. Moses' heart surrendered to our God! He believed. Praise the Lord! The first hurdle of our salvation - Moses' surrender - had been accomplished!" She could feel her face flush with joy. The story had taken her breath and energy, but nothing was more important than Datya understanding the foundation, the early stirrings, of the Great Exodus.

"Oh, Miriam. What can be done so that the people will make such a choice? How can they be persuaded to full surrender?" Datya was distressed. Of course, it was hard on the sweet young woman to realize that the chosen people still walked with much wickedness.

Miriam's job now was to blanket Datya's feeling of overwhelm, with hope. "Many have made that choice, Datya. Your mother has, and I believe your father as well. The widow Ravit, why she is truly a devoted servant of Yahweh. I feel certain she has realized and repented of idolatry. Moses has often shared testimonies with me of young men who leave their families and realize, under his tutelage, that idols were worshiped in some way or another during their childhood. Once they surrender such behavior to Yahweh, he helps them to change, as he did for Moses, as he does for you and I. There is much hope, Datya. For the remainder, you must devote much of your life to prayer. Many of the Egyptian gods gain their power and favor through the weapon of fear. How successful fear is in the pitiful human heart! You must pray courage over our people, Datya, always courage."

As Datya's head bowed low once more, Miriam realized the girl intended to start praying right then and there. Such a tender heart she had. Now was not the moment to tell Datya that to this day Miriam saw the influence of the Nile gods in her own heart. Still, she knew that very soon she would be free forever from sinful behavior. She would finally be at home with her Lord! Moving to the far wall where more of her goods lay stacked in crates and sacks, Miriam began sorting. She would have a servant boy take loads of things to her daughter's family. Her daughter's husband had become a good trader so they needed little, and yet Miriam wanted to send a few treasures at least to what remained of her family. She would also pull out a few bags of dried fruit for Aaron's grandsons. They had faithfully served her needs these many years and she wanted to show them a final act of love. The remainder would be Datya's to keep or distribute as she saw fit. Miriam had long ago ceased thinking of this tent as her possession; all she had was for Yahweh's use and she prayed Datya would feel the same.

CHAPTER EIGHT

Datya had been freed from fear of loss and the trappings of her own will yesterday; it had led to the most restful sleep she had enjoyed in many years. Today, she woke with the fullness of Yahweh's peace. The past week had been stuffed full with thoughts of worry and despair, but today, those thoughts fell off of her, powerless. She did not want to lose Miriam, but for the first time, she felt she would be able to live and serve in her role on the other side of that loss. Nevertheless, she had promised to leave such worries until their proper time. Turning she saw Miriam, freshly awake but still reclining, on the folds of her own pallet. It would remain unrolled today, since no labor was to be done on the Sabbath. They shared a greeting and a smile. It was clear that Miriam was also celebrating the freedom that she was walking in. As the women rose, Miriam began a quiet hum. Datya reached for the timbrel. Most of her favorite moments were found when she and Miriam would sing praises to Yahweh. So few among the Israelites sang. They left it as a role fulfilled by few rather than many. There was no decree or ordinance in the law that said such, but nonetheless singing was out of character for her serious-minded people. They preferred to listen to praise rather than participate. She would sing, no matter. Many were the mighty works and wonders of Yahweh's hand; today she and Miriam would recount them in song!

Datya studied the cadence and notes of Miriam's humming. It was unfamiliar which meant Miriam was calling for a new song! Through her words and rhythm she would weave a new psalm to the God of Creation. How she loved being a witness in these moments! She loved to hear the old songs as well, for Miriam had taught her much through them, but the songs that Miriam created, simply through the leading of God's spirit, were a treasure trove of faith. "Today you will sing a new song as well," Miriam stunned her with the announcement. "Me? Miriam, I do not have that gift. The songs come from you! I can repeat them, but I cannot create them!" Miriam swapped her hum for a chuckle. "Yes, child, so it has always been. Miriam sings, then Datya sings. Are you not also created by the Creator? In His very image? Yes, Datya! You are a creator too, because you are like him! Today will be my last song and also your first. Turn to prayer now; Yahweh himself will give you the words." Miriam left no room for questioning as she slipped quickly back into the hummed melody, her own head bowed waiting for the words.

Datya was tempted to let her thoughts, and her heart, race. Pulling a song together from nothing seemed an impossible task; how could Miriam ask it of her? Yet, hadn't she learned her lesson about allowing her mind to do all the thinking when it was her spirit God purposed to use? Yes, she had learned her lesson, though she suspected she would always be tempted to let her head run away with her calling. Now, she would believe Miriam's claim, that God would give her words. Head bowed, commanding her heart to listen rather than quake, she waited for them to come.

Miriam's hum began to form syllables and the praise filled the leather walls around them:

Stronger than the Red Sea
Mightier than the Nile
King of mankind, your kingdom bring!

Other gods are mere mortals
You stand far above them all
King of our world, you silence idols!

One who conquers kingdoms
All bow before your throne
King of all days, your victory won!

Name that stands for all time
How mighty is your glory
Ancient of Days, our praise will rise!

Our eyes have seen your goodness
What love and care you offer
King of our lives, your name we bless.

When you choose to end my days
Your servant brought home
Oh God of my heart, we trust your ways!

As Miriam's stanzas began to loop, Datya wept. The looming loss broke her heart and yet joy reigned within. The ringing words were wise and true. Datya would trust the One who poured out this wisdom through Miriam. Yahweh's ways were good, with no exception. Once, she had repeated that without conviction, now she believed it with all her heart. Once more, she trusted Miriam too. The aged prophetess was right; Yahweh was filling Datya with a song. Could she sing through her tears? The compassion of a God who would choose such a doubter to be a deliverer of praise overwhelmed her! Miriam's hum was quiet once more. Though it shook, Datya offered her voice to her Lord:

Life-giver, there is none like you!
Tales I've heard of other gods
Have only served to prove,
Yahweh, there is none like you!

Hope-bringer, there is no peace like yours!
Our own pursuits so often fail,

But as your holy calling pours,
I am lifted by your grace.

Creator God, I see your faithful hand!
I can bring nothing to your throne,
Apart from you, I cannot even stand,
But faithful God, I am yours nonetheless!

How young Datya felt! As though she were a baby taking first steps, Datya felt humbled as Yahweh's presence thickened about them. She also felt more steady than ever before. Shifting sands beneath her feet were her way of life, but, as Yahweh lifted her to the solid ground of what she was called to do, she felt as though her feet stood on a rock. Like their own Moses who had so often walked the heights of mountains, she felt as though she had climbed a great obstacle between herself and the God who delivered the Hebrews from Egypt.

With a smile, Datya realized that Miriam had moved on to the Song of the Sea. What a favorite it was!

"Sing to the Lord, for He has triumphed
Gloriously and is highly exalted!
The horse and his rider He has hurled
Into the sea!"

Datya joined in as they sang the psalm over and over. Knowing that Yahweh listened to the voices of two women in the midst of a crowd in a desert, nearly knocked Datya's voice from her. Hundreds of nomadic families had passed them by in the many years of traveling. None had ever shared of a god who would be so familiar and compassionate. None! Once again she was reminded, it was their great and gracious God that made the Israelites a chosen people, not the people themselves.

~ ~ ~

Evening was nearing. Miriam and Datya had worshiped

for many hours. Dozens of men, women, and children had settled around their tent, just listening to the testimonies rise. When Datya and Miriam had rested their voices, the crowd would leave, only to gather a new one when a fresh song would issue. In the quiet place within her, Miriam overflowed with thankfulness for the day. Worshiping with her student had brought gladness to many, but she also knew that, at least among today's witnesses, Datya's ministry had been launched. She would be accepted as Israel's prophetess. Many had not even seen Datya's face today, for only a few could fit into the tent's mouth. Yet, they had heard her voice, felt the anointing. It was the sweetest beginning to the transition that she could have hoped for.

She marveled once more at her student. Datya had lain so much on the altar of the Lord this week. From her will to her worry to her voice to her calling. All had been offered up to Yahweh. Though she still called Miriam "Teacher," she was no longer learning, rather practicing. Miriam was overwhelmed with gratitude for her sweet successor; how wondrously God had provided! The ache in her heart reminded her that tomorrow Datya's joy would be tested. A burden of loss would once again weigh down the young woman's spirit. In only a few more days, Datya would graduate forever from Miriam's care.

Only a few morsels of manna were left for the women to enjoy before the night's rest began. She motioned for Datya to join her. She longed to reveal the truth of the coming days to her dear student, but the truth was, Miriam knew only that tomorrow would be different, and that the end was closer than ever. There was no way to prepare for either one of them. Yahweh knew best, and they had both spent the day agreeing to trust him with their whole beings. They would eat their fill, then wrap once more in wool blankets, still trusting. Tomorrow's answers would be revealed soon enough.

CHAPTER NINE

Until Datya awoke and parted the tent's heavy front, Miriam had no choice but to dwell with her own thoughts in the near dark. While sleep had come swiftly for her last night, it had not remained for long. Many hours already she had spent trying to see the pallet across from her where deep shade hid her student's sleeping form. She didn't need to see the girl to pray for her, of course, but it was a comfort having her so near.

Early in the day a quiet thought had risen to her mind: yesterday had been the final Sabbath she would observe here on earth. She would not partake of another passover meal, nor would she sing at anymore of Israel's feasts. She would not minister to new widows, or bring aid to Israel's poorest families. All of these familiar tasks were finished. Her life had been lived serving Yahweh by serving the people, and now she had nothing left to do. Nothing, save living just a few more days, and delivering what final blessing she could to Datya.

Once more Miriam commanded her muscles to rise, but before she made it much further than her knees she felt the familiar fluttering in her chest. She fought for great scoops of air as she settled once more to the pallet and the ground beneath it. *So yesterday was also my last day of rising, of walking on my own? So be it.* Hearing Datya's body shifting on the earthen bed, Miriam looked again for her shape in the darkness. Today would be hard for Datya, as would the following ones. She was reminded once more, that although Datya would never face slavery in Egypt or the fearful moments of being trapped between a sea and an army, she would face her own hardships. Who knew what sweet, faithful Datya would endure as she laid stones of faith for her people? Of course the hard hearts and doubting minds of the Israelites were hurdles enough!

Datya had begun moving about her morning tasks with tender hands and feet. Bless her, she must think her teacher was still asleep! Her pallet shaken out, rolled, and stored away, Datya moved towards the tent opening. Parting it ever so slightly, she glanced toward Miriam's place as the light of the wilderness poured in. Grinning, her student offered a delightful morning laugh, "Why, Miriam, you've been awake all this time! Why did you not say anything?" Miriam smiled in response. Rather than answering, she simply welcomed Datya to settle close to her.

Miriam knew all too well that many men and women who made it to such an old age often did so with the loss of one of more of humanity's critical abilities. They would be aged enough to know their great grandchildren had been born, but with the betrayal of their eyes, they would not be able to see them. They would live long enough to receive the respect of younger generations but ears that had long since failed meant they couldn't hear the praises of the people. Miriam gave thanks that she didn't face such infirmities. Right this minute she could reach to her student, hold her face between her weathered old hands, and treasure Datya's tender countenance. She could look at this precious young woman and see that God was doing a new thing, a good thing for Israel. Her heart gushed once more with gratitude! How faithful Yahweh was to provide a legacy like this! Her work would be seen to - it would not simply fall to the earth like shattered pottery in her absence.

Though respect had always schooled her to let her teacher speak first, Datya's voice finally broke into Miriam's reverie. "What is it Miriam? May I serve you? Any need you have I will try to meet!"

Smiling gently, Miriam released her face. Did the girl know

how many prayers she breathed on her behalf? Many were the days spent sending continuous prayer heavenward! *This sweet girl! What a servant's heart! Father, bless her for it!*

"Well, dear one, it is time for manna. Surely God has the barrenness filled up with the little loaves by now. I have woken hungry; have you?" Though Miriam's voice was lighthearted, Datya's discernment wouldn't be assuaged. Her concern didn't slacken for a minute. It resided, with full prominence, on the young girl's face. Miriam suppressed a deep sigh. She was a mere human and yet she thought to somehow spare another being pain and sorrow? Life and death, pain and joy, sorrow and peace all reside in Yahweh's hand, not Miriam's! A fresh smile softened her face. Once more, the day began with her own lesson. Datya's would come later. For now, the girl must learn of Miriam's condition.

"Yahweh blessed me indeed by providing a successor with the desire to serve! I am in no great need this morning; do not worry." Miriam gathered her words and sought Datya's eyes. "However, I will need you to gather manna for me, child. We'll have no tears now, but you must know that I can no longer rise from this place." That Datya was mustering questions was obvious. Her mouth had opened to seek clarification, but Miriam raised her hands once more. "See to the gathering, Datya. Will not your questions be better served once we are nourished?"

Though Datya nodded and rose to leave their shelter, Miriam could tell the girl would much rather remain by her side. All the humor in the world couldn't comfort her obvious grief, and yet Miriam smiled. Datya would understand someday that there was great joy in the days ahead for Miriam. How pale suffering appeared when held up to the light of Yahweh!

~ ~ ~

With a shooing motion that the old prophetess had spent years mastering, Datya had been ushered from the tent. The light of day was already brightening the many leather dwellings surrounding her. Some women shuffled away from tents to gather morning manna while many others hurried back with armloads for their families. The prophetess had asked her at the last moment to make her way first to the tents of the Reubenites. Miriam's only daughter, who had survived infancy, had married into the tribe of Reuben. Though she had died four years ago, she had left behind two sons, nearly grown, whom Miriam longed to see once more. Datya was struck by the dismal message she was carrying. The boys were to come today, for they would not get another chance. Thankfully she spotted a servant of the household she sought within moments of arriving among the Reubenite families. Quickly, she secured a promise from the servant that Miriam's wishes would be taken directly to the boys and their father.

Datya longed to rush back to Miriam, to check on her and care for her, but Miriam had also insisted that she check on her mother and siblings once more. She had not ventured to their tent yesterday, for the Sabbath had commanded her focus. As ever, her teacher placed her mother in a position of honor; Lisbet would receive their thoughts and care each day, no matter how pressing the lesson or how fearful the student.

The camps seemed quite endless this morning. *So many are the tents, so long the rows, I must walk swiftly!* Datya sampled her manna along the way, being sure to tuck plenty into the folds of the bread cloth Miriam favored. With only a single portion required today, this method of carrying the manna, on such a long walk, was more pleasant than the large basket she had used the day before the Sabbath. She hoped Miriam would take in plenty of the nourishment. For several days now Miriam had eaten little. She hurried her steps once more, the sun seemed to move swiftly through the sky this day as she rushed toward the Gadite tents.

"Mother! Ziva!" Datya tried to offer genuine joy as she approached her mother and sister. They were working together to sort through the family's belongings. Rumor had spread through the manna fields this morning that Moses suspected a nomadic trade may be available within the coming weeks. None among Israel would miss a chance to trade with passing travelers. So often the families that passed by were so overwhelmed by the sheer masses of Hebrews that they nearly gave away the goods stashed for their own journey. It was unclear whether fear motivated them, or simply confusion. The nomadic trades were another dose of Yahweh's faithfulness. No wilderness could prevent the favor of a God who so dearly loved His people. Was there hope that Datya's kin would ever recognize this? "What trades are you hoping for this time, Mother." Datya glanced beyond her mother's shoulder at the piles of provisions lined up on the earth.

"Oh Datya, I hardly know! Your father has said to start making trades for your household, that we must prepare the items you will need." Lisbet seemed entirely calm, as though they had talked about Datya's future hundreds of times.

Yet, Datya felt stricken. So long she had been kept from marriage so that her life could be poured into preparation. *Preparation for ministry. Not for marriage. What does Mother mean?*

Lisbet's arm encircled her daughter's waist. "Steady, Datya, it is but a step in one direction. We are simply preparing for your marriage, just as we have done for Ziva." Lisbet pointed to the small lump of packs that remained in the very front of the cart. They were not unpacked with each journey, and in fact had stayed there for many months. Each lump of leather wrapped goods contained something Ziva would need for her household: utensils, tools, cloth, even remedies of precious herbs!

Her sister had mere months of childhood left, but Datya had never considered her own marriage! "Datya, look at me, dear one." Her mother's firm, dusty hands drew her attention once more. "Do not fret. Yahweh prepares good things for you! Yes, you are called to ministry; you will serve Him well! But leadership is not all you are called to. Yahweh's anointing is rarely singular. We all serve Him in many ways, as will you." Datya was used to wisdom pouring from Miriam. She had always opened her ears and heart to learn from those words. Hearing counsel from her mother was unfamiliar to her. Most often Lisbet spoke comfort, correction or love to her children. An outpouring of the ways of their God from Lisbet jolted Datya; she had long thought Miriam to be one of the few true worshipers among Israel. Shamed, she realized she had been wrong about her quiet mother.

Drawing away, Datya suppressed the struggle within. "I am sorry Mother. I cannot stay to help you. I must attend Miriam with haste. She will be glad to hear that you and Ziva have set about good work for the day." Datya nearly tripped on Idan who had been playing by her feet. Urgency pressed on her to flee towards Miriam, and forget the worry that was flashing across her mother's face.

Daylight had already harvested more of her time than she wanted to spare. Nonetheless, she could only move so fast through the camp. Many would cast a dark look her way if she let her feet run, though she felt desperate to. She was the next prophetess of Israel! No longer a child! Datya felt certain she could already predict how Miriam would react to this morning's conversation with her family: complete agreement. Truthfully, Datya began to feel humiliated at her flight. Lisbet was right. Miriam herself had always reminded her that she would not live entirely as a prophetess but also as a wife and mother! How she trembled at the thought! From a long-ago lesson, Miriam's voice rushed over her mind once more. "Datya, your days are in Yahweh's own palm. He prepares your path and your position. What can your fretful ways do to change His good and perfect course? Trust Yahweh, Datya. In all things, trust Yahweh."

She wondered if it would always be like this? If Miriam's words would always remain so strong in her memory. How could she navigate all of life's newness without her beloved guide? *Father, allow Miriam's lessons to always be loud in my life; help me to remember!* Had it been only two days ago that Miriam had told her that she too was a student? The prophetess had urged her to pivot from viewing Miriam as her mentor to viewing Yahweh as such. This she knew with all her might she could not do on her own. *Help me, God Almighty.*

Gripping the bulge of manna tightly, Datya held her breath as she stepped inside the tent. Pausing a step behind Eitan, the widower of Miriam's daughter, she focused on the scene before her. Miriam sat upon her palet with her grandsons close before her. Their knees were nearly touching hers as she reached to hold a hand of each. Never before had Datya witnessed a blessing. Her own grandparents had either died in their sleep or long before Datya had been born. Still she knew well the enormity of the moment. Her own father annually rehearsed the blessings that had been spoken over him.

With a voice that rang with conviction Miriam spoke to Acke, the eldest first. "Acke, your birth was remarkable to the midwives, for your mother had an easy time and little pain. Your own cries were muted, as though you didn't mind your bare beginnings. For this reason your parents named you **Acke, 'Peace of the Father.'** Your parents believed you would be a peaceful boy brimming with joy and obedience. I know and declare a further anointing over your life. Not only will you be a servant of peace within your own family, but you will be a peacemaker among the tribes of Israel. Many can talk about peace.

Many can keep peace. But few can make peace. As long as you walk in Yahweh's light you will make peace for both the great and small among Israel." Acke dutifully bowed his head towards his grandmother. He knew the value of her words. Datya echoed a silent prayer that he would always remember them.

With a final kiss to Acke, Miriam angled slightly and gathered up her youngest grandchild's hands. The boy, who was Ziva's age, looked to his grandmother with tears. Carmine was not usually an overly sensitive child, but Datya realized that no one had previously made him aware that his *savta* was dying. "Carmine, you too, will be blessed among men. God's spirit will be with you as it has been with mighty men. Your parents called you **Carmine, 'Garden of God,'** as they marveled at the new life joining their family. Those who surrounded your family quickly refuted your name crying 'there is no garden in the wilderness.' Yet, your parents held firm that you were indeed a gift of abundant, fruitful life from heaven. So you will be as you enter manhood and walk among the tribes. Your life will bear heavenly fruit so long as you submit to Yahweh. This wilderness people will be greatly blessed by the gifts and working of your hands."

Looking up to Eitan, the sheen in her eyes acknowledged their communal loss. "Acke, Carmine, though your mother is gone from us, your heritage as children of Yahweh is the most valuable treasure within this camp. Always honor your father, Eitan, always honor Yahweh, and always honor one another. What rich blessing awaits Israel if Peace of the Father and Garden of God work together as leaders among men!" Eitan had always been much like Miriam. He loved to laugh, he loved to surprise people. He was unlike many of the elders among the camp whose identities were characterized by studious thought and serious behavior. Today, however, Eitan couldn't muster the joy. It was clear he felt the looming loss deeply. Afterall, Miriam had been a tie of sorts to his beloved wife. Still, Eitan and the boys gracefully kissed Miriam and withheld weeping as they departed. Datya knew Miriam would be thankful for the show of strength; she never wanted sorrow to have a single minute more than it earned.

The tent, which felt empty with their retreat, grew quiet as Datya bent to the ground. How she wanted to be a comfort to Miriam, yet the prophetess spoke first. "Now, Datya, today's lesson is before you. There is joy in all things if one will look for it. As we look around we often see sorrow, suffering, disappointment, and failure. Our eyes, sharp like the predatory birds narrow in on the negative. Yahweh's eyes are nothing like our own, for the same experience radiates with spokes of hope, joy, peace, and growth in His eyes. What you cannot see, He sees fully. What you cannot change, He crafts into triumph." Datya wanted so much to honor Miriam with her response. She couldn't be sure she would, so she simply settled the manna on the patch of earth between them.

Miriam was asking her to admit, to vocalize that Yahweh knew best. That His plan was truly good! The words themselves would cost Datya nothing. Meaning it with her whole being, on the other hand, would mean that she must once again lay upon an altar, sacrificing her thoughts. She would have to let go completely of her own vision for the coming days and the years before her. The task was hard!

Releasing her held breath once more, Datya's eyes flooded her hands, working to dissolve the wafer of manna she held. Over her spirit, she felt Yahweh's gentle hand pressing. Could he truly show her a spoke of joy in this loss? Once again, she grappled; what joy could she find in losing her teacher?

In the volume of a thought, his voice reached her. *It is not that you will find joy in it, Daughter. It is that I will bring you joy through it. Trust me, Datya.*

The potency of the heavenly whisper bolted Datya upright. Never before had she felt that Yahweh was speaking directly to her! To her! "Oh, Miriam," Datya wept as she bent over her own arms. Near Miriam's feet, Datya lay before their God. Waves of humility and hope crashed over her own strength, diluting it and finally washing it away. Her strength lacked value, it was Yahweh's that she required. Into the blanket beneath them Datya gave it all up once again. "Yahweh, you spoke to me and filled my heart! I still cannot see the joy, but I trust you!" With Miriam's gentle hands smoothing the wayward strands of her braid, she let her tears fall before Yahweh. Her ideas, her plans, her hopes were draining out of her - she had to let them go, for Yahweh was filling her with new life and new hope - with his perfect hope!

~~~

Hours passed as Datya remained submitted before the presence of Yahweh. Many were the Israelites who assumed that simply because there was a Tent of Meeting and a Pillar of Fire, that God's presence could not be found elsewhere. What they failed to see is that God's presence longed to be revealed to all of them. What a pure recipe! Simple faith and sincere submission were all that were required. And yet many never found their way to true union with God. It was Miriam's lifelong hope to lead her people, one by one, to that very presence. Many were the stubborn ones among them who remained distant from Yahweh, but some, like this sweet daughter, found their way to Him. Rejoicing, Miriam urged her student to rise, to dry her face. Her joy surely shone forth as she declared that Datya would never forget the lessons she had learnt on the altars of Yahweh.

"Now, dear one, there is little time left before the sun sets, and still much to share." Miriam quipped. Datya's spiritual formation was vital, but for now she sensed an urging to return to lighthearted lessons. Despite the evidence of holy grief on Datya's face, joy was present as well. The teacher and student grinned once more at one another; despite it all, here was an-
~~~

other chance to learn and grow. Neither would let it slip away.

"Firstly, Datya, let us have a little more air," Miriam gestured to the tent's flap. With the kind of ease that Miriam had not known in years, Datya leapt up and widened the opening as far as the leather would stretch. After securing it, she sat once more across from her teacher. With faux mysteriousness, Miriam alluded, "You know, dear, don't you, that the Israelites have lost all sense of time and direction?" Laughter filled the space between them as Datya's dark brows rose high into her forehead. "Yes. For long ago, Yahweh's righteous anger declared the Israelites would endure forty years of wilderness wanderings for their foolishness. Since that day, our routines have shifted like the sand. Families have changed, and lost, and loved, and died. Passerbys bring news of the far-away world, but we've seen nothing of it ourselves. We wander, we gather manna, we tend to our herds, but we go nowhere in particular and never settle. The hard hearts of the Israelites have also become confused and disoriented with time." Miriam's mirth thinned as she recalled the rebelliousness around her. "Some say the forty years passed us by decades ago, and yet we still wander. Others say only half of the allotted time has passed. Many are the arguments; who is right? Who is wrong? The faithless and flustered remain in the dark. Many doubt the great faithfulness of Yahweh. Many doubt the Promised Land itself!"

Miriam lowered her raised arms and released her clenched fists. She had ever been one to talk with her hands. All the more so when her stiff-necked people were getting under her skin. "Well, Datya, one among us is not confused. On the very stones he chisels our history onto, he has also marked the time. Day by day. Year by year. Moses has kept a quiet tally. Would you like to know how much time has passed, Datya?"

Following the girl's rapid nod, Miriam revealed the truth. "Only one cycle of the moon remains, Datya. From full moon to full moon is all that remains of your time in the wilderness." Though she had originally longed to see the Promised Land herself, Miriam had long ago left that desire to be lost among the wild hills. It was enough - it was more than enough - to be a vessel of the Lord's work through her life. Still, for Datya's sake, and for the sake of other servants, like faithful Joshua, Miriam was eager for the days to pass swiftly. "It is no great secret, you know. Moses doesn't keep it from the people. Any who ask may see or be told of the tally. Moses shares the truth of the count with people nearly every day. But confusion reigns by the works of so many who believe they are right and Moses is wrong. Doubting Moses would not be so beastly a thing, except that Yahweh is with him. Doubting Moses is doubting our own savior!" *Oh, Yahweh, I plead once more that you would bring wisdom to my foolish people. How much they lack when they walk in their own ways!*

Though her student's voice wavered, she raised a question. "How can we be sure, Miriam, that Yahweh will take us in? How do you know that the desert days will end?" Taking Datya's sweet hand once more, Miriam's voice delivered truth. "Make no mistake, Datya. The Israelites have trouble tracking the time, but our great Heavenly Father does not. Every word he speaks will reign true. Every promise will be kept. Every judgement will be metered out. The Promised Land is right around the corner, Datya."

After sampling nourishment from Miriam's troves of dried food, Datya called a passing servant in to help move Miriam's pallet closer to the tent entrance. Night was beginning to claim the horizon. Despite the brightness of the distant Pillar of Fire, Miriam and Datya could still observe the vast display of illustrious stars dotted above the camp. Miriam's face lit once more with delight in the near dark; this too was a lesson for her sweet student. Silent moments soaking up the Creator's wonder had always been a boon to Miriam's faith, as they must become for Datya's.

Battling the temptation to fill the space with instruction, she watched as Datya looked to the lights placed so lovingly by their Creator. Did the girl see in those small specks just how large Yahweh truly was? Did she understand the size of the hand who had crafted the endless skies? Did she realize that she was situated in those very palms, for all her days? Settling to close the day in prayer, Miriam began to claim all these things and more over the heart of her student. How she would need this amazing, majestic Master in the coming days.

CHAPTER TEN

Datya awoke to the sounds of men's voices calling to one another in the distance. The voices seeped into the tent from the direction of the herds. It was birthing time for many of the sheep, camels, and oxen. Listening to the frantic shouts, Datya overheard that a mother ewe was having trouble; her shepherd was seeking help to bring the little lambs into the world. For a moment the man seemed frantic, then calmer as nearby shepherds came to aid and advise, only to once again sound the alarm. Datya wondered if the little lambs would make it. *How many will there be? Will the mother be alright?* She had little experience with caring for animals. Her father owned a small assortment but paid a childhood friend, turned shepherd, to care for their animals amongst his own.

Once when Datya had been little, her father had brought home a weakling lamb from the flock. He had said it was too little to even stew, nor would it survive to produce more sheep. She had begged her father to let her nurse the little lamb. With reluctant agreement, Cohen had bent down to look his little daughter in the eyes. He had told her the sheep couldn't be saved, that it would be better if he took it away. The memory of that little lamb still stung to this day; how she had wanted to save that soft, patchy baby. How she hoped to see it grow. Her father had been right, as usual, the lamb had only lived a few hours before it's body caved in, lifeless and cold. It had never nursed beneath its mother, never slept in a patch of sunshine. Datya had wept over the little lamb, while her mother fretted over the state of her soiled robes.

Her father had once again stooped to her level, scooping the lifeless lamb from her arms. "He had a better death than any lamb before him, little one, do not cry." It was some comfort to Datya, knowing that she gave the little lamb a few hours of love. How like that lamb was she! She had been born a weakling into a world of wolves, but she knew that all of her hours spent on this earth, she would be held in God's arms. Wondering if Miriam felt the same way, Datya turned to ask her teacher. They'd left the leather opening to their desert home ajar last night to harvest the cool breeze blowing in from the far off hills. Wincing, Datya quickly crawled across the space between her and the prophetess. Sweat was beaded around Miriam's beloved face, though the dawn light was still cool and pleasant. Her hands clenched and relaxed, clenched and relaxed by her sides. *She is in pain!* Gently wiping away the perspiration while searching for words that could comfort or help Datya whispered. "Miriam, what is it? I am here." Eyes fluttering, Miriam's response was mangled and tense: "It will pass, child, just wait."

Once more, from beyond the dunes and tents, Datya could hear the shepherds. They were rejoicing! She couldn't make out what the problem had been, but the mother ewe and three baby lambs were all doing well! Though she wanted to boldly make her way out close enough to see the new little balls of fleece, she held fast to Miriam's side. *Yahweh, help her! Help me; I do not know how to pray for her!* No recent day had pitted her heart so against itself. With one ear tuned to the happy little birth and another witnessing the agony of aging, Datya's heart wavered. If only her dear teacher could face these final days without such suffering! Feeling a hand tugging her down, Datya shook her head free of the warring prayers and worries.

"Now, Datya," Miriam's breath was as loud as her voice as it slowly evened out. "Hastening to fear once more?" Miriam's gentle, smiling face looked up at her student. The sweat was gone, the pain was gone, but with it, Miriam's strength seemed as slight as that long-ago baby lamb's. "I am sorry you were frightened. Entering this world is a messy, painful, often terrifying process for the newborn. What you don't realize until you get much older, is that leaving this world can be much the same." Miriam chuckled as though her recent torment was nothing more than a desert pebble to stumble on. "Alright, Datya, let's not waste the dawn. I'll be just fine here, resting against a pack while you fetch us some of Yahweh's bountiful bread." Giving way to Miriam's contagious grin, Datya let go of the former tension. Wise words from the prophetess floated once more to memory *'Never give sorrow one more minute than it has earned.'* With careful shifting and hauling, Datya mounded up the softest satchels in Miriam's possession to be a comfortable support. Shaking her head at her mentor's mischievous mirth, Datya ducked through the opening into the sunshine.

Wilderness air wasn't always easy to take in. Often it was hot or full of dust, or, sometimes, one's guilt was so heavy that taking any sort of deep breath felt intolerable. Today, Datya knew she needed the air that Yahweh mercifully filled the skies with. She knew she needed her Creator to pour life into her. It warred within her very nature to be joyful when the loss of Miriam was so near. Nevertheless, the wisdom of her teacher rang true. Mourning began after the loss and only then. The prophetess was known throughout all Israel for this very perspective and Datya suspected, in the coming years, the same would be expected of her.

Thankful that Miriam had given her permission to omit the daily visit to her family's tent before she left, Datya hurried to gather abundant manna to break their fast. It took no time at all to gather enough flakes to make two women full. Most days, Datya savored this task, making the act of providing nourishment for herself, an act of worship as well. Today, she commanded her feet to move urgently over the outlying land as she offered her thoughts to God. *Yahweh, I know I must submit to Your plan, but I cannot quiet my heart from its longing for more time with Miriam. Help me to find peace; help me to prepare to say goodbye.* Her mind felt weighted with a weariness she had never known before. It seemed the prayers of the week had been a kind of toil. Was it the loss that pressed on her? Or was it simply this strange new season of no longer being a child, but being a woman among Jacob's descendants? A prophetic woman at that. Or was it neither? Perhaps, it was simply the dawning of her anointing that burdened her. It was a great gift to be called to this work, but for the first time, she felt a kindred awareness of the weight Moses, and Joshua too, had so long worked under.

Returning once more to Miriam's leather home, Datya poured mounds of manna into the shallow dish Miriam held on her lap. Raising a wafer to her lips with one hand Miriam offered Datya a wineskin with the other. Knowing they would not munch long in silence, Datya looked to her teacher through half-closed lids. She longed for Miriam to share all the secrets of Yahweh's ways with her, and she longed to know Miriam's thoughts on Israel's future. Custom dictated that she wait for Miriam to speak, a precept she nearly always obeyed, but today impatience gave way. "Miriam, I long to know what's coming. I mean, what lies before you? And before Israel? How can I motivate their faith if I am as lost and blind as they?"

~~~

Exhaling the blended, spicy scents of coriander, honey, and wine, Miriam once again let laughter erupt. How delightful her young student was! Truly the girl believed Miriam had insight beyond that of the people around them. Often Yahweh awoke messages of hope or judgement in her heart, and yet, many more times, Miriam simply had to walk by faith, just as the many sojourners around her. "I think, sweet Datya, that we'll discuss Joshua, Son of Nun today." Datya's face lit with confusion and surprise at Miriam's announcement. "Yes, Moses' young
~~~

steward will bear the revelation you are looking for." With her winsome declaration, Miriam settled deeper upon the packs supporting her and closed her eyes to several moments of silence.

Poor Datya would think she had fallen asleep, but, this story, being one of her favorites, was best presented slowly. Afterall, it's not everyday the God of the Skies and Seas orchestrates such a dramatic victory over such a fierce foe. Certainly, Datya was well aware of the skirmishes in which the Hebrews had found themselves pitted against the wild, violent Amalekites. They had talked before of that early victory when Joshua had battled back the enemy, but today, Miriam would start at the very beginning. Ah! How she loved this fervent, high-stakes story. Yes, it must be told slowly!

For the second time, Datya's patience failed her, "I don't understand, Miriam, how can Joshua's experiences be of any use to me? He is not even a prophet!" The girl's frustrated expression threatened to release another of Miriam's grins. Datya was certainly very familiar with Moses' chief apprentice. Joshua had even tutored Datya's own father, Cohen, long before Datya's birth. Their families had remained close and she had grown up calling Joshua her *dohd*. The man truly had been an uncle to Cohen and Lisbet's three babes.

No wonder Datya was confused; she was familiar with Joshua's fun and caring side, but she lacked understanding of his warrior position. "Joshua is a man of victory, Datya, for he has faced and conquered many opponents during these wandering days. Under Moses' command, and Yahweh's protectorate, Joshua leads the people into victory. Your work is much the same, though you do not use swords and spears, rather words and worship." Datya's face revealed she was working hard to sort out her teacher's revelation.

"Within months of Israel's Red Sea Crossing, a vast group of godless nomads rose from the South and made a target of our people. They were descendants of Amalek, a vile and evil king who had made war his pleasure." With Datya's patient nod, Miriam knew the young girl had heard all of this before. Yet, there was no mistaking Yahweh was whispering 'Tell the tale of Joshua and the Amalekites,' to her spirit. Continuing, Miriam's tone unleashed holy words. "Since that time, Yahweh himself has declared that Amalek would be utterly destroyed, vanquished from the earth, that his memory would be worth less than even the dust beneath our feet. But in those days, during those doubt-riddled wanderings, Amalek's blood coursed with savage strength through his warriors. Their attacks were swift and ruthless, aimed most often at the widows, stragglers, the ill, and the herds. We had been brick makers, Datya. Builders. Farm hands along the Nile. None among us was trained to fight nor protect. Yet, something had to be done." Miriam winced thinking of the many bodies that were wrapped and sunk into the earth after a visit from Amalek's marauders. Even now, the dark memories thickened her pulse with revulsion.

"We had many months of traveling before we would pass beyond Amalekite territory. Our people could not survive so long a journey under the threat of constant sabotage. Finally, Yahweh spoke. Moses, Aaron, Hur, and Joshua were given detailed instructions. Though I expected the men of the camp to quake and rebel upon hearing that they would become soldiers for the day, our wonderful, wise God filled the camp with a venerable courage. It seemed to flow out and over them from the Pillar of God's presence." Remembering the thickness of God's spirit in camp, as the great battle approached, Miriam's form trembled, just as it had on that day. God's own spirit was a mighty thing for a people to experience. The people shook under the power of God's spirit dousing them with courage they never could have mustered on their own. "As we approached the place they call Rephidim, the attacks of the Amalekites began to overwhelm us in frequency and severity. No more than three days had separated any of the consecutive onslaughts. Hope among the people had dammed up tightly; all memory of the Crossing seemed dammed up as well. Terror reigned - some would say, rightly so, for of all the foes in the wilderness, none were feared as much as Amalek's descendants."

Datya's own face mirrored the fear the Isarelites had tasted not so long ago. Desperate families had fought to move from the ordered positions towards the inner rings of the camp. Mothers drove themselves to exhaustion to keep their wee ones from dropping even a pace behind the body of the moving camp. Widows who had previously been tenderly cared for were suddenly abandoned as neighbors gave in to the gut-clenching fright of the slaying enemy. Israel had not honored one another. The swiftness of abandoning the joy of the Red Sea Crossing and taking up the panic of prey had caused Miriam's own head to spin. "What a pitiful sight we must have presented to Yahweh, nothing like the priestly people he had called us to be! Moses' own worries for the tribes began to climb. Already, they had been a difficult people to guide, but, with panic in play, what hope had our leaders of successfully traversing this untamed land?" Sympathy shone from her student's eyes; Datya had always been sensitive to the grievances of Moses' position. He had only spoken to the girl a handful of times in her lifetime, and yet she was his staunch supporter, a faithful, prayerful little partner of his work. How blessed that aged man was to have this young daughter's favor, though he didn't know it!

Eyes closed once more, Miriam settled deeper into the story. How well she recalled that long ago morning. Though she'd had to wait outside the tent with Hur, she too had felt the rising waves of God's spirit mustering the camp. Yahweh was getting ready to move. "The tribes had gone two days since an attack. One of those had been a Sabbath. Moses had sent messengers telling every family and patriarch, "Fast and pray for deliverance." That Sabbath was marked by hands and knees in the dirt and voices raised loudly to the sky as men, women, and youths cried out to Yahweh. All knew that the following day would surely bring the rage of the Amalekites. Before the next dawn, and before even the manna had formed, Moses gathered the elders. We encircled the Tent of Presence, and many of the worshipful women of Israel joined me as we prayed and lifted praises to our God. Finally Moses, Aaron, and Joshua stepped from the tent. While Moses often covered his face amongst the people, there was no need amongst the faithful of the leaders - we were overwhelmed, but also uplifted by the glory shining on his face." Strange tears always filled Miriam's eyes upon viewing Moses cloaked in God's glory. They were tears of joy and awe, but they often stung too, with a touch of holy pain. She felt them now, as she recalled that early morning declaration. "He had been with God and he was bearing a message of our deliverance. Shouts of triumph arose as the darkness of night lifted off the camp." Her own face glowed, all these many years later, as she described Yahweh's saving power, as He poured out rushing peace over her people. "Moses spoke directly to Joshua, sending him to gather men who would spend the day as warriors. It was then that our small crowd noticed the staff. Moses had left behind his everyday staff, exiting the Tent instead with the Staff of God! The very staff that had humiliated and devoured the gods of Egypt! In that moment, not a single elder or prophetess among Israel doubted the victory that was surely coming." Glancing to her student's face, painted with wonder and anticipation, Miriam gratefully realized that the account was winding deep roots into Datya.

Upon seeing the Staff of God resting in the humble crook of Moses' arm, Miriam had been filled with a vision. Yahweh's guiding Pillar of Cloud had lifted from in front of the camp, and begun to thin out in the sky. It's folds and winding substance stretched and uncoiled until it was a great blanket in the sky. It was God's own presence hovering above the fields of Rephidim. Under it stood two armies. One led by Joshua, the other by Amalek's grandson. The part of the Cloud that hung above Israel's mighty men seemed full of light, and yet shaded the men as they fought. She saw that the Cloud suspended above the Amalekite troops sunk heavily upon their shoulders, as though they battled through seawater rather than air. Great streaks of light pulsed through this portion of the Cloud, and it seemed to roll and quake above their prideful heads. As Miriam relayed this vivid memory to Datya, she reminded the girl that such visions opened up the spiritual world to simple-minded humans. "God may give you one vision in your lifetime, Datya, or he may give you hundreds. Remember this, each vision is only possible for you to witness and bear because you are an Image-Bearer of Yahweh himself. This, Yahweh declared at the very foundations of the world when he created the first seeds of *enosh,* Adam and Eve." Tears clouded the vision of both Miriam and her student at the reminder; the wonderful God who had brought *enosh,* mankind into existence cared enough to reveal all manner of spiritual sight to his servants throughout all time to come.

Joshua's obedience had always set him apart among the tribes. All knew that he had never questioned Moses, and seemed to have unshakeable faith. Those closest to him had seen his private battles where doubt had once stood tall. Nevertheless, he was known from tribe-to-tribe as "faithful," and "righteous." "Joshua carried out the command within the hour. Sending dozens of Moses' swiftest attendants, Joshua called for every man his age or older to gather what blunt or sharp object they could and move with all haste to the front of camp. The younger men were to disperse among the camp and guard the rear. Never before has a small army assembled so expeditiously. Nor any since, I suspect." Datya's eyes, as round and large in this moment as they could possibly be, drank in the retelling. How Miriam loved sharing this treasured testimony with her pupil! She couldn't help wondering what manifestations of God's glory Datya herself would witness in the coming years.

"Moses began trekking up a shrub-studded hill a few miles

beyond the camp. With Aaron and Hur by his side, he arrived at the top in time to see Joshua's hastily amassed army begin to advance against the ruthless troops. With the grasp of a young man, Moses lengthened his arms past the edge of the cliff, and slowly raised them above his head. In those mighty, toughened hands, the Staff of God reigned high above the battle. Though the camp could not see their leader's presumptive victory stance, the warring men, of both sides could. No doubt, the Amalekites knew of Moses - the man who walked in the very spirit of the plague-casting God. Never before had the people of Amalek submitted a single drop of fear to the name of Yahweh. I wonder. No, I know they did at that moment. The Staff of God meant nothing to them, but, deep within, I suspect their fiercest men began to tremble. The victories of Yahweh in the surrounding nations - and yes, in Egypt, herself - had been too great, too wonderful to dismiss." Many of the elders had gone to that plateau with Moses, staying out of sight of the armies, but close enough to see the muscles and veins of Moses' arms struggling as the sun lengthened in the sky.

Moses's strength outlasted elders, who settled into the dismal shade of dried-up shrubs. Miriam herself had held her breath more often than wise as she listened to shouts, clanging, and clamor below. "The Staff battled down the pride of Amalek until they were warring with a stub of their former ferocity. Meanwhile, Joshua's troops moved through the slain enemy that was falling at their feet. Near the noon hour, Moses's arms, deathly pale in their grip, quavered to keep the Staff from collapsing. All the elders jumped to their feet, but what could any of us do? Moses' task was to uphold God's instructions for the battle. Aaron could not take over, I could not take over. Moses must raise it, and raise it well. A support was all any of us could offer, and the men swiftly offered one to Moses in the way of a heap of flat stones. Moses' stiffly lowered to his throne, though all knew that it was Yahweh's presence that was so heavy on the rock. Quiet, faithful Aaron took his brother's shaking arm and stretched it once more towards the sky. On Moses' opposite side, Hur followed suit, and once again the banner of the Lord was propelled high above the battle." Miriam shuttered, remembering the nearly sudden death screams of the opposing army that had risen to the top of that hill as the Staff of God once again claimed it's lofty position.

With the courage to stride forward, Miriam had found a vantage point that confirmed the victory. Joshua's troops surged forward. Amalek's fell in grisly lines, their bodies torn apart as though the wickedness had been ripped from within them. "Swords and spears continued to strike, inching the enemy backwards. Even weaponless men locked their mighty arms around Amalekite warriors, quickly diminishing each new opponent." For mothers, and those who loved like mothers, the temptation to spare their little ones from the gore of war was strong. Watching the pale grimace rising on Datya's face made Miriam want to withhold the violence of that day. But how could she know of the vast threat, the great effort, and the final triumph if her teacher avoided the story's harshest details? "Most of daylight was spent before the barbarians turned and fled towards far dunes. Joshua's exhausted men slowly made their way back through the grime and blood. The women had spent the day erecting tents in a makeshift encampment. The warriors, victorious though they were, would spend many days removed from Israel." Shuttering at the horrid smell of the camp, and the remembrance of grown men weeping over what they had endured, Miriam told of how hundreds of their women had hauled and tugged barrels and buckets and skins of water to the men.

Washing away the stink of the day had taken hours, but washing away the impurity of participating with death had taken much longer. The warriors who had fought had later been quick to accept Yahweh's commandments at Sinai regarding ritual cleansing and purification after being such close witnesses of death. For his own part, Moses had stayed upon the hill.

He no longer had the Staff raised over his head, but he had summoned his pupils to search out perfect stones for an altar. Once again, the young boys who lived under his tutelage carried and curated heavy stones to and fro. Moses had overseen the exact placement of every single one, until a large altar arose overlooking Rephidim. "Though his voice was as aged as his aching muscles and skin, Moses cried out at that altar "The Lord is My Banner!" His voice had carried down beyond the mountain, even miles away it was heard, as though God himself lent it volume. All knew that Joshua and the mighty men had won the day by Yahweh's hand alone!"

Though Miriam had stayed put, camping on the hill with Aaron, Hur, and Moses, the majority of the elders had scurried down. With urgent feet that sought out their tents, their families, anyone who would listen, to relay the message: Yahweh is a Banner over Israel. "Overwhelming relief swept Israel, much dancing and singing had erupted among our people, Datya. I wouldn't be surprised if the Egyptians themselves could hear the jubilant roar of the slaves-turned-desert-outcasts. How many were the nations and rulers who had scoffed at our God! How often we had been snickered at. The nations believed our people a lost cause, saying 'Surely, they will die out in the vast wasteland!' What fools, Datya! Yahweh humbled the peoples of the earth at Rephidim - through wild, humble Moses, and through stout, brave Joshua. Through the prayers of women like you and I, Yahweh reduced the threat of the Amalekites to ashes!"

Eyes closed once more, Miriam pivoted into prayer. *Yahweh, I know my sweet Datya knows the value of your victories. She can see the fierce love you have for your people, but many of her generation overlook the tremendous way you triumphed over the Amalekites. They forget or devalue your favor. Stir them up, Lord. Sift away the distractions and doubts that make them complacent.* Looking up, Miriam realized that Datya had followed suit. The young woman's lips moved with slight whispers; she too had realized the grave state of the hearts of her kinsmen. She recognized how they traded faith and favor for the insatiable desire for goods and status.

Watching her spiritual daughter pray, Miriam quietly sank further into her plush support. The retelling of Joshua and the Amalekites was a critical tool to hand to her pupil, but it had been costly. How she hated the fluttering, drip-dropping feel coursing through her chest. One moment breathing was as natural as ever and then in the next, spasms reigned until she could scarcely funnel air into her chest. She knew in her heart that the days she had left could be counted in hours now. Then the pain would be no more, but she couldn't deny the twinge of fear that came with each suffocating spasm. Many were the men and women who died in an instant, or in their sleep. They had no time to dwell on the silly questions that Miriam battled now. *What will death be like? Will death be the last word of Miriam, will my work end like a candle being blown out? Ah, Miriam, how foolish you are to spend your last hours on such thoughts!*

Reaching out to Datya, Miriam followed the nudge within once more. "You must continue this prayer, Datya. For your generation, you must pray for their faith every day. Always beseeching the Father to cancel doubts, to build great paths of faith, to make His spirit strong amongst you, as he did the day the Amalekites tasted his wrath. This is your lesson for today. Joshua knows well and good the wonder of that long-ago victory, but if he never asks for another one, his faith will grow cold. Tell the stories of the triumphs, Datya, from the Victory at Rephidim, to the Red Sea, to the Plagues, to the amazing way the Lord knit the lives of the Patriarchs, but look forward too, dear one. The miracles that haven't happened yet are the ones that will propel Israel into the Promised Land and keep her there, if her people have the valour to pray and hope for them" Defiantly, Miriam leaned forward. Struggling to breathe or not, she would not break her connection to Datya's awe-filled eyes until she was sure the young girl understood. "Mark these words in your heart. Keep them close for all of your days-"

"A message for the prophetess!" The winded voice that suddenly broke into the folds of the tent sounded young, and familiar. With a bemused nod she gestured to Datya to rise and greet the messenger. The boy's hasty announcement seemed urgent, though Miriam hated to halt such a vital lesson.

Upon raising the tent's front wall and thoughtfully tacking it far to one side, Datya ushered in the young boy. Younger even than Ziva, Miriam immediately beckoned to the little one whom she recognized as one of her many great nephews. Aaron's daughters and daughters-in-law, had produced many sturdy boys for the youngest generation. All were well known throughout the tribes for they carried all manner of messages, often day and night. Elders of the camp, judges, leaders, all relied on boys, like Aaron's grandsons to spread news amongst all the men and women. Drawing him close, Miriam kissed the boy's forehead and offered him a wineskin of semi-cool water. "I have a message for you," the boy seemed suddenly timid. She may be his great aunt, but Israel had so steeped her reputation in intrigue that he only saw her as the great prophetess, one for whom he had an important mission. Chuckling, Miriam beckoned the sweet boy to deliver it, this instant! Her humor scurried away into the sand as the boy spoke again, "I am sent to tell you that your brother, Aaron, high priest of Israel, has not moved since morning. He remains stricken to his pallet, and is not expected to rise again." The boy had been trained, likely from just a few years of age, to deliver all messages with urgency, but withholding all emotion. He seemed like a small adult as he delivered the news about his own grandfather, even mastering the tears which had mounted a sting in her own eyes.

Miriam struggled to hear her nephew, as though he were

far away. She had silently kept her eyes on her own passing through this uncomfortable week, but she had been blind to other deaths to come. Datya seemed less shocked, as though she had sensed it; Miriam would have to ask her about it later. "Aaron's sons Eleazar and Ithamar continue to serve in the Tabernacle, but the remainder of his descendants are gathering to him. His speech is much altered, and he cannot rise, but, already, he has begun administering final blessings on those who come close." With each heavy statement, the boy's professional demeanor seemed to crumble a bit more until her student wrapped up his little body as he began to sob. Loss was nothing new in the desert, but Miriam suddenly faced a stark revelation: Israel was about to enter long, suffocating days of mourning. Despite the familiar pain gripping her heart, Miriam stretched to take the boy into her own arms. At his age, he likely seldom felt such embraces, but she knew that this was the best way to meet the little one's hurt.

Though the boy soon became so quiet that Miriam wondered if he had fallen asleep, her own thoughts could not be so easily tamed. She longed to go to her brother, to stand before Israel and testify of his service, character, and lifetime loyalty to Yahweh. Her own body racked with weakness and agony, she could do none of those things. Jostling her nephew to rise, she kissed him once more. "Now, little one, you must deliver a message from me. Aaron is to be told the Chief Prophetess among Israel has been seen at her tent, singing of the great servant Aaron, proclaiming his faithful service to the tribes!"

While sending the messenger on his way, she also commissioned Datya for a task. She was to go and find two or three of Miriam's servants to come and remove Miriam to her makeshift doorpost. Many years ago, when her daughter had already married and Miriam no longer had great need, she had begun lending out her servants to other households. More often than not they were sent to help young mothers or struggling widows.

She had continued to place her household servants into other homes until she lived alone. Many puzzled at her decision, for who among this dense crowd lived alone? Yet, she stood by her generous act. Periodically, when a need arose she would briefly recall a servant or two. Now, Datya would fetch those servants, for Miriam could neither stand nor walk. Be that as it may, nothing would keep her from testifying for her beloved brother's sake.

Two servants, both middle-aged men now, who had been born into her household entered timidly and approached her. Moving an elderly patron was likely nothing new to them, but many among Israel, both slave and free, had a lingering fear of touching the prophetess. Whether they recalled her brief encounter with leprosy or they were simply caught up in the superstition surrounding her prophetic work, she knew not. "Move swiftly, men, just carry me beyond the leather opening and then you'll be free to return to more pleasant work." She would have bubbled up with laughter if thoughts of her dear brother weren't pressing on her. As the men gently lifted Miriam up into the air, Datya quickly relocated her pallet and several mounds of cushioning packs. How strange it felt to be suspended in the air, moving about through the power of others' muscles. All her life her own feet had propelled her and her own hands had worked to meet her needs. Now in her last days, she could do neither. *Thank you Yahweh for keeping me from pride. I can submit to being carried about if it means I get to testify one last time.* After being lowered to her pallet, Miriam insisted the men return that evening to carry her back inside. "It will be the last time I ask it of you," she whispered, though she wasn't sure the bowing men heard her.

Settling deep into prayer Miriam sought the Lord. *Father, give me one last song. For Aaron. Help me to tell the people of the Magnificent God that called quiet, plain Aaron to the high priesthood!* Miriam's eyes were slow to open. The day had taken a toll on her, and truthfully, the desire to lie down in sleep was overpowering. Yet, she had a song to sing. Many had gathered around her. Aaron's tents would be welcoming close family, and other elders only. Others who heard of his condition would flock to Miriam, looking for peace and comfort. *How little I have to offer these people. And yet, Yahweh is here. If I give him my voice, he will minister to the people.*

Ignoring the weakness that strove to keep her quiet, she opened her mouth, singing of the steadfastness of Aaron. With a melody woven of old stories and new notes, she exalted his faithful service by Moses' side. She sang of Aaron's staff devouring the devious snakes which had hissed into existence by means of the Egyptian's dark arts. Breaking into a quiet hum, Miriam recalled that evening as Moses and Aaron had sat in her small mudbrick home. With exuberant hands flying they had both recited the intense session in Pharaoh's court, stumbling all over themselves to get the story out. Miriam too had been elated by the tale. So long had her people waited for such signs and wonders! The Hebrew masses had struggled to embrace the joy. The oppression had been so endless and so fierce that even a miracle could scarcely kindle their hope.

To the gathering witnesses, Miriam lifted her voice describing the beautiful tabernacle coming into existence. Men and women had labored over every detail, while Aaron had immersed himself in learning every aspect of Yahweh that he could. Day in and day out he had poured over Moses' secret stones, looking for every clue to Yahweh. Aaron pursued the fulfillment of one question: Who is Yahweh? He wouldn't rest until he was woven through with the character of the Saving God. Almost since the moment of his return to Egypt, Moses had been quietly interviewing every elder and man among Israel who had even a smidgen of knowledge to share. He especially hunted for the history of the time before Egypt. Many accounts were recorded for Moses' written history, but Yahweh himself revealed all of the missing details to Moses. All of this knowledge

Aaron devoured. He had been a faithful observer of their customs all of his life, barring his now-forgiven lapse at the base of Sinai. In Egypt, he had been considered devout, but here in the wilderness, as he actually came to know Yahweh, he had been transformed. People saw him shed the last bondages of slavery, and the sanctified man that stepped forth as their high priest was nothing like the man that had apathetically cast a golden calf for the freshly freed Israelites.

Though the sun was nearly sunk, Miriam would not allow her voice to give out. All who remained active in the camp, or at least those nearby, would hear of the way Aaron had mourned Israel's sin these many years, and how he had tenderly overseen their victories. As her servants returned to carry her once more beyond her curtained home, she begged a boy who was hovering nearby to fetch her word of her brother. "Go and seek the tent of Aaron, the high priest. Bring me word of him, and offer him my loving blessing."

Unwavering, Datya had stayed by her side through the long day, surely deeply enmeshed in the thoughts of oncoming loss. For Datya, it was a brewing storm that wouldn't stay quiet; harsher even than the fierce heat of the wilderness' rare storms. She had seen Miriam perform mourning songs hundreds of times before in their years together. She had been there through the aching weeks as Miriam mourned her own daughter who died so young. Today had been different, hosting a new, heartbreaking lament. Today, Miriam had finally pivoted to face the ending of her own life. Datya would not have missed the change in her demeanor.

"None of the tutors in all Israel have a charge as sweet as I," Miriam murmured as the young woman thoughtfully took her hand. She meant to lend her strength. Miriam was silently stunned by the reversal in their companionship. In the past, teacher had offered student aid and support, but here, in these closing hours, the student was offering what strength she could to her beloved prophetess. So often Miriam thought of her as the awkward, shy girl who had first been delivered into her tutelage. When Miriam could get the tiny, dark-haired child to speak, she had often tumbled over her nervous tongue. Miriam's tendency to see the mirth in such a struggle probably startled the little one even more. Nonetheless, Datya had grown in her shadow and had absorbed all the methods and wisdom of their shared kingdom work. Truly, she had developed into a young woman who was a treasure in God's service.

Though Miriam knew in her heart she had one more sunrise to witness, she also knew that if there were no more, her ministry was in capable hands. Datya would never be the vessel of perfect ministry, but her spirit belonged to Yahweh and her life had been crafted and curated with the skills of their calling. Miriam felt a wonderful namelessness. She was no longer a leader, but a citizen. She sensed the mantle was passing. Tonight, she would go to sleep as a former prophetess for the first time in her life. Did Datya know? Did she understand that she was the Chief Prophetess of Israel now? Miriam just managed another solemn prayer over her dear sweet counterpart before sinking into what rest would be allotted to her this night.

CHAPTER ELEVEN

A grimace, the dozenth in as many minutes, dislodged the dust that had settled on Datya's face. Miriam was in pain once more. Her sleep was deep, but the pain managed to course through her skin and muscles, convincing her body to twist and tighten. Datya knew not what to do. Hours had passed and the darkness still remained. How long had she sat at her teacher's side? How long had she been begging Heaven to pull away the mantle of pain? The night had been young still when Miriam's gasping breaths urged her closer. The young woman had carried her pallet as close as she dared though she had long since abandoned reverence for a sweet kinship. Now the mat that cushioned Datya most evenings was just inches away from Miriam's shoulders. Those same shoulders now tensed with raspy breathing and the frequent tremors of pain. What caused the agony tormenting her mentor, Datya could not even guess at. Somehow she knew that the dawn that had not yet made an appearance would be Miriam's last, and it crushed her.

Able to offer only a gentle stroke or pat, or at times press Miriam's arms gently to keep the writhing from causing further injury, she felt despairingly helpless in the dark of their desert dwelling. For not the first time Datya questioned herself: *Should I fetch help? What would Miriam have me do?* The silence gave the same answer that her teacher would have, had she been lucid. There is nothing anyone can do. It seemed one of Datya's final tests would be to walk closely with Miriam on her way out of this world. Leading her teacher to life's exit was an unwelcome task. So long, Miriam had been a step ahead because she was guiding Datya, showing her the way. Datya's duty had been to quietly model the prophetess, to faithfully quote her, until all was learned and every detail molded into the foundation Datya required. With this swift and severe reversal, Miriam no longer paved a way for Datya, but struggled through the remainder of her own journey.

How foolish she had been to imagine that Miriam's death would be wrapped in the same grace and charm that her daily life was! No matter how great the personage, death was a cumbersome, bitter load to carry. Even the most graceful among Israel would succumb to their body's pitiful attempts to exhale the last of life. Datya's hope faltered. Her test stared her down, though she herself could see little; it remained a burden she could not pass up, to simply be at her beloved mentor's side. She could offer nothing more to Miriam than the knowledge that she remained, through it all, until the last moment.

Despite resigning herself to be a faithful attendant through the day, she knew Miriam would request news of Aaron, if her body allowed her to wake with the dawn. She could not seek out the news without depriving Miriam of her presence, so in the stillness, she waited long hours for any passing foot step. Finally, still long before the manna, Datya heard rustling, nothing more than a featherlight disturbance in the sand. Dashing from the tent, she was thankful for the half moon that cast enough light to see the passerby. Melting in relief, Datya rushed forward as she recognized her sweet friend, Ravit. For a long moment, Datya simply laid her head on the shoulder of her friend's embrace. Tears didn't belong to this hour, though Datya felt much inclined to weep. Ravit, stable and compassionate, held on. The woman's dream of nearly a week ago filled in the answer to the unspoken question: *Whatever is wrong, Datya?* Both knew these pre-dawn hours were the beginning of death's labor pains for Miriam.

Releasing her tired voice into the moonlight, Datya commissioned Ravit. "I must have word of the High Priest before Miriam awakes. She will need word of her brother. Will you seek out his servants and discern his condition for me, Ravit? I cannot leave her for even a moment." Already, Datya felt anxious to slip into the tent to resume her vigil. Ravit consented and filled in the curious question of why she roamed in the darkness. A Gadite woman was giving birth, and her other little ones needed looking after. Ravit had been sent for and was willingly on her way to help. She would carry the two with her and fetch word, quickly, of Aaron. The would-be sisters shared a quick solemn hug for they both knew they were now living Ravit's vision. Deaths were coming and neither of them could stop even one.

Datya returned to Miriam's side with haste. She longed to tack up the front wall for the faint light of predawn and the breeze it would scatter through the stiff tent, but she knew Miriam's private battle deserved closed quarters. Bending low, Datya tenderly shifted Miriam's aged head into her lap, fighting sobs as she had been these long hours. Her beloved mentor was hours away from death, and Datya had never felt more lonesome. Miriam would tell her to pray, and yet her mind was too focused on the raw evidences of pain to do anything but worry. Still, what else could she do? *Yahweh, help me! You have judged my heart wrong! I am not strong enough for this loss. I cannot bear it.* Many times, Datya had felt an answer to prayer in the immediate. God would calm her with a testimony or remembrance of the past, or he would remind her of his majesty, or one of Miriam's own sayings would float in and Datya would be calmed. Today the darkness matched the silence. She couldn't stymie the tears that began to fall, many of which sunk into the scattered strands of Miriam's variegated hair.

Though the hours had seemed endless, Datya knew that dawn was moments away from kissing the earth. For the Israelites, at least, dawn ushered in a heavenly aroma even as it brought light. Outside, the morning air was thickening with the wondrous scent of honey and coriander even before the first wafer appeared on the ground. In the looming loss, Datya's breath quickened at the wonder of her God. Only true power and true love could stir up such a delightful miracle in the day to day dust of the Israelite life. *How strange you are to me, Yahweh. I ask you to change your plan. I beg you to restore life, yet you answer with a sweet scent. What do you mean by it?* Though she questioned him, she continued to hold Miriam as the answer enveloped her. Yahweh meant comfort by it. She would indeed lose Miriam. And, it would be painful for the woman she cradled. But God's very presence would be wrapped around them both through it all. Datya was at once at war with the thought that God's presence was an even better gift than getting to keep Miriam would be. How hard it was for her humanity to accept that! Still, the whispering truth remained. God wove it into her heart as she held her dying mentor. The God who split the Red Sea held a young, weeping woman, and would hold her even until her own end so many years away.

~ ~ ~

Long before she could convince her lids to part, Miriam recognized Datya's hands plying soothing touches to her head, shoulders, and arms. She pressed with a tender lightness that endeared her all the more to Miriam, and amused her. Her delight rose in stark rebellion against the agony inflaming every inch of her body. Ah, but if Datya stroked a little longer, Miriam's thick wrinkles may even out once more. She would be youthful! Her body, too tired to chuckle, wouldn't give in to the tidbit of humor, though Miriam's mind would seek it out until the last moment. Sensing her student was wandering the fields of prayer, Miriam lay quietly in place, praying for strength through the pain. It had been a come-and-go thing for many months. Sometimes many days went by before a spasm gripped her;

sometimes, like this night, they wracked her with a constant, destructive pace.

Yahweh had met her in a dream many months ago providing all the answer that she would have for the suffering. He had told her that her death would be like the birthing pains of new life. She herself was entering a new life, a foreverness with him, but it would not feel that way. There would be agony, there would be fear, there would be a struggle, a squeezing. He would be the prize at the other side of the last breath, and Miriam would no longer know or remember the pain. This vision, she had shared with no one. Most of what Yahweh revealed to her was for the public, it was milk for the people. This had been for her alone. She scarcely understood it, and, once more, grappled to believe it. She could not fathom a prize, like a sweet newborn, awaiting her beyond this pain. Yet, Yahweh had said it would be so, and he had never given her reason to doubt.

Wondering, not for the first time, if she should share the divine revelation with Datya, Miriam felt relief course through her. It seemed this torrent of agony was finally loosening its grip. Praying for strength, and peace, Miriam's mind headed toward sleep once more. Against her will, her body demanded a true rest before welcoming her final day. *My final day. Yes, Yahweh, let your will be done. I trust you. Help Datya, Lord, help her.*

~ ~ ~

Datya's face hardly knew what expression to cast. Ravit had returned, quietly entering the tent with her two trustees. The eldest, toddled in the folds of Ravit's robe. While the youngest snored and snuffled, tied with a swathe of linen to Ravit's body. She bore good news, and her demeanor lent Datya courage. Aaron had rallied during the night. Though he was still unable to rise or walk, his speech had cleared. He sent "the greatest blessings and honor to Israel's mighty prophetess," and more tenderly, "my beloved sister is to be told that Aaron bows in gratitude for her faithful, godly companionship since my boyhood." Though Datya sagged with relief at the good news and touching messages, she also sank into her fear, the dawn had arrived but Miriam had not woken up.

She had sensed a fading of the pain and struggle more than an hour ago, and had hoped that the Prophetess would awake. She had even dared to secure a small opening in the tent, hoping the caress of morning light would revive Miriam. But the older women had sunk deeper into sleep. Her breaths were light, and only occasionally, did the thick, dangerous warbles escape with it. Ravit reached for Datya's hand and gave it a sturdy squeeze. How often the young woman had spent her time and energy comforting others these many months since her own loss. Datya convinced her mouth to offer the lightest smile to her friend. Though Ravit may not know it, the youthful widow had her own ministry every bit as much as Datya did. Here sat the incoming Chief Prophetess and, dubbing her affectionately, the Chief Comforter of Israel. Datya admired her friend, and thanked God for the revelation that both ministries were of equal value in his sight.

Many of their kinsmen liked to accuse Miriam of pride, declaring she was puffed up with position when she ought to be contrite with humility. These same people threw the same insults at Aaron and Moses. If only people knew that Miriam, and Datya, saw every Hebrew as a minister of their own gift. Chief Prophetess was a title given over many years of faithful service, but Miriam would gladly never hear it again and still work to build faith and tear down doubt in the community. *Yahweh, help me to have such humility. Help me to remember that you call all to service. You have said we are a priestly people. All of us. Show us the way to humbly honor the gifts and callings we each possess.*

Ravit's charges were getting restless, the little one's face was twisting this way and that, looking for it's mother. Likely it would soon recognize that it was strapped to the wrong chest. Sharing a bittersweet smile, Ravit departed, dropping a last kiss on Datya's bent head. No doubt, she would care for these little ones through their mother's long struggle and all the while intercede for the prophetess and her broken-hearted student.

Ravit, like a substitute mother, had thoughtfully gathered a linen-full of manna for Miriam and Datya. She had left it close by so Datya could sample the nourishment without leaving Miriam's side. Datya prayed that Miriam would awake and taste some. *Miriam's last manna.* Her heart sped up at the thought, the sorrow causing the beats to skip like startled footfalls. Her beloved teacher would partake of God's sweet manna for the last time today. Resisting the surge of anger over the selfish muttering the same manna would produce tomorrow - a day when Datya would learn to live without Miriam - Datya commanded her lips to take the bread. She would need strength to see her teacher through these last hours.

Working hard to cancel the renewed threat of tears, Datya's heart leapt to attention. Miriam was waking! As though no pain or sorrow stretched between them, Miriam's mouth slowly curled in an almost-smile at Datya. With a calm that belied her pain, the dying woman stretched her hand into the pile of manna. Popping it into her mouth like the little Hebrew children running about the fields, Miriam's smile grew. It was pale, it was thinner than it had been, but it was lovely. Datya breathed a prayer of gratitude. She would have remained faithfully by her side had she not woken up, but one last day with her teacher meant more than even the manna miracle itself.

Hours ago, she had doubted she would ever again hear Miriam's voice, but it was welcome in her ears as a new comfort was issued. "Datya, dear one, none in Israel make it even to adulthood without knowing loss. Sorrow and suffering swirl around us, and they won't be foreign troubles in the Promised Land either. If every one among Israel must taste grief so soon in life, how much more so does a leader arrive at their position by passing through a fire?" Miriam opened the day with wisdom that snuffed out Datya's self-pity. The command was subtle but clear, one last day to learn, to grow, at least under Miriam's tutelage that is. The prophetess had taken to reminding Datya that her life itself would be a study of God's character. There would be many passing teachers in her life, but Yahweh would be the constant source of wisdom and guidance.

A bursting array of needs was beginning to swamp Datya's thoughts. All at once she wanted to rehearse every story Miriam had ever told, to beg her to tell them once more. She wanted Miriam to sing, every song of majesty and wonder and power that she'd ever known. Thinking also of Miriam's mischievous side, Datya surprised herself by longing to spend the day in high humor with Miriam, laughing at the mirthful tales that were Miriam's favorites. She wanted too, to soak up the testimonies of Miriam's life, to hear of every private and public way that she had lived and served in the anointing of God's spirit. She could not ask for all of these pastimes, nor even one, for that same spirit pressed on her to listen. Miriam was still her teacher, she was still a student. Though quietness had always come easily to her in the past, in this moment, clamping her voice down was a hurdle.

Miriam, full of wisdom, and knowing some of the same longings, chuckled at Datya. How Datya longed for the sound to fill up the tent instead of disappearing so swiftly! From beyond their walls, both women began to hear excitement, neighbors scuffling about, voices raised, many people whose pounding footsteps suggested something was happening that should not be missed.

~ ~ ~

Curiosity had long been Miriam's chief source of trouble. She was known just as thoroughly for her inquisitiveness as she was for her devotion. Thankfully, neither woman would have to taste the frustration of not knowing for long, as a messenger boldly stepped into the tent. Miriam recognized the boy immediately. He was close to Datya's age and had been a ward of Moses for many years. Orphaned after his parents participated in a rebellion, Moses had adopted the boy as an act of mercy. Through his tutelage, he aimed to show the people that all could faithfully serve Yahweh, no matter where they came from. Though the young man's parents had paid a tragic punishment for denying Yahweh, the boy seemed to be filled with a quiet anointing of favor and faithfulness. She had always respected what Moses aimed to do through the boy, though she suspected the lesson was lost on the bulk of the Israelites who had likely long ago forgotten the boy's origins.

"A word with the prophetess?" The boy spoke into the quiet, waiting for permission to deliver his message. With his head bowed, he could not see the delight on Miriam's face. Even Datya withheld a chuckle. It seems the serious customs of the Hebrews would never quite penetrate the joy of the prophetesses, who had learned that humor was as much a gift from heaven as manna. Taking pity on the young man, Miriam lilted, "Speak, I am eager to hear what you have to say." Miriam meant to put the young man at ease, though she herself churned with nervous dread. Was she to hear news of her brother's death when he spoke?

"I am sent from Moses himself. He builds an altar this day. All the people of Israel are gathering to sing praises to Yahweh for the gift of Miriam." Strong though she was, nothing would have prevented the onslaught of tears that quickly made her dark eyes swim. The sweet man. The old, wild, sweet man. Her younger brother had so often left her to do her work in whatever way she would. She had often felt he was less than interested. In moments of clarity, she realized that Moses had placed his ultimate trust in her, and she was blessed that he refused to interfere. That he would be so moved to honor her among all Israel stole her breath. Though Moses' love for her was great, his willingness to display it was a rare thing indeed. In her shock, she had nearly forgotten the boy who ventured to speak once more. "Moses intends to send his best cart for the Prophetess if she is willing to meet the people," and in a flustered whisper, "one final time."

The poor boy! Here he was on assignment to bring a message to Miriam, the Prophetess, and in so doing had to approach her about her death. No messenger among Israel would have vied for his role, but he'd managed it with solemn respect. With an encouraging nod, Miriam dismissed the youth to summon the cart. She knew not how her body would handle the travel, though the distance was within eyesight of her tent. Miriam took Datya's hand, "Datya, catch that young boy for me please. I must ask him to also fetch word of Aaron. I must know if he lives."

~ ~ ~

"Forgive me, Miriam, I have already received word of the High Priest," Datya tripped over her words, ashamed she had neglected to share them sooner. "Word arrived during the night that Aaron is well. His body remains pinned to the earth, but his speech and mind are clear. He too sends you a message." Watching her mentor's face blend with joy and tears once more, Datya relayed the sweet sentiment Aaron had sent by way of Ravit. She knew that the blessing both brothers were speaking over her today would minister to Miriam more than even a healing could. Long years she had cared for the older and the younger, as a surrogate mother, as a co-laborer, and yes as a prophetess. All in Israel had benefited from Miriam's ministry, perhaps none so much as Aaron and Moses. Datya breathed a prayer of thankfulness that Yahweh stirred Aaron and Moses to honor their sister.

Already the women could hear the approaching creek of a cart. Datya could feel the tremor of the packed earth below her as one of Moses' fine oxen drew near. She could see the beast's steady breaths rising and falling in his muscular build as he stopped just outside of the tent. He had approached slowly, likely led by a servant who spent day and night with the animal. Datya was assured that Miriam would have no finer way to travel. Placing her own pallet on the hard wooden surface of the cart, and then Miriam's atop of it, Datya stood aside for the two stewards who lifted Miriam to her new perch.

Trekking to the side of the cart, she refused to move beyond an arm's reach from Miriam. Custom perhaps dictated that she allow Miriam to arrive alone, that she quietly blend in with the gathering masses. Custom wouldn't rule her this day, as she walked beside her faithful mentor. Miriam's final day would include Datya's closest service no matter what. Faltering in her footsteps, her eyes flashed with shock moving first from the crowd to Moses and back to Miriam. Miriam, arriving by cart with her back to the scene, could not see what she saw, though she would hear it. Hundreds had already gathered around Moses. There he stood, on a small, but raised flat patch of earth. Datya had seen this bit of earth as she gathered manna the day after they stopped in this wild encampment. It had stood out to her then as a lovely place to erect a tent, but it never occurred to her that an altar would rise there. Beyond the hundreds gathered to witness the event, ten times that amount seemed to be streaming in from the many varieties of patched homes in the distance. Beyond Moses himself, a reclined figure lay propped against a leather bound load of supplies. Datya knew, even at a distance the figure was Aaron's. Tears sprang to her eyes even as Miriam's exasperated whisper reached her ears, "Well what is it, child, what do you see?" Though she craned her head, the older woman could not see more than a small patch of the people represented.

Datya struggled to return an answer as she dwelt on Aaron's presence. For him to allow himself to be seen in public in such a condition, for surely he had to be carried just as Miriam was, in honor of his sister was so humbling. Many men among her father's tribes would refuse such a condescension.

~ ~ ~

Finally, Miriam's oxen was directed to pivot, angling towards the flat mound of earth. The cart itself was hauled directly past Moses' nearly finished altar until it came to a stop just behind him. Miriam's seat was one in the same as her transportation. In her lifted position, she could see the vast hordes of the Hebrew faithful gathering to honor her. Thankful though she was for them, her eyes fixed on her beloved brothers. The younger she had so often worried over and cared for. The older, so similar to her own self, he often felt like a mirror of her, a part of who she was that could not be dismissed. How appropriate that their lives were closing so near to one another. In her heart, she knew that Moses would follow in hardly no time at all. She did not envy the people the burden of mourning that was coming, but she marveled at the life of service that Yahweh had crafted from the three children of slaves.

Datya had sunk to a place just behind Miriam's shoulder, between the ox and the head of the cart. She would be close by in the event that Miriam needed her, but she planted herself in the background, staying as much out of sight as possible. All too soon the people of Israel would have their eyes locked on Datya the Prophetess and Joshua - the two leaders who would rise to meet the new season of need among these vast tribes.

Miriam reached her hands forward as Moses approached the cart. After he bowed low to the ground he met Miriam's hands with his own. Grasping them first warmly, then pulling her in towards him. With his hands firmly on her shoulders, he held Miriam in a tender wrap. Placing a kiss on her forehead, he looked once more at his dear sister's face. She read his thoughts in an instant. Oh they had butted heads more than once, but none had been knitted together so intensely as the pair. From the moment Miriam had watched her brother's basket bob towards the favorite bathing place of the Nile princess, Miriam had felt tied to Moses' life. Likewise, when Moses returned from forty long years in his own wilderness, Miriam had been the counsel he most needed, the embrace he most sought, the quiet, continuous source of valour he needed to face Pharoah. Always, she had been there for him. In his infancy, she had cared for him. When the princess had lost interest in her adopted son, Miriam had found time to entertain and soothe him. When he carried the bruises of Pharaoh's staff, for Pharaoh had made Moses' troubled youth a thing of entertainment for his violence-loving courts, Miriam had ministered to every wound. When he had become a murderer, Miriam had sent runners in every direction with food and aid. Though none had found Moses as he fled to the far reaches of a foreign land, he had heard about the tale many years later and wept at Miriam's faithfulness. When the elders gathered to stone him for simply obeying Yahweh's edict to war with Pharoah for their freedom, Miriam had intervened, sending men twice her age and status scurrying to their homes in shame. Miriam had been a faithful sister. Even on the day of their worst argument, which they both seemed to recall with amusement now that the pain and embarrassment was decades old, Miriam had acted out of concern for Moses. Above all, she had always tried to spare him from his own heedless ways.

A silent sob tore from Miriam's throat as Moses released his hold on his sister. Both knew, and Miriam shuddered at the thought, that this would be their last embrace. He took precious time away from his ministry today to bring honor to his beloved sister, but Miriam knew he would not be free to await that final moment by her side.Trying, yet again, to focus on the promise that good awaited her beyond her final breath, Miriam watched Moses approach the stones. This view, of her strong, willful brother speaking to the people on her behalf was to be her last of the man they call Moses.

~ ~ ~

Beyond Moses, his stewards were double-checking the final layer of stones. They must have hunted for perfect selections day and night since Miriam's reported turn for the worse. It was a small altar, but just right to send a signal to Yahweh. A signal of thanks for the gift of the light of Miriam, for she was a light in Israel as surely as the night's Pillar of Fire. Though his back was presented to them, the words of Moses resounded clearly. "Children of the Most High, Yahweh showed you his favor by preparing and presenting the servant, Miriam to you. How she has cared for you, O Israel. She has wept at your graves. She has labored over your needs. She has ministered to your faith, and yes, worked to erase your doubts. No other god among the nations gives such a gift to his people! But here, you, the wandering people, have such a fine shepherdess!" Moses angled a gesturing palm toward his sister. Normally strong and mighty when facing the wayward people, in this moment the tremor of his voice was felt by all. Moses had always felt loss and grief personally. He never ignored the call of mourning when a leader or patron of Israel was lost. All the more so with one so dear as Miriam.

Of all the many men, women, and herds who had left the narrow road from Egypt only three remained: Moses, Aaron, and Miriam. Before continuing, Moses looked around at his brother Aaron, as though to say, "These words are for you as well." Then he looked briefly at Miriam, honor and love flowed from his features, before turning once more to the people. Some unseen signal had passed to several of Moses' wards. Quietly, they anointed the altar with wood and oil, kneeling low as they waited for Moses to signal the lighting of the altar.

Datya had often wondered at the supernatural volume of Moses' voice. None but God had a voice that could be heard by all of the thousands of Israelites, but Moses' voice often reached a large majority of them. It was something like a continuous miracle; no one really talked about it, but it must have dawned on others' minds. His commanding voice launched over the people: "The nomads of the desert, the nations who have passed us to and fro on our journey have sat in amazement at the telling of the tale of the Great Exodus. Talk of other gods is silenced swiftly as the description of the great walls of the imprisoned water of the Red Sea lands on foreign ears. Many nationalities walk away from an encounter with our people quaking with fear and trembling at the thought of this strange, all-powerful God, Yahweh. They say to one another, "This great man Moses drew the Israelites out of Egypt as one draws water from a well!" Not so, children, not so! God alone drew you from the clutches of Pharaoh. Moses was a messenger of the Almighty, an errand boy, simply performing a task." Pausing with the grip of mighty grief, Moses gestured once more to his sister. "Moses himself had to be drawn out of the water. At the mercy of a treacherous river, happy, floating bait for predators at large, infant Moses was helpless. Yet, I was drawn out of the water and so named "Drawn Out." I might have preferred to be named, and thus become "Mighty Warrior," or "Faithful Herald," or even "Godly Man." But I was poor, half-drowned Moses, "Drawn Out." Yes, a princess pulled me from the water, but she loved me not. Left to her care, I may have died like the brothers of my generation, but a girl stood on the shore between death and me, between sorrow and me. You know her as the Prophetess, but the princess ordered her as a slave to care for the river-drenched boy. My own mother nursed me, my dear sister carried me to and fro, watching my every moment. As surely as the princess drew me out of water, Miriam faithfully drew me out of all manner of trouble and sorrows. Faithful Miriam remained by my side until I was a man, and she would have remained there indefinitely had I not abandoned her." Datya herself wept as Moses gruffly quenched a sob to continue his tale.

"Yes, I abandoned her to slavery, while I sought the freedom of a desert shepherd. I wed. I seeded sons. I grew and prospered as Miriam and her family toiled. But Miriam's faithfulness was not to go without reward. Israel's need was not to go unnoticed. A burning bush, alive with the Spirit of Yahweh himself sent pitiful Moses back to Egypt. He spoke much to me on that mountain, children. We were secluded away from view, as he poured his spirit into me, though I would have heartily refused him. Though he spoke much to me only two words motivated my feet toward Egypt with haste: Draw out. It seemed I had been drawn out not because I was a beautiful Hebrew baby but because I was to go and draw out Israel from the clutch of her oppressor. Only by our God's great mercy was the feat accomplished, and yet hear this! The greatest miracle you have ever known, salvation, would have had to come another way entirely were it not for faithful Miriam who patiently drew her brother out of much more than just a watery death." At the last anxious syllable, Miriam and Datya both saw the trembling of Moses as grief washed over him. Truly he was engulfed in mourning laced heavily in thankfulness for his devoted sister. He would not let Israel walk away with anything less than a pure understanding of Miriam - a true champion of Israel, just as much as he.

A slight nod, missed by most, signaled the fire for the altar. Moses' voice rose once more, though to Yahweh this time rather than the people. He spoke a quiet, fierce gratitude for the Prophetess, and blessed Yahweh's name for the gift of Miriam's presence in Israel all these years. The fire was swiftly burnt up and Datya heard the tinkling sound of chiseling. Looking to the altar, she saw the messenger from this morning tapping away at a low stone. She dared not approach to view the holy words - words, in the form of symbols, she knew she could not decipher - but she suspected they echoed Moses' prayer. God had indeed been good to the Israelite people in providing a shepherdess like Miriam.

As the etching of the stone continued to meet Datya's ears, she thought back to Miriam's revelations of Moses' work with the great stones. Realizing for the first time that this chiseling sound was not foreign to her, Datya understood that many times she had passed by Moses' work-tents, hearing the very same sounds. Though Israel did not know it, much had already been recorded of their history. She struggled still to understand how their speech would be marked down, and, even more so, how those markings would be a retelling. Nevertheless she was filled with a quiet gratitude for Moses' commitment to the bewildering, but wonderful project. How precious their history was! The testimonies were more valuable than rare stones. All these years, elders, prophets and prophetesses had carried the words in their human minds and given them new life with their mouths. Now God's crafting and curating of the world would be set in stone, just like Miriam's service was being inscribed to the altar before them. She wondered if Miriam's name and work would find its way onto Moses' stone tablets. Hadn't Miriam said only yesterday that Joshua's victory over the Amalekites had been recorded?

Elders were streaming in from the crowd to speak first with Moses and then with Miriam. Miriam had sunk into the boards of the cart, depleted of strength but unwilling to depart just yet. She received every whispered thanks by bowing her own head as best she could. These faces had doubted her at times in the past, but today they shone with reverent love. Miriam had failed them often, whether by ignoring God's urging or joining in on their doubts, but many more times she had blessed and encouraged them. All knew that she was a key fertilizer of faith, critical to the weak and wandering hearts of her people.

As Miriam's posture sank more and more into her cushioned perch, Datya raced to fetch one of Moses' young men. She was adamant, Miriam would be heading back to her tent no matter her protests. The line of elders approaching was diminished now, and the remainder could pay their respects as the patient ox slowly marched away.

As the crowd parted for Miriam's removal, Datya could see their tent only a few turns of the wheel away. Large deposits of gifts had been left framing the opening. With Miriam's last breath only hours away, she likely needed none of those things. Still she would be moved and blessed by the thoughtfulness of the people she loved so thoroughly. As the ox was brought to a halt, Datya looked up to smile at her teacher. Home felt like a sweet relief after the tiring but wonderful morning. Her smile faded at the sight of Miriam's sleeping face. The dark, dusty wrinkles moved with little tremors as her breath moved shallowly in and out. Datya signaled the servants who had followed to lift her with care. Though she would have gladly clambered into the cart to retrieve the pallets to be placed inside, three other servants moved swiftly to the task. The weakness that woe breeds threatened her and Datya felt herself losing her grip on the earth. In the next moment, Ravit stood directly behind her, tightly holding onto her shoulders. "The weight of the grief is too much to carry, Datya. Come inside." Thankful for the strength of her compassionate friend, Datya shuffled slowly into the tent where Miriam's sleeping form had just been lowered.

Ravit gently guided Datya to a cushion, all the while whispering, "God knows, dear one, God is here. God cares." How had one morning depleted her strength so much? She needed to be strong for Miriam, to nurse her in her final moments, but here she was, trembling, barely able to walk without the assistance of Ravit. Then she knew, as though Yahweh himself swept into the tent bearing the answer. It wasn't the grief that weighed her down. This morning was a memorial for Miriam and also a transfer. She, Datya, daughter of Cohen, was the Prophetess now. The weight of Israel's warbling faith had deposited itself on her spirit. It was a new weight, an unfamiliar burden and Datya struggled to breathe around the tightness of it.

Longing to see Miriam's eyes stir once more, to ask her if she once felt this weight or if she had always carried it, Datya looked to her mentor. There was a slight smile on her latent face, as though she was pleased with Datya though she slept. Lamenting tears drenched the contours of Datya's face. The silent truth rang loud in her heart, Miriam would not wake again. Even Ravit's thoughtful stroking of her hair was not enough to soothe the ache crashing through her. Even the waves that had toppled those once frozen walls of the Red Sea did not impact the Egyptian armies as severely as this pain rolled over her. She had not been able to say goodbye. Certain Ravit would be horrified by the loud, garbled sobs that surged from her, She attempted to shake off her friend's care. "I will remain, Datya," Ravit promised, the kindness of her voice lost in the wake of despair.

Datya fought her grief as surely as Joshua had battled the Amalekites. God's anointing had been with the warriors that day, bringing victory despite the great wrestle each and every man endured. Though she knew Yahweh was with her, that same anointing felt far off, as though it had been diluted by her tears. Miriam's voice would never again meet her ears, but she still lived! *How can I serve her, Yahweh? What should I do?* Her first question as a prophetess was one acknowledging that she was frightfully lost, and had no idea what was to be done. It seemed a horrible sign to her already quaking heart.

Still, Yahweh had never left Miriam, and Datya was assured of the same faithful guidance. *Sing, daughter.*

Looking sharply at Ravit, Datya questioned her, "Did you hear that?" Ravit's bewildered look was answer enough. Yahweh's voice had been audible to her own ears, but to no one else. *Sing what, Lord? My heart is rendered in two. How can I possibly sing?* No voice returned these questions. Miriam herself could not be asked. Praying once more, Datya opened her grieving soul to heaven. *Fill me, Father. My voice fails me, but yours never will.*

Just as Moses had, Datya started at the beginning. Singing the ancient dirge that had first been heard among the Hebrews during the early days of oppression. Joseph had only been gone a century, and Miriam and Moses were centuries away. She sang then of the world, wrapped in dark arts and ancient evils that Miriam had been born into and the small fragment of Yahweh's light that was all that was left in Israel. She sang of Moses' flight, of Miriam's long years of intercession, and of Moses' return. She sang of Miriam's praise as the Red Sea crashed back to its bed lightly misting the backs of the finally free Hebrews. She sang of all Miriam had done for the people in the forty years of wandering. How the people had writhed in anger at their discipline, and how Miriam had persuaded them back to righteous faith. Hours passed with Datya's voice often cracking and leaking its sorrow. She would bend over Miriam's hand, kissing it and washing it with her own tears only to rise and begin again. Yahweh had said sing. This was the anointing he was pouring out over Miriam's death; Datya would not let silence reign.

Many times Ravit moved between Datya and Miriam as concerned for one as she was for the other. Often they lifted Miriam and held her upright between the two of them to ease the fragmented breaths that Miriam seemed choked with. Light was fading fast, and though Datya knew that Ravit had not slept the night before, she could not convince her to go and rest. She was surprised, but endlessly grateful when her mother, Lisbet, slipped into the tent. Miriam had added faint moans to her uneven breaths and Datya's heartbeat raced with the desperation to see the pain end. Her mother bowed low and she too kissed Miriam's hand, then moving behind her daughter she hummed along. Datya sensed that both her widowed friend and her mother beseeched heaven in this moment to welcome the prophetess and to bring peace to Datya.

With alarm, Datya felt her song closing. Part of her wanted to believe that if she just kept singing Miriam would always be here. In the midst of the next syllable Ravit's hand stilled her, and she looked down to see the woman who had molded her so tenderly. Miriam's last exhale was rising to the top of the tent now. Bending over her, she held her tightly. She wept and whispered all the love and gratitude that had been stirring inside her. Miriam could no longer hear her. Miriam was gone, but she couldn't cease this final outpouring of devotion. Feeling her true mother beside her once more, she turned and caved into her mother's arms. As though she were a little girl again, Datya held on as sobs tore from her aching spirit. Devastation reigned and warred, overpowering her in exhausting waves. Never had she imagined the horrible, tearing pain this loss would bring.

CHAPTER TWELVE

Wasteland air thickened within her. As Miriam's body rolled slowly away, Datya felt sure that the rise and fall of her own chest would never resume. How could she breathe around such a great knot of loss? Moses had sent the very same cart and ox that had delivered Miriam to yesterday's celebration. This time the ox bore a forever sleeping Miriam towards an even more remote region of this endless desert. A procession of friends, family, and faithfuls followed the final journey of Israel's greatest prophetess. A cave had been found many miles from camp. Miriam, along with others who had died over the last few days, would be sealed into the cave and left behind. Datya's tears refused to purge from her aching eyes. The panicking dust seemed to bind itself to her, in a stone-like cast, as she watched Miriam moving further away.

Ravit and her mother had helped her tenderly clean, perfume, and wrap the cherished prophetess, but they could not walk this last way with her body. They had been with her when she died. They had cared for the remains of her life. The law was clear; the three would trek towards the outer edges of the camp and settle in the isolated purification tents. Moses had thoughtfully sent stewards ahead of them to stock a tent with a week's needs, but, for Datya, her only need was currently fleeing the camp wrapped in burial linen.

Interrupting her vigil, Ravit filled her vision. With her customary gentleness she urged Datya away. "We must leave the camp now. Miriam would not want you to stand helplessly in her wake." The admonishment jarred her, though her friend spoke true. Many witnesses would be watching Datya in a test of sorts. How would she handle such great loss? Would she crumple, cower, and fade from memory? Or would she muster strength and step into the role that Miriam had so often prophesied over her? Examining once more the crushed, bruised feeling of her heart, she could not imagine how she could deliver even a fraction of the steadfast hope Miriam had represented among their people. Her grief was vast and seemed every bit as wide and long as the wilderness the Israelites wandered. Would it take Datya her own forty years to find the way through?

Moving forward, Datya's footfalls touched the bare earth even as she clamped her eyes against the world. Her mother and Ravit each held an elbow, steadily and patiently guiding. They knew the way, just as surely as the watching Hebrew families knew where the woeful threesome were headed. She simply could not look into the eyes of the amassed witnesses along the way. Most shown with a compassion that landed on her with an unintended sting. Datya wanted Miriam, not comfort. Some of the watching eyes danced with doubt. None could fathom how a youth with less than twenty years could be any sort of leader among Israel, let alone Chief Prophetess. Nevermind that Miriam herself had spoken to elders of Yahweh's virtues at an even younger age. Nevermind that Miriam had approached a powerful, foregin princess to rescue Moses long before she was even as old as Ziva! The doubting Israelites were conveniently neglecting those memories along with the simple truth that Yahweh himself had chosen Datya. She had been lifted out of a humble Levite family to serve Miriam and to be trained and moulded for this role. Miriam would want her to declare this swiftly to her doubters, looking each one in the eye.

Datya herself ashamedly leaned toward agreeing with the doubt-filled, desert-worn tribes. Truly, who was she? Even on her best days, when she was not swamped by grief, what could she offer even one of these people? She had failed, so far, to manage the rocky relationship of sisterhood, and yet she was expected to suddenly step in to make a difference in the spirit of the Israelites? Reconciling the truth that God had indeed called her to this work and the truth that she was woefully inexperienced was a task that her mind could not conquer no matter how often she made the attempt. Asking her people, most of whom did not even know her name, to trust her with their faith was a sheer-faced mountain in her path. Miriam would dash up to such a steep rock and start climbing right away, one foothold after another. For her own part, Datya could think only of passing the mountain by, letting the work fall to someone else. Her head drooped deeper into her shoulders as the shame of what Miriam would say about her cowardly thoughts dug into her. Courage or no, experience or no, Miriam had moulded her to claim that mountain, and to make a difference in the lives of their kinsmen. Somehow, though she couldn't discern it now, she knew that the trek to the purification camp was the first foothold up.

Keeping her vision silent as she moved through the camp was a faint-hearted way out of facing the curious people who were flocking to get a glimpse of her. Denying her hearing was another matter. How she longed to be able to shut her ears as well. The song of mourning rising through the camp invaded her grief. Not even a hundred footsteps moved her a speck further from the volume and the din of heartbreak. Her people had never done well with loss. Oh, they loved to accumulate, but to lose one precious thing, or one treasured person was akin to cutting off a mighty limb. Mourning Miriam would mean a constant flow of theatrical grief. The sound of the nearby mourners forced Datya to clench her teeth tight together, her jaw nearly bursting with the effort. No doubt Ravit and Lisbet felt the rigid way her body resisted the death song. Years she had spent sitting at Miriam's feet listening to the history songs and the songs of Yahweh; that was what she wanted to hear, not this hopeless dirge.

The lonely tents where purification weeks were spent began to cast shade on Datya as she approached. With willpower she had thought she lost, Datya forced her eyelids to part. Only a few people filled out the spaces between the neglected tents. Likely these people had witnessed their own losses this week, or endured a sickness of some sort, though she had not been told of the other deaths. She had been too focused on every moment with Miriam. Oddly, word had not arrived to Miriam either, or at least, not that Datya had witnessed. Miriam had ministered to the grieving families of Israel throughout all of the wilderness years, and it had been full-time, consuming work. Though Moses had many appointed men who foresaw everything from removal and burial of bodies to widow-care, from possession disputes, to inheritance management, it was Miriam's job to comfort the grieving among Israel. Many widows had come under Miriam's guidance to perform this service for the families of each and every tribe. Miriam herself often met with grieving loved ones two or three times per week. Datya felt her throat tighten into a dry struggle as she realized that this duty would fall to her. How could bringing comfort to others become a part of her daily work when she felt anything but comforted? How could she mop up someone else's drenching sorrow when she felt that her own gloom would never lift?

Ravit steered her towards the tent that Moses had prepared for them. It was the nicest tent in this desolate, forgotten camp by far, more than enough for the three of them. Datya could see also that Moses had sent two servants to remain with them for the week. While it was thoughtful, she rebelled at being served by hands unknown to her. In fact, she would not have minded if she was sent even further than the already distant purification camp, to a desolate, truly alone place. Approaching the leather walls, Datya felt as though she were sinking in place. For the last week, she had been entering into and staying in a tent that was fairly soaked in the presence of God. Prayer and praise had drenched the walls of Miriam's tent for the entirety of her desert lifetime. This tent however looked newly stitched. It had never housed a prophetess. It had never burst with the songs of Yahweh. It had no presence, no life, no hope.

Despair loomed. *At least in Miriam's tent I could feel you, Yahweh. How can I bear this?* Prayers in the same vein had been flitting upward from Datya through the long hours of the night, and as the day had carried her and Miriam further apart.

Do you think Miriam's prayers never rose from a place of sorrow, Datya? She was no stranger to grief, and yet, amidst the pain, she sought Me faithfully. Yahweh's conviction swept through her with breath-taking fierceness.

Datya hung her head as she settled onto the stiff, provided pallet in the new tent. Her God was right. She had approached her purification place thinking that none could give her the comfort she needed when in reality she needed correction more than comfort. Neither Miriam nor Yahweh would want to see grief pull her from the presence of God. There was no doubt that what she needed would be found at the knee of Yahweh, if she would seek it.

Start right now, Datya. I'm listening.

Her gaze roved the newly stretched and tanned leather that had been stitched into a dark home around her. This week could produce either a stirring of God's presence in this forlorn tent, or the cold bitterness of self-pity.

With her choice made, she pressed her body into the dust of the earth and released a tightly held sob that had amassed through the day. *Yahweh, thank you for never leaving me. Thank you for your calling. I cannot see past the loss. I have no vision for life without my teacher, my friend. Help me, Lord.* Gentle stroking followed the lines of her dark linen-bound hair down her back for long hours as she alternated between weeping before the Lord and pleading for hope. She knew not if the ministering hands belonged to Ravit or to her mother, or even to one of the loaned servants. Nevertheless, the single pair of hands never left her as she grieved on a humble, private altar.

A feeble light lifting from a shallow dish of oil was all that Datya could see as she raised her head. For many hours, her arms had cradled it inches from the dirt beneath her. At first her lips had moved in silent prayer, but prayer must have given way to sleep. "A messenger was here, Datya," her mother spoke from beyond the edge of the pitiful light. "Miriam was laid on a small mound of stones within the cave. The men Moses sent checked thoroughly for additional entrances and blocked up all that were found. Many stones were needed. It took all day. Her body will never be disturbed." Her mother's voice trembled, but remained thick with kindness, as she relayed Moses' words. "Moses wanted you to know." Lisbet had come close to Datya now and resumed the kind and thoughtful stroking down her weary back. Datya looked up at her mother with timid eyes. Her mother was known by her girls as a master of efficiency. She never seemed to struggle under the load of caring for a nomadic family. She was never flustered during the long months of separation that were a product of Cohen's duties for the Tabernacle. Lisbet worked hard, and managed her desert dwelling to the height of Hebrew standards. However, she had never coddled her children. Affection in Datya's childhood had often been words, and a kind look, but rarely a hug or a thoughtful touch. Even young Idan, who still took to the milk of his mother, was never held or stroked as Datya was now. Datya's eyes misted with the knowledge that she had judged her mother cooly. Here Lisbet had spent the entire day simply comforting her eldest daughter, quite ignoring any other tasks that could be tackled.

Apprehension gripped her as Datya questioned her

mother, "Where is Idan? I have not seen him, yet he nurses still? Will someone fetch him for you, Mother?" Lisbet's eyes were soft pools of comfort for her daughter. They swam with tenderness. The type of smile that comes with such love tempted at the corners of the older woman's mouth. "I knew I would not leave you to face Miriam's death alone. Yesterday, before hastening to you, I placed Idan and Ziva in my sister's care. He was so close to weaning, and so adept at devouring manna - I feel sure he will be fine without my milk." Her mother appeared confident, but Datya worried about the suddenness of her decision. Still, her little brother would be happier with his passel of cousins rather than idling in this outcast place.

Datya wanted to reach out to her mother. To hold on to her and thank her for sacrificing time with Idan and Ziva to be with her, but she hardly knew what to say. "It is no great sacrifice, Datya," her mother, proving wisdom once more, seemed to read her mind. "I have often felt as though you did not need me. You have always had a quiet strength, and your way has been known since you were so young. For many years it seemed," Lisbet's voice struggled with the confession, "that you just did not need me. Not like Ziva and Idan. Not even like your father, though I suspect you get your strength from him." The ministering hands stilled as tears tipped from her eyes filling out the lines of her face, etched by the desert sun. "When you brought the timbrel home only a few days ago. When your father whispered to me that Miriam was dying. When I knew the loss that was looming before you, then I felt you needed me. I would choose nothing else, Datya, but to be here for you."

Datya reached out to her mother feeling both the weakness of having not eaten for a full day and the succor that only a mother's ministrations can give. Bending her body onto her mother's sturdy shoulder Datya once again gave way to confessional prayer. *Yahweh, I grieve a mother, a spiritual parent that you placed in my life, and yet here my own mother's faithful love is revealed. I have neglected that source in my life, and yet you have not taken it from me. Thank you for parents such as mine, Lord.* The knowledge that she would not have to step into her season of prophetic work alone coursed through her. Moses had Joshua, and Aaron, and once good and kind Hur, the very men who had held up Moses' weakening arms so long ago. She would have a wellspring of support and love from her mother, sweet Lisbet, who, Datya realized, was more dear to her than she had ever known. She would have Ravit too who would surely be a faithful friend as God wove her ministry through the fabric of twelve needy tribes.

Once again startled by the knowledge that something wasn't right, Datya questioned her mother. "Where is Ravit? Nighttime is nearly here; she should be with us." Her mother chuckled then, surprisingly long and hearty considering the events of the last several hours. Lisbet was apparently tickled at her panicked look and frazzled questioning. Datya could not participate in laughter. It would be some time before mirth could break free, but she admitted a small smile. As her mother began brushing grime from Datya's face and tucking hair and robes back into their proper places, Datya felt soothed, the worry receded once again. "Ravit foresaw your need, Datya, for comfort and care, but she saw need elsewhere as well. There are many mourners in this place, dear one; Ravit left you in my care and has been ministering to the others." Datya nodded, though she hoped her earlier demeanor hadn't been dismissive towards her friend. Sweet Ravit. Her tender heart lurched towards needs everywhere she went. She wasn't well known in Israel, her family had been quiet, ordinary people, but she was highly praised by those who did know her.

Shame and grace warred within as she waited for her friend's return. Shame that she had ignored the brokenness around her upon entering this camp, but also, grace - her ministry would consist of many years of service, none would begrudge her the time she needed to mourn Miriam. The knotted loss lodged once more in her throat. Miriam. An entire day of her life had passed by without her now, an entire arc of the sun without the shadow of Miriam's wisdom. Miriam had made worship a heartbeat in this camp, when the tendency had been to worry. She had built altars of praise that still remained criss-crossed through this land. No nomadic family ever passed them by without hearing of the God who parted the Red Sea. Datya's mind pulsed with the thread of one thorny thought: as hopeless as she felt without her mentor, how much more dismal was Israel's future without Miriam's steadfast faith standing pillar-like among them?

Her mind was as proficient in worrying as Miriam's mind had been in believing. Even now the tent's stifled air reminded her that hours ago God had commissioned her to fill these walls with prayer. He had gently told her he didn't expect them to be prayers of joy - the ones of worry, grief, and even anger would do, for they had their place. Still, rather than praying, Datya was nibbling her cheeks with angst for tomorrow, anxiety for Israel. *Forgive me, Yahweh. Did Miriam ever struggle with worry as I do? How can I serve you when my mind is riddled with it?* As Yahweh's silence responded, Datya's heart fluttered with the fear of all that stretched before her. *Pray, Datya! Pray! Yahweh has commanded it. Miriam would agree! What would she pray?* Her mind hurdled back to the beginning, the earliest days with Miriam when lessons were briefer than a meal. Miriam had taught Datya to pray, one by one for the tribes. Datya's tiny voice had repeated the prayers faithfully through her days and evenings. Even as a small child she had never wanted to forget a thing Miriam taught her. Her father, Cohen, had always been amused by her simple prayers for the tribes. He often said, "Too bad your voice is so small, Datya, for those prayers would do much better if you shouted them at the tribes themselves." Accompanied always by a hearty laugh, he hadn't meant to mock Yahweh with his words, only to point a finger at the stubborn nations who seemed unmoved by many righteous prayers.

As Datya thought about those early days where practicing prayer had been her most intense assignment, she dwelt on the current call to intercession. She had gone to Yahweh for comfort and yet, with gentle insistence, he had exhorted her to pray. Why? And why did he stir those long-ago memories of her infant-like prayers for the people?

Your ministry starts here, Datya. It starts now. Yahweh's voice rushed through the tent with authority that disturbed the normally stale air.

As near-darkness settled, Datya struggled to grasp the revelation. She had thought she was beginning a purification week, but God was showing her that it was a different beginning altogether. Yes, sharp grief made for a rough foundation, but coupled with the grace of a God who never leaves and the knowledge of his faithful power, she was standing in a stronger place than she'd realized. Yahweh was showing her that this near-empty tent was holy ground. Grief or not, Datya was to begin her ministry to the people from this outcast camp, and she was to do it, through prayer.

Though the sorrow remained, she bowed low to the earth once more. This time, as she felt the fullness of her pain, she would remain awake. She would launch her service to the Tribes from the lowest place among them, a dark, lonely tent in a place reserved for the sick and unclean. Ravit had returned and knelt within arms reach. Seeing the concern filling her loved ones' eyes, Datya whispered before closing hers, "It's time for me to pray."

How, Yahweh? I don't know where to begin. Face deep in the dust that had been her lifelong home, not even the smallest prayer would leak from her. Repeating "Lord, Lord," over and over was some sort of heavenly request, but she sensed God urging something more, something different.

The earliest prayers. The beginning. Datya sensed a faint echo of the laughter Miriam had employed so often, drifting towards her. Far away, like a memory, but she ached to hear the sound continually. Yes, her teacher would agree. Start at the beginning. Searching her memory carefully, Datya, feeling like a baby in her spirit once more, released the long-ago Prayers for the Tribes that Miriam had taught her.

Father, for Reuben's families, long has self-control been their downfall. I ask for your spirit to pour out among them, that they would be filled with righteous desires. Teach them through your holy discipline, Lord, and let the families of Reuben's tribe bear good fruit.

Yahweh, for Simeon's offspring, always they have pushed forward with their own will - often being the first to argue for their own way. Fill the men and women of Simeon's tribe with a grace that washes away willfulness and pride. Become their source of righteous living.

Lord, Levi's descendants are blessed and cursed. My father's fathers did not always honor you and many met the rod of your discipline. Stir them to true holiness, Lord, that they might walk in your blessing and leave behind the curses of sin. Many can quote your law, but many more struggle to honor it. Purify my family for your service, Lord.

Father, Judah has proved your goodness and power before, but they have also doubted You. Restore the hearts of Judah's offspring to full faith; anoint them to lead us in praise, and to be an example of your might to the nations. Abolish the strongholds of doubt that dim their voices.

Yahweh, the sons of Zebulun have grown thick and tangled with the vine of pride. They excel in their tasks and talents, and pride reigns. Topple idols among the tribe of Zebulun, Lord, so that they can serve the Holy God in spirit and in truth.

Lord, the tribe of Issachar has traded your favor for mere survival. They sin against you with a longing for Egypt, and yet your love still washes over them. Give them a hunger for the Promised Land, Father, and show them the goodness of your way.

Oh God, your purpose and plans for the offspring of Dan were great and mighty, and yet they were tossed aside. Dan's people have taken their eyes off of you and inspired all of Israel to do likewise. Shower holy discipline over their people once more, Lord, bring repentance among the tribe of Dan.

Father, from among the families of Gad, many warriors have arisen. With fierce strength they protect our people, but with equal pride they ignore the source of their victory - you. Call them to submit to you once more and show them that your authority is what blesses our people.

Lord, your abundance has showered the people of Asher. I lay before you in awe of the miracles and wonders that you've done among Asher's families. But their faith is shallow, Lord, and like Miriam, I cry out for you to reach the deep parts of their hearts. Stir them to be a fountain of your mercy.

Father, all among Israel know that you blessed the offspring of Naphtali with flowing words, with wisdom, with grace and stature. Often their wise words have fueled faith, but just as often they have used their cunning speech to stir troubled waters. Give them a pure heart that seeks to serve you, Lord; cast away the false wisdom of Egypt that still lurks in their hearts.

Yahweh, I lift a thankful heart for the many blessings you've poured upon Israel through the children of Joseph. Provision, protection, joy, and abundance abound through the leadership of Ephraim and Mannaseh's descendants. Father, even amidst great favor, Jo-

seph's tribe remains cool to your presence, aloof in their pride. Urge them to humbly seek you.

Lord, you established Benjamin's people as the fiercest among Israel. They are strong warriors and wise - men and women of valour. Trusting in their own strength, they so often pull ahead of you, and find themselves lost and misguided. Plant conviction to remain in your presence in their hearts.

Datya sunk her body further into the dust of the earth. Her loss was humbling in its own way, she felt as low as she ever had, but her heritage doused her with a thorough humility, commanding her to bow before Yahweh. How foolish the tribes so often were! The Hebrew men and women stood out as wise and wonderful among the nations. One only had to pass by a handful of pitiful nomadic families to spot the difference. God was surely in the people of Israel! Yet, they so often launched their days from a bed of pride, stoking the fires of vanity and fame. Some, Datya believed, even relished in their wonderful ability to survive such a long, desperate journey. They were the first to brag upon their abilities to the passerby, conveniently forgetting that without the God of Heaven supplying simple bread, every day, they would have died long ago. She had no idea why Yahweh was urging her to pray over the tribes once more, as she had done as a girl. Certainly she and Miriam prayed for them regularly, but more often than not, they prayed about specific needs and situations, rather than for entire families. *What next, Yahweh? What would you have me intercede for?*

Though Datya longed to hear Yahweh's voice in the audible and sure way she believed Miriam had, mostly she had to sit very still and quiet and listen with all her might for a whisper that may or may not come. Miriam had always told her that her ears would grow stronger as decades of prayer passed by. Though she loved to pray, it often seemed like a mountain of responsibility for a smidgen of reward. And yet, each time she did hear her Lord speak to her heart, Datya felt almost breathless by the tender gift. Her heart seemed to melt at the realization that such a mighty God would stoop down to answer the prayers of so lowly a person.

Now, waiting for God's direction the answer was maddeningly one word: *again.* Again? With exasperation, she acknowledged that her heavenly Father loved mystery as much as Miriam had loved humor.

Still, the following, faint whisper, seemed to hold the telltale clues. *You have this week, Datya. Pray.*

Though there was no altar besides the dirt itself, she submitted to it. Her mother and Ravit had long since engaged their pallets for the night. Datya knew that sleep would come for her as well, but until that moment she would pray for the Tribes. Lifting them up, just as she had before, Datya called out for the God who had never left them, to come and be the God who stirred their hearts to faith and favor.

CHAPTER THIRTEEN

As the sunshine did its cleansing work, Datya felt her smile tug free once more. The little one, that had quickly become so dear to her, head full of dusty, tangled curls, ran swiftly, eyes darting to find a perfect spot. The sweet child bent to gather a newly spotted stone and then launched into a full run, back to Datya. The two had spent the morning this way. Little Evita, had latched onto her on the morning of her second day in the purification camp. It had been Evita's third day. She and all her *achai*, her siblings were there with their mother. The children had awoken only days before to find their father, no longer breathing and the mother weeping over the hem of his robe. The man had encountered a venomous snake while working among his herds. His sheep had been protected, but he himself had been pierced with the deadly fangs even as he throttled the baleful viper. Though Yahweh did sometimes provide a life-saving miracle, such had not been the case for impish Evita's father. Unclean from their final farewells to his body, the family had moved into a half-shelter in the purification tents. The pitiless dwelling their extended family had spared for the cleansing week was a three-walled patchwork shelter that looked as though it had been old at the start of the Exodus. Even if a fourth wall could be stitched to the tattered edges, Datya doubted it would do much to damper the wailing that came from the broken-hearted woman inside. To be a widow in Israel was a fearsome thing, to be a widow with several small mouths to feed was a state with little hope.

Ravit, whose kindness couldn't be withheld, was spending long hours with Evita's mother, Noya. The woman grappled bitterly as she desperately sunk into new widowhood. Datya's heart broke for her, though she felt dry of any words that might help. Ravit's personal widow-walk was apt to be a better comfort and so Datya had offered what help she could by watching the little girl who was young enough to still seek play in the midst of such great loss. Evita had fetched new stones for their project all morning. Often she would carry back a clump of clay believing it to be a fine new pebble only to have it crumble in her hands. The stones she did find were sorted, dusted off, and added to a tiny altar they were erecting in the shade of Datya's tent. In the beginning, Evita had named each new stone. There was a stone for each of her *achai*, her brothers and sisters. Two stones were named for her parents, though she had cried as she lovingly settled the stone for her father. Soon, she ran out of relatives and simply added the new stones too fast to name. Datya had quietly named one for Miriam.

The little altar had no spiritual significance; it was a game really, to entertain the girl. For Datya, it was a remedy of hope. The smiles she received coupled with the healing warmth of the sun muffled her grief, though even the sweetness of her young friend couldn't mute it. She watched Evita stoop once more above the little pillar of pebbles. "I found three this time, Datya. Where should I put this one?" In her sweaty palm Evita held a round pebble, smaller than her fist by half. In appearance it was different from their other finds, as though someone had designed the rock by hand, like a work of fine embroidery. Each fleck of light on its surface seemed an unspoken whisper confirming the tiny stone was a special find. Closing her own fist around the priceless pebble, Datya stooped to look in the little girl's eyes. "This one you keep darling, to remember this altar, to remember your *abba*." As Evita marveled at the wonderful stone, Datya fetched a strip of linen from the tent. Wrapping it tightly, securing it with a knot, Datya braided it into the girl's sash about her waist. Dangling next to her petite friend it reminded her of Ravit's similar keepsake: Koppel's tassel kept within her belt. "Keep it close always, Evita. Remember that Yahweh was with you in the desert. Your *abba* would want you to remember that." Evita's eyes lit with a mix of wonder and tender tears as she put her hand over the tiny treasure. Doubtless there were thousands just like it, if one cared to search them out, but to Evita this one alone connected her to her beloved *abba*. Young though she was, Datya whispered a prayer that the girl would keep a memory or two of her brave father.

"You do good work this day, Datya." Her mother seemed to have watched the morning's activity, though she had been ministering to other women in the camp, women who had been through illness or tragedy. "It's just playtime, *Immi*, hardly the work of a prophetess." A secret, the kind the elders always seemed to possess, lurked in her mother's smile. Datya received a new batch of stones and sent Evita off once more on the hunt. "Yes, just playtime, and yet…" Shifting to face her, Datya encouraged her *immi* to spill out what was on her heart. Taking her hand and strolling along behind the scampering girl, Lisbet gracefully filled the air between them with sage counsel. "Yes, just playtime, and yet, you are teaching her about building an altar to Yahweh. You two play at hunting for stones so that her mother can rest and heal, and yet, already you have spoken hope and brightness into her little heart." With kind, but insistent pressure Lisbet held firmly to her arm. "Better your ministry starts in the service of a sweet little child, Datya. If you are willing to put your love and efforts into the child of a widow, Yahweh will trust you to use your gifts for Israel's greatest needs." The words, so like a mantra of Miriam's "Serve the least, Datya," poured over her, a comfort that stung, since they would never have been shared if Datya and Evita hadn't first experienced harrowing loss.

Her mother was right, but Datya resisted the sagacious speech. This brief encounter with the innocent joy of girlhood didn't seem like any great work. It was no hardship at all entertaining the miniature angel. In fact, Evita's playful trust was a balm for Datya's own grief. How Miriam would have loved this sweet-hearted creature! Her mother's presence was clearly not ready to release her attention until she understood. "You know, Datya, many among Israel would say that 'Lisbet's work is just mothering.' Perhaps you have thought this yourself a time or two." Her mother gently raised Datya's head though she had dipped her chin, hiding the shame coloring her face. She had often thought that about her mother, about many mothers. "Feel no shame, Datya, I do not need the appreciation, or notice of others. Yes, I am just a mother. Cooking, cleaning bodies, sewing garments, and instructing." Humble humor traced the twinkling of her mother's eyes as she announced, "But perhaps there is something my observers have missed? Why, my work has been raising Israel's next prophetess! What do you think of that?" Lisbet chuckled, but Datya still felt the burn of abashment. When would she ever learn that Yahweh was in all things, great and small. Even the lowliest servant among their people could serve Yahweh through their work. An orphan's first little prayer meant as much to the ear of Yahweh as the fervent petition of a great prophet. Only days ago, Miriam herself had alluded to this very principle when she talked about God's heart for all people, his passion to replace enslaved thinking with the heartbeat of his holy kingdom.

A deception she hadn't known she carried fell from her as Datya realized that her mother abided in this heartbeat. In service of her family, she had fulfilled Yahweh's good call every bit as much as Miriam had. Truly, Miriam had been correct when she told Datya that Yahweh would become her mentor. In watching Ravit minister to Israel's widows, in growing closer to her steadfast mother, even in entertaining little Evita, Yahweh had taught her much in her three days of cleansing. Even a morning that had been set aside for play had birthed new knowledge.

Evita, who was showing the signs of exhaustion wandered closely between the two walking women. Walking with her mother and the darling girl reminded her of the days when her lessons with Miriam had been short. Ziva had been younger then, rambunctious yes, but certainly not the daughter of trouble she portended herself to be these days. A check dug at her heart, Yahweh was not delighted by her favoritism. It was acceptable, and even good to receive Ravit and little Evita as sisters of her heart, but not in place of her own true sister. When this week finished, she must love her sister better. Her mind surprised her with a brief, walking vision wherein she stowed away today's lessons as keepsakes tied on her belt, for easy remembrance, just as Ravit carried her husband's memory and Evita now carried her father's. The vision cleared as swiftly as it came as the three set off in search of Ravit.

Moses had provided more nourishment and supplies for the three women than a dozen would need. He had sent everything from cloth for new garments, and a servant who was skilled in stitching, to dried fruits and fragrant wines. In part, Datya felt a bit sick at such extravagance in the wake of Miriam's death, but she knew Moses had meant the gifts to bring care and comfort. If Moses intended to set her to work among the tribes as soon as this week concluded, she would need sustenance, and the treats did inspire her appetite. Ravit and Lisbet had heartily agreed with the suspicion that Moses' wife had made the actual selections from their troves of surplus. Moses had always made shrewd trades and the pair had plenty to spare, but even still, Datya could tell that some of the finest of their wares had been sent. She was overcome by the generosity.

She had been in Moses's presence many times and had met his wife a handful, but she had never felt especially close to either of them. The gifts reminded her that Moses was not always the aloof leader that his reputation described. Amongst the supplies had been many sacks of dried fruits, the kind that the elder Israelites had spoken of in remembering the Nile. Those elders had mostly passed away, and few among Datya's generation had the opportunity to taste such treats. They surpassed even the ones Miriam had lovingly shared with her over the week. Datya, Ravit and Lisbet had thoroughly enjoyed sampling them on the first full day of the camp. Now they made it a habit to mark the middle of the day with a handful of the fruit for each of them, and many of their bereft neighbors, including Evita's family.

Evita's mother, Noya, had eaten very little, even though Ravit had bravely sent a messenger back to the main camp requesting meat broth be sent for the sick and weak among them. Perhaps today Ravit would manage to get the poor woman to accept some of the sun-dried fruit. Noya, who still had a tiny infant who depended on her milk, must be goaded to think of the baby's needs despite her sorrow, just as Datya had learned to save her mournful thoughts for private moments so that Evita received her best attention. Perhaps that comparison was unmerited. Datya had lost a teacher. Beloved as Miriam was to her, it had not been the painful severing of losing one's spouse. Nor did Evita depend on Datya for strength and life, as the baby depended on Noya. No, the comparison was not fair to the grieving woman, but they must work to make her see the infant's need nonetheless. A relief swept over her, Ravit could be trusted with the task. The young widow would know how to reach Noya, and wouldn't stop with her efforts until mother and baby were both well cared for.

At the tug of her mother's hand, Datya looked up to see Ravit standing in the opening of a tent, just a few dozen steps in front of them. Thankful to have found her friend at last, Datya paused. Alarm coursed through her. A messenger stood with Ravit, and his face bore the fearsome signs of a grave missive. Datya planted her feet so forcefully in the packed earth that Evita, who didn't realize they were stopping, ended up pitching forward then stumbling backward since she still clung to Datya's spare hand. She didn't want to move. She didn't want to go to her friend, to hear this word whatever it may be. Her own sorrow was endlessly deep, and here she was surrounded by hurt, pain, and sickness. *Yahweh, no more. Send the messenger away.* Even as her stomach churned, and the hopeless prayer fluttered from her, Datya felt the crush of panic as it rose within her.

Evita knew that the time had come to sample the 'treasure' as she called the ruby and gold colored strips of fruit. Tugging hurriedly on Datya's hand, she urged her friend to take another step. The little girl probably hadn't even noticed the messenger, and certainly had no inkling that bad tidings were on the horizon. But Datya knew. In the next moment Ravit's head lifted, her searching eyes met Datya's and the truth flew without words through the air.

Datya knew what the approaching herald would say. Was it not enough that he'd already delivered the blow to Ravit? Why was he coming this way with his dreaded news? With a bowed head he addressed her. The morose rasp of his voice matched the earlier doom Datya had recognized on his face. She recoiled; the unwanted sound reached her ears. "I was told to bring this message directly to Datya, the Prophetess." More than anything, she wanted to reject the title along with the message. In the face of fresh sorrow, being anything but a prophetess sounded like the only way to avoid a new layer of pain. "Moses requests your prayer for the people. The High Priest, Aaron died at dawn; many hearts are awash with despair." As the emissary's footsteps retraced their desolate path Datya's mind spiraled. Aaron. The faithful third pillar of Israel. Of the wise braid that had tethered Israel securely to Yahweh, only one remained now. Ravit had come close, but Datya could not look at her. Both knew that Ravit's dream was unfolding before their eyes. Moses, Israel's righteous leader, some would say savior, was all they had left. The question seared a cavernous fear onto her heart: *How long will Moses remain with us?*

Once more Datya took her steps with her sealed eyes. *Aaron. Dead.* The two traitorous words slunk back and forth amongst her thoughts with each step. Wisdom would say that Miriam and her brothers were aged further than most, that their deaths should be no surprise. But to have the deaths follow so closely was unbearable. Evita, who had overheard the messenger's report, seemed to finally understand. She clung to Datya's robe, her own nervousness trembling through the fabric, as the three older women entered their tent. Datya settled near the back wall, hoping her mother would care for their young charge for a time. *Yahweh, I do not understand your timing. Why take Aaron and Miriam so swiftly?* Miriam's voice echoed about her once more, "One prayer that will always be met with silence, Datya, is the one you send up questioning God's timing. It is not for us to know, but to trust." As she bowed low under the grief, her tears did not have far to fall to meet the earthen floor.

With one sticky hand clutching her share of 'treasure' fruit and the other carefully bearing a small stone, Evita came near. Sweetness laced the petite voice, invading the grave silence of the mourners, "Don't cry, Datya. We can build an altar for the High Priest too." With a sticky kiss, the girl embraced her older friend and dropped the first stone into the dust in front of her. "I will help you," though Datya tried desperately to retain the flood, she cried all the more as the thoughtful words wrapped around her.

With sudden conviction Datya captured the little one in a thankful embrace, nearly casting the remaining fruit on the ground. Her mother had been right when she pointed at Evita as a first, important task. Datya could lie here worrying for Israel, or she could get up and minister to the heart of one of Israel's little ones. The choice was clear. Even had she never been named the next Prophetess, Evita deserved her care and attention. The young girl found her own cheer as she played each day among the lowly, outcast tents, but, whether she understood it or not, tragedy had touched her young life, and would surely influence her coming years. Breathing a prayer for strength and wisdom, she guided the girl back into the sunlight. "Let's start on Aaron's altar, shall we?" The grin that enveloped Evita's face was proof enough that this was good and godly work, and Datya would perform it with all her might.

~~~

A plume of dust scurried as Evita landed strikingly close to Datya's head. "Rise, Datya, let's gather the manna for my *immi* and *achai*." Groaning with realization that the young one was making good on Datya's promise to spend Evita's last day in the camp together, Datya struggled to push her woolen blanket up and off of her. Though she had bent to the work of remaining cheerful through the days for Evita's sake, she often dipped into an aching sorrow through the nights. Each dawn, grief seemed to weigh her down to her pallet. Mornings had become their own little hurdle. How strange to wake with a changed purpose. Once she had been a carefree Levite girl who woke each day to dutifully receive her lessons. This was the pattern of her everyday life for so many years. While her new pattern was still hidden from her, for this week at least, she had been waking to entertain a young child, whose mother was awash with the agony of loss. Yesterday, she had even invited Evita to spend the night in their tent so that they could spend the whole day together. *What was I thinking?* Though Datya dearly loved her little charge, she was also fond of time just to herself in the morning. Walking amongst fresh flakes of manna and praising the God of the sunrise were two of her treasured healing habits, but this morning she would share them with the tiny bouncing creature that Yahweh had lended her for the week.

Datya smiled as they traipsed through the camp. Nearly
~~~

every tent opening was graced with a small pile of pebbles. Miniature altars Evita had lovingly stacked as she prayed for the people around her. Her prayers were little more than, "Yahweh help her not to be sad anymore," and "Yahweh, help him to get all better." Datya had no doubt that the Heavenly Father was blessed upon hearing each sincere entreaty, and doubly so by the rickety little altars dotting the camp. After their first altar had been completed, and then the one for Aaron, Evita had tirelessly spent her days gathering stones. Most of the other members of the purification camp were used to seeing Evita bent over a batch of pebbles attempting to build a perfect platform. She wondered what the girl's family would say about her new habit and hoped that trouble didn't lurk for the little one. Still, in her own precious way, Evita was serving those around her with kindness and love. Miriam would be delighted with the creature's tender heart and generous offering. There was no doubt Yahweh would honor her sweet gesture. Hadn't Miriam told her there wasn't a pair of lips on this earth that God wouldn't listen to if the bearer was sincere?

Long hours had been spent watching Evita go about her intense project, but Datya had not wasted any of them. She had faithfully fulfilled the command of her first day. The tent Moses had sent, outside and in, had been thoroughly steeped in praise and prayer. Letting Yahweh speak in every quiet moment, she had prayed over far ranging topics: the herds, their health and breeding: the tents, their constant need for new hides and skilled fingers willing to stitch them together: the camp's many ongoing arguments and doubts: the Promised Land, for she remembered Miriam's urgent whisper that the Crossing Over day was almost upon them. She even prayed over Moses' work with the Great Stones. Though she had originally worried about the necessity of the work, and their future acceptance, she now believed that Moses was truly led by the God of Abraham to develop the carved words for her people. A permanent history seemed like the best foundation for a permanent home - something her people had never tasted but longed for desperately.

When she wasn't praying or praising the stones Evita found, she was singing. She tried to be sensitive to the aching hearts around her, but refused to lift up the sound of the traditional mourning dirges. Instead she gave voice to the melodies of hope and wonder that Miriam had favored. Miriam had been ruled chiefly by joy. Many had accused her of being inspired by rebellion, claiming her name 'Rebellious Woman' fit her flawlessly. But the truth was, Miriam wept at the way her heart often surged against the accepted practices of her people. Rebellion wasn't her goal; godly joy was. Anyone who listened to her songs, truly listened, would know that. Daily, Datya planted those songs in the wilderness air as she and Evita walked the sorrow dredged length of the purification place. Each melody went up with a hopeful prayer that it would bear fruit for those who heard. She lovingly, and triumphantly, squeezed the little girl's hand when she heard the tiny voice singing along. *She has picked up the songs, and she is so young!* Only a few days had passed since Miriam's death and already Yahweh had let her pass on the gift of Miriam's songs. She hoped the little girl, who would shortly return to her place among the tents of the Asherites, would always remember the words, and the loving joy they inspired. Perhaps, through the little girl's witness, Yahweh would even raise up a prophetess from Evita's tribe to partner with Datya in her work!

Often, they strolled beyond the last tents into the barrens around them. Though Datya always kept the camp in sight, she and Evita both seemed to long for the open air. Together they traipsed across dusty paths, around scrabbled together shrubs that hadn't borne leaves in many years, and through the shadows of wind-piled dunes. The little girl especially loved catching sight of wilderness critters, hares, mice, or hawks, or walking along a strand of curious pawprints. More often than not she would lift her face up to stare intensely at Datya and ask,

"But who made these?" For Datya, this was the one moment a chuckle could break free, and she knew, undoubtedly, that Miriam would have laughed aloud as well. "I don't know, sweet one. If we walk just a bit further perhaps we will find the owner of the prints!" At that, Evita usually surged ahead while Datya started a new song. Creation was a wellspring for her words.

This morning's walk had followed their usual pattern and, once again, Datya was stirred to praise as she surveyed the earthy colors around them. While she knew this land could never support cities, it was beautiful in its own way. For the thousandth time, Datya half-wished and half-prayed that her own stubborn people could see the allure of the landscape. *Perhaps if they'd silenced their grumbling a little, they would see what I see.* Frustration rose within as Datya mused. The people so often look to the sky as they walk in the shadow of the scavenger birds and think, 'This land supports only death!' But if they would just look to the earth, like Evita, they would see the scampering tracks that lead to life. Yes, life, and a wide variety of it. In only the few days that they had spent together, she and Evita had found paw prints of every shape and size scattered near and far around the camp. Though they seldom saw the scurrying critters, they saw plenty of proof of the Creator and it had filled both the younger and the older girl with much hope.

"Evita! Come, Angel!" Datya's voice rang out loudly as she realized they had wandered a bit far. The sun had already climbed to the highest point and Evita would be agitated if they missed their chance to snack on the midday fruit portion. In addition, Evita's mother may need help preparing the family to return to their main dwelling tomorrow. As the curly-headed girl rushed back to her, Datya grinned. God had been generous in providing such a sweet companion for this week. She had grieved as was proper, but she hadn't sunk. The miracle of childhood had supplied her with an unexpected, cheerful hope. "Let's put haste into our footsteps, Evita, for I do suspect that Lisbet will eat all the fruit if we tarry!" The little girl's giggles flooded the dryscape as they hurried along. Datya had not yet told Noya, but she planned to send the remaining bags of fruit with the family. She hoped it would be some small blessing to them, especially the children, even as they faced an utterly new living.

~ ~ ~

"You've done well this week. What a difference you have made in the midst of their pain." Her mother's words startled Datya as they watched Noya and her children begin the long trek back to the Asherite tents. With such young ones, it would take most of the day to walk past the many miles of tents belonging to the other tribes.

Datya had been dwelling on what difference Evita had made for her own sorrow; in truth, she hadn't felt like she'd managed to soothe Noya's pain even an ounce. "Evita was a true gift to me this week, Immi, but I wish I could have done something for her family." Though she normally forbade herself sighing, Datya allowed a sigh to break free as the family grew more distant. She had not felt like a prophetess this week, observing Noya's near constant tears and remaining helplessly mute in the woman's presence.

Datya's mother had apparently viewed the week with a different scope, "You were all a Prophetess should be and more this week, Datya. You may not know it, but you minister to Yahweh himself when you humbly serve a lowly little one like Evita." With the dry chuckle that comes from a lifetime in the wilderness she continued. "And don't think I don't know just how much of Moses' possessions you sent along with them. I'm no fool, Datya." She looked to the earth, an unspoken admission of her mother's suspicion. Of course, her mother was too wise to miss the real reason Datya had insisted on sending along one of the servants. Even before her husband had died, Noya's family had likely never been able to afford hired hands. It was true that their neighbors may raise some questions when Noya's brood returned with a well-packed servant and more possessions than they had ventured out with. Datya had not been able to withhold the generous act no matter what Noya's neighbors would say. Surely Moses would not begrudge the kindness, afterall, he had sent them as a gift and was not expecting their return. By the time the woman's indentureship expired, Noya's grief, and her children would be older, and they would manage.

The dawn was only an hour or so old, but Evita's family had faded. They were likely already trooping past the first tents of the main camp. Evita and her *achai* would love passing so near the sheep herds. Though the shepherds wouldn't tolerate the children coming near, or being rowdy in their midst, they would still be able to see and hear the sheep which stretched on for a few miles. Lambing season was blessing the camp with wonderful new white tufts of joy; yes, Evita and her siblings would find much laughter and wonder as they passed by. Datya, turning to face the cleansing camp, felt less than joyful as she realized that her own final day in this place would be spent without the little angel who had so soothed her.

"Ravit! Wait, I will join you." Ravit looked up from the entrance to a dwelling several paces away. Hesitantly, she smiled at Datya, then put a hand to her lips, gesturing quiet. Though Datya had largely spent the week apart from her friend, she longed to throw herself into gentle ministrations as Ravit had done.

Drawing close, Datya barely caught her friend's whisper. "You may join me, Datya. You may watch and pray, but do not approach the bed." In the dimness of the tent, Datya struggled to keep her eyes on her friend. She struggled too with the scent which reminded her of the few times her family had caught and prepared an edible bird. With a twinge of fear, Datya realized that the smell alerted her mind - death hung here. Overwarm and alarmed, Datya huddled close to the entrance while she watched Ravit draw near to a crooked man whose body heaved and sweated with some unseen malady. He was bare of any kind of cloak and his tunic bore stains of blood and all manner of waste. *Fool! She is not comforting a widow! You rushed ahead, and here you are facing death, the very thing which sent you to this place!*

She tried to settle her stomach and hold herself upright, but even as she looked at the wretched dying man all she could see was Miriam on the morning of her last day when she had endured such terrible pain. The way the spasms had seized her body, pinching her into a tightness that stole her breath away. The afternoon, when the sleeping breath of Miriam's last hours grew more and more shallow. For the entire week, Datya had battled back these same memories shunning them to a distant corner of her mind, but as they played in front of her now, nothing could dispel the sorrow and grief that trapped her.

Ravit was speaking tenderly to the man. When she had first entered, Datya had thought him old, as aged as one could be, but after staring at the horrid scene, Datya realized he was likely her father's age. How sickness could change a person into something so mangled and twisted, Datya couldn't fathom! As Ravit crooned, only a few words made it to Datya's corner, "The message has been sent. Word has arrived... Your family, your cousins will come. Be still, don't fight." And around stifled tears, "Peace, friend." Though Ravit's words had been issued to soothe, Datya watched horror and pain fill in the sunken lines of the man's face. Another emotion, even more heartbreaking took up residence. Datya remembered seeing the same agony on Miriam's dear face when her daughter had died. Devastating grief. The man languished with disease, and even more so with grief.

In the darkness of the tent, it was clear no one but Ravit was attending the man. The odor of a body that could no longer care for itself, coupled with the fever that seemed to be burning him, assailed her. Odor itself was nothing new to her, for the herds musk and waste always rode the wind into camp, and of course her baby brother was yet too young to privately deal with his own waste in the designated places. Many nights, their family had been assaulted with his pungent little scent. But the smell of death turned her stomach in a new way. Miriam had suffered and died so quickly, all the while she or Lisbet had been gently bathing her skin. There had been little odor, and the women had perfumed her immediately, preparing her body for burial long before decay could taint her memory.

Ravit approached her, but stayed an arm's length away. The man had drifted into a burning, tormented sleep, and Datya's questions flew fiercely. "What can you be thinking, Ravit? You will not be able to leave now that you ministered to this man, and touched his sickness! Do you even know the man? When will his kin come? Why are they not here with him already?" With maddening patience, Ravit let Datya spill her frustration. It stemmed from Ravit's foolishness and also her own. Why hadn't she asked Ravit where she was going before blindly following along?

"I know you mean well, Datya, but I can no more disobey Yahweh than you can. He called you to be a Prophetess, and tomorrow you will head home to begin that work. He burdened my heart for this sick man." Looking back to the crude packed-mud birthe that supported the crippled form, Ravit's impassioned plea continued, "He was cast out from his home for fear of contagion. Though he is a true Israelite, who deserves to die at home, no matter the risk, his family has abandoned him here. I cannot." Datya's heart softened with her friend's revelation. Of all the sins, disrespecting an elder, your own relation no less, was detestable! Truly, Ravit had a heart of gold to risk even more time spent in the purification place for his sake.

Remorse flooded her, but Datya could not quite let go of

the selfish thought that her friend would not journey home with her. She had envisioned having Ravit close by her side in the coming weeks, now, it seemed she would be alone. "I don't understand Ravit, why has his family made such a dishonorable choice? I heard you tell the man they were coming, will you leave him to their care then?" For a moment, Datya doubted that Ravit would answer her. With alarm, she realized that something grave was amiss.

Ravit's head hung heavy and despair settled between them. "When I return..." Ravit's voice was thick, distressed. Clearing her throat, now swollen from tears, she tried again with a bit more strength. "When I return, I will have to ask my father-in-law to take a sacrifice for me." Datya's breath stilled and she looked sharply at her dear friend. Her statement meant one thing: She had lied to the man whose sleeping breath raked coarsely across the leather walls. "I could not bear to deliver the true message. His kin answered my plea for their presence in anger. They have disowned him, refusing to see him. It has, in fact, been many years since a kind word or look made its way to this man. Not even his looming death stirred their compassion. All these long years, he has lived without their love and he will die without it too." Tears blended with her own compassion as she glanced back once more. "My only hope is that he will pass into the next life before he wakes and sees that they have not come. Before he realizes that he will never see them again." Ravit was weeping now and desperately trying to tamper any noise that escaped her.

Datya's fury was surely evident in her eyes. Her father had taught her above all to care for the elders every day of her life. Their wisdom was a valuable treasure! Why, honoring one's parents and relatives was a clear law in the Tablet of Ten! All in Israel knew the grievous penalty for disobeying God's sacred commandments! This mystery baffled her, and filled her with fear for her friend's sake all at once. What could explain this grim refusal? "What could they be thinking, Ravit? No grievance is so severe to dishonor this man so. Maybe Moses should intervene. He could command the man's family to attend him. At the very least, they should be compelled to send servants for his care!" Datya finished, suspecting her questions would not find satisfactory answers. What kind of forgiveness was a forced one? If the law did not motivate them already, Moses' words, and even his discipline wasn't likely to. But what could the man have done? Any transgression that would garner such treatment would likely have been punished by death long ago.

"No. Nothing will make them come, Datya. I will be here for him, but none from his own people will be, though the iniquity was not his own." With a tone akin to fright, Ravit revealed the cause, "Datya, the man who lies here is Abel, Son of Palti, Son of Raphu." Datya's gasp burst into the tent causing the man to release a moan, though he slept on. Weakness and rage filled her. Though the man's piteous state still drew sorrow from her, she understood the plight of his cousins and kin now too. The long-ago sin of this man's father had marked them among Israel. They were not outright hated, but they bore the stain of the spy, Palti, maybe forever.

Ravit's noble compassion would not be approved by a large portion of the camp, thus it was no surprise that the man's own family refused to attend him. Certainly, he could give no blessing from his cursed state, none that the men of his family would want, anyway. What words could such a wretched man offer those he left behind? No, indeed the sin had not been Abel's own, but he had surely borne the stain of his father's wickedness since that ill-fated day.

Datya felt her own body stepping back into the wall of the tent even more. It felt wrong, immoral to be in the man's presence, regardless of his personal innocence. *I can not believe Ravit comforts Palti's son! I did not even know that a child of the forsaken spy of Benjamin's people still lived!* This man must surely be the last offspring of the evil-hearted spies who had brought such woe and fury upon the Israelites. Noble Caleb still lived and of course, steady Joshua. They had been the youngest, and it turned out the wisest of the spies sent into the Promised Land so long ago, and they would see it soon. Though the wicked spies themselves had died by Yahweh's decree after their faithless report, their offspring and all those who shared family ties to them had been treated with derision in Israel. Datya's revulsion must have shown on her face. She could see Ravit searching for words, but she doubted her friend could say anything to banish her ill thoughts of the dying man.

Did you not pray for mercy, not so long ago, Datya? Where is your own racham? Yahweh's conviction wrapped thickly about her and drew her eyes reluctantly to the dark, dying form before her.

"Forgiveness is courage," the memory of Miriam's voice bound her to Yahweh's directive. Miriam had spoken the words over her when she was very young, and had bravely found the courage to forgive an older cousin who had been mercilessly cruel to her. The memory was distant and vague but the lesson was bright as though it had been learnt yesterday. Miriam would tell her to lead by example, to speak forgiveness, for it was the only gift that would soothe this cursed son.

Yahweh's whisper was pressing it on her heart so fiercely she felt as feverish as the ailing man. This man was a forsaken tie to a hated generation, and yet Yahweh's stirring was clear: Forgive his father's sin. *In your strength only, Yahweh. Help me!*

With courage supplied from heaven, she stepped away from the leather wall. It had soaked up the suffering scent of Abel's illness, and was no haven to her. Compassion took control as she looked to her sorrowful friend. "You may tell Abel, Son of Palti, Son of Raphu that the Chief Prophetess has visited his bedside. Her blessing arose in the tent with a message of forgiveness for Palti, and a message of mercy for his son, Abel. He is no longer the son of a spy, but a child of God, released and redeemed from all former stains." Her words, the first she had spoken on behalf of Israel, felt like they belonged to someone else. They almost tore from her, but it was right that she would spend her first words, on Israel's behalf, for the cause of redemption.

Ravit renewed her tears as Datya stepped as close as she dared and lifted her voice in the Song of Forgiveness that Miriam had taught. The work of mercy had been accomplished in her heart, a spiritual act more meaningful than these words, but she sang them whole-heartedly for this fragile man. He had paid more than enough for the sin of his father. He had been hated in his father's stead since youth, for surely he had been younger than her when his father died for his treacherous words. Abel had never married, for who would have the son of one of the ill-fated spies? Never bore a son, nor daughter. Never loved or accepted. He had never had peace in life, but she hoped to give him some small measure in death.

CHAPTER FOURTEEN

Brilliant, but blessedly gentle, sun flowed over Datya, Lisbet, and the serving woman who would be leaving with them today. Two of Moses's youngest stewards stood in the distance, remaining far from the sounds, smells, and sights of sorrow and sickness. They had been sent to escort the Prophetess home, but they would not come into the Purification Place. Happy was the Israelite who managed to avoid this place through a long life, so they say. Her own heart had shifted. She no longer saw it as the platform where the disgraced landed. She saw it rather as a wellspring of God's mercy. Yes, many had entered in their own brand of suffering, but many received something precious while inside.

Evita had discovered a tiny remembrance of her father here. Ravit had awakened, more than ever before to her calling here. Lisbet had regained a daughter here. Then there was Abel. Datya's blessing had been a sincere offering, but she still shuddered at the thought of Abel's wretched father. Abel had received forgiveness on behalf of his father here and a mercy he had thought would never come. He had died under Ravit's gentle care before the sun fell to its depths yesterday. Were those final, despairing breaths eased because he had been given a message of mercy from the Prophetess?

Datya had not thought to ask if the man had been well enough to know of Miriam's passing. When he received the message, did he evision it coming from Miriam's lips? Or did he know the Prophetess was now a hopelessly young Levite girl?

She answered to the title with reluctance this morning. Would it always be so?

And what had she received in this place? She would walk home, to her family's tent, rather than Miriam's, with a new-found confidence that she could obey the Lord's directives, just as Miriam had. Stepping towards Abel, Son of Palti, Son of Raphu and speaking Yahweh's words over him had taught her that. It was a gift more palpable than Evita's keepsake stone, for Datya had entered this place in fierce denial that she could ever be what Miriam had hoped for her.

Without comment, Datya and Lisbet bundled robes and garments into the outstretched arms of Moses' waiting stewards. Turning, they strolled back to the tent, to gather the things they would carry themselves. Their goodbyes had been said yesterday. Datya had wept as Ravit stood beyond her reach. A friend's embrace was needed desperately when one faced something so new, like the work Datya was about to begin, but the embrace would have to wait. Ravit would endure another week in the purification place, remaining in the tent Moses had sent, for he would not want it returned. It would pass to each new person or family who came to this place in need. Even now her friend was far from her, watching Abel's wrapped form leave the camp on the opposite end from Datya and Lisbet. Ravit would likely be Abel's sole mourner.

Pausing with her final load, she watched the men carry Abel's wrapped body, stiffly and without the ceremony that usually accompanied the newly dead. It was clear the men who'd been selected for the task knew well the name, the legacy of the man within the linen bundle. Their stoney faces held no echo of the redemption she had poured out on the man. She had the right to speak for Israel on such matters, had seen Miriam do so before, but that did not mean the hearts of her people would change overnight. Palti's family would likely carry the taint for long generations though his own line ended when his son took a final breath. Her prayers that the Benjaminites would let go of the harsh feelings for Palti's dying son had been too little too late. How freeing it would be if her people left behind the loathing they'd felt for the ten foolish spies here in the wilderness rather than carrying the millstone of it into the Promised Land.

With her mother beside her and one of Moses' stalwart apprentices to their head and one behind, her steps carried her further away from Abel, from the purification place, from Ravit. How she wished she could leave behind the ache of Miriam's memory as well. Yahweh would bring healing to her heart someday. A tiny portion of that work had begun in this place, but she still felt the severity of the cut that had removed Miriam from her life. She was eager to be home, with her family. It seemed the proper place to take this pain.

Perhaps as she healed, some improvement could be made between her and Ziva. Despite the longing to return, sorrow made her footfalls maddeningly slow. How could she bear days passing void of precious walks with Miriam, no lessons, no prayers or songs except the ones she offered herself? Could Datya bear time's march without her teacher? Miriam's voice had been the one that nurtured her, comforted her, moulded her. Even now it stirred within her, memories rushing back to her as she traversed the no man's land between the camp proper and the far-flung outcasts.

Would Miriam's voice carry her the whole way home? Then what? How long would it stay with her? Could she count on the audible memory forever or would it fade? Would it fill her with hope as it loomed before her like the great mountains that they sometimes passed only to shrink to nothingness the further she walked through life? Losing the sound of the beloved voice would surely break her; it was her only lifeline in the lonesome work that lay ahead. The days ahead certainly would be lonely. Few would understand her work, the need for her service and the ways that she would go about it. She would be both desperately needed and severely judged among Israel. She would become great, but separated, as Miriam had been these many years since Egypt.

~ ~ ~

Miriam would have a thing or two to say about Datya's worry, of that she was sure. Datya would accept all the chastisement she could muster if Miriam would but stand before her now! How she longed to replace the stiff, unknown back of the steward before her with the loving outreached arms of her teacher! Even the presence of her mother close beside her did little to calm her. While little Evita was still with them, Datya had felt a small healing. Now a scoff sounded within, the healing had been a mirage! Her spirit was torn apart. She was awash with grief. Grief for Miriam, grief over Ravit's absence, and grief, even for Abel, son of the wretched spy of Benjamin.

Memories of moments with Miriam stirred, offering some small comfort that she would have gladly traded to hear Miriam's voice in front of her, and not from foggy confines of her mind.

"Well, little one, would you like to hear a tale about spies and mystery today?" Miriam's voice floated through her mind. It sounded distant, as memories do, but Datya cherished it. She had been so young when Miriam had first recalled for her the tale of Israel's foolish spies. Of course, in recent years, Miriam had dug deeper into the story, sharing the family histories of the spies themselves, but that day, she had laid the groundwork. A web of words had woven about Datya as she sat, listening quietly. How amazed she had been at the way her teacher described the commission that started it all, the fury of Moses when he realized the evil that had been committed. Speaking first with her mouth, and at another moment with her eyes, and still more with her weathered hands communicating in the air between them, Miriam had delivered the truth behind the legend. She would never forget a single word spent that day.

"The Red Sea Crossing was a wonderful thing, Datya. Even the earth shook with the power of the foaming waters. Sea life, normally invisible in the murky waters, had suddenly appeared all around us in the high, impossible walls. No doubt, the Egyptians felt a similar surge of wonder until those same walls choked the life from every soldier. Our people were stunned, Datya. Despite the grim horror cast upon the shores, we had been delivered and what a mighty sound went up from us! Never since that day has Israel raised such praise!" This, Miriam had said with a tremor of sorrow, for she witnessed many miracles in the forty years following the Red Sea Crossing, but the tribes brushed them away as minor and insignificant. Often, they had rejoiced for only a handful of days before their faith withered once more like the sun-dried snake skins that littered the wilds of their barren path. Their faith had been watered down, as though the wilderness itself were a strange malady, capable of muting the most zealous heart.

"Yes, it was wonderful and terrifying," Miriam had continued, speaking intensely to Datya's young self. "We had no idea in the midst of our celebration what lay ahead. Our goal had been freedom, leaving Egypt. Yahweh had accomplished it, but what would become of us now? There were too many people, Datya, hoards unending of needy bodies and souls. Could Yahweh make a provision for us? Would he? Or was our freedom his singular goal as well?"

A smile wove into the memory as Datya remembered questioning her teacher, "But what of the covenant, Miriam? Surely the people remembered the promise to Abraham, Isaac, and Jacob?"

Miriam had lovingly palmed her small head in reply, "Oh

child, I am afraid the Israelites hardly recalled it at all. Still, our feet were ordered to move. 'Make distance between yourselves and the false gods of Egypt!' Moses had ordered. So we walked, Datya. I walked, with my kin. Your grandfathers and their families walked. Egypt faded and the land changed all around us. Had it been weeks? Or had it been years? So much was the dust on our feet, that it was hard to tell!" At this, Miriam had lifted her tunic, bringing one bare foot out for a good shake as though the dust of those first days was still pressed against her skin.

Datya's youthful giggles bubbled through the tent quickly, but just as swiftly, she had sobered, wanting Miriam to tell her more. "Some of our travels saw good happening for our people. Miraculous water! Foreign friends laying down their gods and choosing Yahweh! Many days of travel saw danger and darkness, like the ill-fated day foolish men convinced the High Priest to cast an idol for the people." Here Datya had gasped. This story, Miriam had already told her, several times in fact, but the thought of the iniquitous golden calf had always alarmed her. She remembered wanting to hide just at the mention!

Miriam's voice had curved around the story, flowing with the heights and lows of each moment. "Finally, we approached a land that seemed to hum with a call. All felt it, heard it, within their souls. The lips of the people couldn't be quieted as they sang a song to Yahweh in response. A great river sliced across a lowland in the distance. Moses and the elders fasted and prayed, meeting together from dawn until the stars rose. Then one morning, we heard his silver trumpets blast the call to gather. The elders and patriarchs from every tribe made their way to hear his words. Some of us fairly danced with a divine hope that had begun to warm us from head to toe. Others quaked, sensing a temptation, a struggle ahead. When all were assembled, Moses, his face veiled from his time in the Presence, uttered the command. 'Choose from amongst yourselves, the wisest, the strongest. Every tribe will send one spy into the land before us. Yahweh has revealed that this is the land he calls us to. We will enter and take possession when the spies have returned to us!'" For the retelling, Miriam had done her best to portray her brother's solemn voice, but she had finished with the chuckle she was known for.

"But the people standing before Moses never entered, did they, little one?" Here, she had shaken her head. It almost seemed to her that the earliest memory she had was a parent or uncle or aunt mournfully wishing for the Promised Land. No, their people had not entered, because of Palti and his fellow spies.

Her teacher hadn't made her wait long to hear what happened next. "A week passed, then the assembly came together once more to present their chosen spies. Each man had been selected from the very strongest and fiercest families. They were the finest men Israel could offer both in body and mind. All of Israel radiated with pride as they were each called before Moses and Aaron."

Miriam's voice had thickened with herald-like importance. Datya had closed her little eyes, trying to envision the brave parade. "An elder of Reuben stepped forward calling, 'Reuben sends Shammua, the son of Zaccur!' Simeon's people followed with a loud cry, 'Shaphat, the son of Hori!' 'We offer Caleb, the son of Jephunneh,' the elder of Judah's voice dripped with pride. Not to be outdone, a clamor rose from Isaachar's people, 'Igal, the son of Joseph!' 'Can the land be explored without mighty Joshua, the son of Nun?' This voice rang out, of course, from Ephraim's people. The elder of Benjamin thundered, 'Benjamin offers Palti, son of Raphu!' 'Fierce and wise Gaddiel, the son of Sodi joins the company,' Zebulun's people puffed with the declaration. From Manasseh's descendents, the children of Joseph, Gaddi, son of Susi was announced. The elder of Dan lifted his voice above the noise, 'Ammiel, the son of Gemalli!' The

Asherites had quickly answered with 'Sethur, the son of Micheal will serve Israel!' Naphtali's spy was announced next, 'Nahbi, the son of Vophshi!' Finally, the proud heirs of Gad declared their chosen man, 'We send Geuel, the son of Machi!' How she remembered being stunned by the list of names, men she had never met from tribes she rarely mixed with. She had felt the pride of the elders swirl around her. Even so, the tale was just beginning and her teacher quickly set to telling it.

"Our people had been restless in that camp, Datya. Can you imagine? Our people were perched on the edges of their new home. They could see it's hills and rivers in the distance. They heard the sounds of its wildlife at night. They saw the long dusty paths travelers had carved to the cities. Still we remained on the outside looking in. Excitement had been brewing. All felt the spies were a formality, a signaling if you will. Every man and woman among Israel spent their days preparing to enter in, to make a new home. The spies, all of whom had worked closely with Moses since the Exodus, were dispatched. The people knew the taste of waiting once more. Everyday that passed we waited, sometimes with a collective silence, but more often with the excited murmurings of hope." Miriam's gaze had looked beyond her, as though she were stilling waiting, hopefully, for some news.

"Finally, three spies returned. Moses ushered them into his private encampment. Though the people longed for a report, none was given." Miriam had clutched her hands in mid-air in front of her as she relayed the anxious days of waiting that the Israelites endured. Datya remembered how her tightly bound fists struck up towards the sky as though Miriam were still aggravated at the delay. "In four days time, all but two of the spies had returned, and still Moses told the people nothing. 'The report will be made in whole, or not at all,' he had told the impatient tribes. We waited many days, nearly a whole moon had passed. Some feared the lost spies had been captured. Some lamented they were dead, long since devoured by the wild animals prowling our new homeland. Moses offered, with his quiet, fierce confidence, 'They're alive and making their way back to us.' How restless we were then, Datya! Never have our people enjoyed the virtue of patience, but in those waiting moments, I know not how Moses kept peace."

Miriam had dropped to her knees at this point, looking Datya in the eyes. Even then, Miriam had been well aged, though she had a youthful, lively way about her. Looking back, Datya realized just how much Miriam had indeed begun to shrink with sickness through their last year. How had she not noticed death approaching? The Prophetess always seemed mighty, tall, her authority filling the tent. Voice low, she broke the tense waiting: "They returned at night, and though the night watches were commanded to silence, murmurs of the return had circulated most of camp within moments of dawn. Still, Moses gave our people no word. The spies were cloistered in his camp. Elders came and went. Days passed and nothing was revealed. The people were speaking openly against Moses now, and even Aaron, demanding that the High Priest put an end to the secrecy."

Miriam's face was so sorrowful in the next moment that Datya's young self had reached for her teacher, aiming to comfort the ache she couldn't even comprehend. "Finally, Moses called an assemblage. The elders and patriarchs of the tribes met to hear, from their own mouths, the reports of the spies." The Prophetess dropped her head; Datya had no longer been able to see into her eyes. "Two spies were eager, 'We must move into the country; God has provided a good thing for us!' Their welcome words were drowned out by the bellows of cowards, men who had gone up as brave spies and returned as beaten whelps.

Datya had learned later that chief among the cowards had been Palti, Son of Raphu, spy of Benjamin. How young had

Abel been when he found out about his father's treachery? His father's faithlessness? Had he been old enough to understand and burn with the shame? Arguments lasted through a night and a day, but those who stood with the two wise spies were overruled by the crowds. Finally, Moses sent the final report. It was read among the tents of every tribe, though most had discerned what it would say before it arrived.

His proclamation read: "Israel, mourn! A gift from Yahweh was before you and has been rejected! Mightier men than your own have stolen it from you, and you have let them as though you were lowly animals at the foot of champions! What a foolish thing you have done!" Miriam had whispered these words, as though the force of them all these years later was still too much to bear, but Datya could well imagine Moses' scribes thundering with the message amongst the tents. She had witnessed many such messages during her young years. The exact words of the remainder were lost to Datya, but she recalled the summary: Israel would remain lost, homeless and desolate for forty years.

Forty years, and the instant death of the ten cursed spies, was the price Israel paid for cowardice. As the memory faded, Datya began to wonder if the camp had been told yet that the forty years was nearly complete. Did the people know that the price had been paid in full? Did they know they would shortly stand on that long-distant horizon once more? Would Israel respond with fearless faith this time or would they be lost forever in the shifting wilderness?

~~~

A gentle hand landed on the broad part of her arm, startling Datya from her hazy thoughts. "You are far from me. What troubles you?" Her mother's voice sounded dry as though she had walked many days behind the dusty herds. More likely, it was the fumes of the tannery fires which corrupted the air around them. Soon they would pass by the handful of patchwork
~~~

tents inhabited and worked by fellow former slaves. The Israelites benefited greatly from their presence and skill. All were thankful for the variety of tribes who had fled with them from Egypt, but none had proved quite so useful as the families who worked the tannery camp.

The Israelites needed the tanned hides for their tents, for their garments, for storage, and for trade, but they found it foul work better left to others. Other than cooking and shepherding, most of the Israelites she knew detested any work which caused them to handle carcasses. The tannery camp, fast approaching, was distant from the regular camp, though not so far cast as the Purification Place. She had rarely been forced to breathe in the strong odor, for the tannery tents were well away from the camp proper. Smiling reassuringly at her mother, she let her mother's question go unanswered. The truth was, she wasn't exactly troubled, but she felt an uneasiness within. Astir with some work that she couldn't quite fathom as of yet.

More long-dormant memories drifted in to soothe her troubled mind. Though she had little reason to visit the tanneries on her own, she had been here a handful of times with Miriam. Miriam had felt an additional calling to share the stories and songs with the people who were not descendants of Jacob, but had been absorbed into their people. Some of those families chose to embrace all of Yahweh's precepts. Others had spent these forty years in the Israelites' shadow, but separate in worship and in the peculiar ways they lived. Miriam had loved these people. She refused to shun them, though the largely boorish expressions of her people suggested she should. Her teacher had listened to their stories, then shared some of her own. She had listened to their songs, then lifted up one of her own. She had prayed over their newborns and their dying. When they would let her, she would offer long hours of love and compassion in their midst.

Datya had been startled and uncomfortable on her first such mission with Miriam, but had quickly grown to love the people as well. The children were different from the Israelite children. Lively, colorful, cheerful, the foreign camps among them had much to offer, but most of Israel disagreed vehemently. They had not learned, as Miriam and Datya had, that God had called more than just the Israelites out of Egypt. He had called all who suffered under Pharaoh's hand, and it was his good and holy purpose that all who desired would become a part of his new nation. They would be called the Israelites, the descendants of Jacob, but Yahweh extended the invitation to those of any parentage, so long as they would declare him Lord of All. As Miriam had said, so shortly before her death, "Our God builds his people through adoption."

All around her and Lisbet were the men and women and youths who spent their lives on the hide-tanning process. Datya could not help but wonder if these people had finally begun to trust Yahweh. She and Miriam had not visited in many months, and she knew only a handful had been open to Yahweh's law at their last visit. Deep within, Datya felt a whisper, though if it was Miriam's voice or Yahweh's she couldn't say. The conviction was clear, her service was as much for these tired, set-apart souls as it was for her own kin. Though she was passing from their presence, heading into a camp she couldn't yet see, she promised Yahweh, quietly, that she would soon return and show these people Heaven's love. She would return to them, take their stained and worn hands in her own and deliver words of hope and love.

"I am sorry I seem distant, Immi. I have been thinking of Miriam. Dwelling on her stories and her songs." Her mother took her hand, looped it through her own arm and walked closely by her side. Lisbet understood the sorrow. Her love reached into Datya without words. She wondered now if her mother had always been this tender. Had she simply misunderstood her *immi* all these years? God in his mercy was knitting their souls together, nevermind that their relationship had once been cool and dissonant. The gift was not lost on her. Miriam had gone into her ministry with her own mother long dead. Datya would have Lisbet's support for many years to come. A knowledge stirred deep inside her that a great need for her mother's friendship was coming. How strange it felt to be straining to see what lay ahead of her while at the same time keeping a constant view of what was behind her: the days of her life spent with Miriam. The gap between the past and the future would only grow. Would she be able to keep both in her view? Or would trying tear a fissure in the foundation of who she was and what she was meant to do?

As the volume of the tannery families was starting to fade behind them, an idea struck. "Immi, Mother, do you suppose Father will have commissions for the tanners sometime soon? He hasn't ordered the culling of his older ewes for quite some time. Do you think he may set the shepherds to it?"

"Perhaps, Daughter, but he has not spoken of it. Our small herd is usually far from his mind unless the shepherds report a problem. Whatever has you thinking of such?" A curious and amused face accompanied the response. Of course her mother would be startled by the suddenness of her request. She had ever been the calm and predictable child; a sudden desire to commission the tannery camp was out of place for her.

Feeling a joy she hadn't expected, with a fresh, miniature mission tucked in her heart, Datya conscripted her mother. "I would very much like to visit with the families of the tannery camp, Mother. All the better if we plan our visit with a bit of purpose. We can fetch hides from the shepherds if Father gives the order, then bring them here to be worked. We'll have a wonderful visit with the families, perhaps we can get to know them better! And, of course, we'll need to make our way again when the hides are ready! It's a good plan, Mother; will you speak with Father about it?" Datya's breath finally commanded her to pause for it had plenty of catching up to do. Although it was needed in the next moment as she turned to her side to face her mother. Lisbet's eyes were wide, her bewilderment at her daughter's sudden enthusiasm evident.

Finally, taming her shock Lisbet could raise only questions. "If it is important to you, I will ask him, Datya. I am sure the herds would benefit from a culling, as you say. But why the rush to revisit this place? I saw the way your breathing stiffened as we approached their tents, and the way it eased as we found clean air once more. I saw too, the way your throat worked to keep your morning manna in its place." With upthrust hands, Lisbet studied her, "Why are you making plans to return to the tanners?"

She wanted, desperately, to give her mother an answer that belonged to a prophetess, to the Chief Prophetess, no matter how new and untried she was. As much as she hoped to speak in wisdom, her only answer was, "Yahweh tugs my heart to them. He has placed a stirring within, a knowing that they are to hear his name from my lips." Her hand pressed tightly against her mother's as if to say that her statement was true and sure, as though her hand stamped, albeit gently, her authority on the matter.

Though many tents and families separated them still from their own dwelling, she longed more than ever to be home. The ache of Miriam would stay well lodged within her, but she knew that her work was beginning. How could she minister to this vast people from unsteady ground? She needed to be home, with her brother, sister, and her thoughtful mother. Quickening her footsteps, she pulled ahead of the lead steward. Moses' two apprentices could easily ask the other Levite families to point the way to her tent, if they decided not to keep up. For her sake, and for Lisbet, who had swiftly matched her new pace, it was time to go home.

CHAPTER FIFTEEN

More often than not, the traveling pace and rationed grazing meant the mother does of the goat herds produced little milk. What creamy sustenance they did create went to their suckling babes. Occasionally though, a few of the Israelite women would have the opportunity to set up a shared tripod and the massive swaying butter bag beneath it. Often, youths and widows would be pressed into service as soon as a fresh portion of cream was brought in from the herds. The butter bag, like a leather wine skin, only much larger and heavier, was suspended between the tripod, filled halfway or less, bound tightly, then swayed, rocked, and swirled back and forth for many hours, sometimes even through the night, until the cream set up. Datya had taken many turns with such work when she had been little, before her daily lessons had lengthed.

One pleasant memory saw her kneeling beside the setup under the watchful eye of an elder widow who had seemed ancient to her. The older woman had told Datya that in Egypt the butter churns had been twice as big, worked by pairs of slaves, and they had been made of pottery. In her youthfulness, she had been startled by the thought of working something so large and heavy for so long. All for the sake of butter, rich and luxurious as it was, that would be gone in a matter of days. In more recent years, even the largest batches had not lasted until the next morning. The cream of the herds was never generous enough to keep butter in good supply.

Standing dumbstruck in her memories, Datya could not

overcome the surprise as she rounded a neighboring tent to see her sister sitting at their own tripod, calmly and gently rocking the cream filled bag. Ziva had never willingly sat to such work, and had often been whipped for her blatant refusals. She could see no matriarch enforcing her sister's efforts, and of course her father was far in the distance. What on earth had happened in the short week she had been gone that made Ziva so willing, so compliant?

Her mother's chuckle sounded close behind her; her disbelief must be evident in everything from her expression to her posture. Still, she couldn't nudge her feet forward, no matter how they ached to find a seat. Seeing Ziva set to patient work, for little reward was almost as shocking as the scent of the tannery kettles. "I suspect my sister can be thanked in part for Ziva's behavior today, but the girl is still young. It is natural to struggle a bit as childhood fades and womanhood begins. We'll both have to wait and see if Ziva makes her transition a little smoother from now on." Lisbet stopped short of the unspoken "or if she will be back to her usual wild ways tomorrow." Her mother's near whisper was intended to spare her youngest daughter embarrassment; but they would be hard-pressed to keep the questions from their faces.

Lisbet's sister emerged from their own tent at that moment. Idan let go of her tunic, nearly stumbling as he made short work of the distance to his mother. He buried his sweaty head in his mother's tunic as she knelt down to receive him. Compassionate pangs darted through her heart as she watched Idan's sweaty hands reach their way into their mother's long plaited hair. He would break curls free that Lisbet would later tuck away once more, but Datya knew how much their mother's thick tresses comforted the little one, as it likely did for all sweet babes with their own *immis*.

Passing a grateful smile at her aunt who held her own

toddler perched on her hip, Datya moved closer to the butter work. Ziva had yet to look up though she had surely heard Idan's squeaks as he alternated between messy sobs and joyous giggles. Still nothing had raised her head. *Is she unhappy?* All the unpleasant memories and moments in the world couldn't keep Datya's concern at bay. It was only right to care for one's family, even if that same family often stirred up fights rather than love. Yahweh's law itself propelled her feet towards her sister, but something more than that too: a longing for a rebirth of their relationship, just as she'd experienced with her mother over the past week. The lesson was slow, bittersweet that mourning often grows new life in the sore soil of a broken heart, but she was committing it to the tender places within her spirit.

Perching opposite Ziva, she reached out to clasp the cream filled bag as it tipped towards her. From the slight slosh inside the bag she could tell only an hour or two of the work remained. The consistency could only mean that her sister had been faithfully tending the work since the earliest fingers of the sunrise. Holding onto the bag for a moment longer than necessary, Datya waited for her sister's eyes to lift. She wanted to catch them and offer a smile at her sister, to tell her without words that she was happy to be home, reunited with family.

When Ziva looked up, Datya was startled by the mix brewing in her stormy eyes. Grief lined her face. And, was there a touch of fear? Still, Ziva offered a half-smile in return as Datya released the bag in her direction once more. Back and forth the girls sent the bag, giving it a slight rotation with each nudge. After a hundred passes or so, Datya stood and circled the bag around and around in the center of the tripod, then let it unwind between her hands. As she sat to resume the passing she prayed quietly for her sister, feeling a vague instinct that it was best not to interrupt the silence.

After an hour or so, the butter was still unset, so Datya

guided her worrying once more into prayer. *Yahweh, what pins Ziva to her place today? Never have I seen her so still, except on the holy Sabbath. Is she ill? What should I say?* Though Yawheh's voice was silent, a conviction began to form in her mind: across from her sat another avenue of her work. Ziva would always be her little sister, not a mission to add to her agenda, not a problem to solve, but a fellow child of God to love and cherish. Datya had not been a Chief Prophetess the last time she saw Ziva. She had simply been a prophetess in training. Now her eyes set upon her sister in a new light. Formerly, she had allowed frustration and emotion to bury her compassion and kindness to her. Now, Yahweh's pressing on her heart was clear: Ziva must be a recipient of love and care, from her as a sister first and secondly as the Prophetess.

Datya battled self-reproach, though there was ample mercy in the conviction. Her own thoughts and behaviors had been harmful to her sister, even though she had always viewed it the other way around. Was this why her sister sat in so distant a posture? Did she worry that because Datya was now the Chief Prophetess, that she was somehow less a sister? The grief in Ziva's attitude bore a resemblance to her own sorrow, and yet she hadn't been to her sister what Miriam had been to her.

Be it now, Datya. Love her, as Miriam loved you. Yahweh's heart had been in pursuit of Ziva's all along. She had missed it, when she may have aided it. Her eyes had been on the people, instead of the person who could have received her care in days gone by.

She had wronged her sister and the knowledge drove her to her feet. Ignoring her turn to redirect the nearly finished churn, she hastened to Ziva's side and dropped to her knees. Tears dripped onto the dusty fabric of Ziva's tunic as Datya bent to pour her love over her sister. "Forgive me, dear one. I've been a shallow offering of a sister in the past, but my heart does love you! It always has, and always will!" Unsure of whether or not she should mention her new position, Datya's words ground to a halt.

Ziva was stiff, if a little wide-eyed. Was it doubt that lined her youthful face? "Datya, I... I fear..." Emotions sparred across her face.

"Whatever it is, you can say it to me. I would comfort you, Ziva, if you would share your burden with me." Though opposites in every other way, the girls' eyes were a perfect mirror of one another, and both sets were beginning to overflow.

A sob she'd been holding in for who knows how long burst out, bringing the painful words with it. "I fear I have lost you! I have wasted time being a bully because I was jealous of your freedoms, of your path! Now, you will move on. You will reside in the Prophetess' tent and counsel day and night with elders and all manner of Israelites."

Ziva had contained the sob, but her words continued to spill over. "Your work will separate us. We are little girls no longer. Why did I waste the time?"

Datya's arms flew around her little sister. She looked over Ziva's shoulder at her mother and her aunt who, between the two of them, were surrounded by four little ones now. They smiled at her through their own tears as Datya hushed her sister with a gentle grasp on the girl's braid. "Oh, Ziva. I thought you knew. I am staying right here for a while." After Ziva's hiccup she added, "I thought perhaps, there may be a few ways you could come alongside me. Help me step into the work slowly. Will you try, Ziva?" Ziva nodded, her head still cradled in Datya's hands, and both girls wept, and giggled as the embrace continued.

Lisbet walked past her daughters, quietly unlatched the butter churn, and began untying the laces and wraps that kept the cream inside. She would likely share all but a small portion with the families around them, and, of course, with her own sister. Retreating to a respectful distance from her girls, she offered the loveliest smile Datya had seen in a long time. It was warmer even than the many doting smiles Miriam had bestowed. None could say if the waters between Datya and her sister would remain peaceful, but for now a mending had begun to weave between the two. It felt like victory, joy, peace, and hope and it overflowed Datya's own heart.

~~~

"Datya! Datya! Come quickly!" Datya dropped the small, knotted wad of cloth that she'd been tossing back and forth with Idan and found her mother's eyes with alarm. She'd been playing with Idan to allow her mother to do some fine beadwork commissioned by the wife of a wealthy trader, but at the sound of her father's imperative call, she knew she must hand over his care and rush to find her father. Datya nearly collided with Cohen as she fled the tent. What on earth was her father doing here? He never returned from his duties early, and it would be many more weeks before his rotation had ended. She had not expected to see him, outside of ceremonial work, before then. The elder looked at her admonishingly, even though his own hurried strides and startling call were partly to blame for the collision. "Whatever are you doing here, Datya? A messenger was sent to the tent of the Prophetess and returned without you! Your presence is required, and they came to me to determine your whereabouts! Now I've left my own duties to search you out."

Datya gasped at her father's rebuke. She'd assumed that keeping a presence with her own family for the time being would offend no one. After all, there wouldn't exactly be a line of needy people waiting for the counsel of a Chief Prophetess who was younger than most of them. Though, in truth, she had not sought permission for her decision. Whom could she ask?
~~~

There was not exactly an authority figure to run to with questions. Aaron had loosely watched over Miriam's work, but he was gone now too. Had his son been consecrated to the High Priesthood yet? Datya had only met Eleazar a handful of times, and knew little about him. He was serious like his father and yet had a brooding quality about him. Would he oversee her ministry? Of course, Moses too was an authority above her, but she could hardly traipse to his tent each time she had a concern. She knew Moses well enough to know he would have little patience for her questions.

Looking sharply at her father, Datya realized that only Moses' command could pull him from his work; it must be Moses himself who had called for Datya. *What could this be?* Datya's thoughts began to race and thunder. *I am not ready; he must not require me yet. I… I don't know what to do!*

As though her father could read her thoughts, he softened a bit and placed his hands on her shoulders. "Calm, Daughter, are you not the Chief Prophetess? Moses, himself calls for Datya, Prophetess of Israel, and Joshua, who is surely Moses' successor." At this, Cohen's face beamed with a friendly pride. That Joshua was the unspoken choice to lead Israel someday, was a point of pride to Cohen. His friend, more like a brother than his own, had been elevated to a great role, even over Moses' own sons, who for their own part didn't seem to mourn the lost glory.

"Come now, Prophetess," Cohen's voice fell on her once more, and the sound of the address puzzled her. Was she no longer his daughter? What message would Moses deliver that could cause her father to be so formal? Resisting a frown, Datya gave a simple nod. Slipping quietly into the tent, she uncovered the shallow tray at the head of where her mat lay nightly. Lying in neat folds was the brand new tunic and robe her mother had secretly prepared for her. It was stitched with fine lines and colors, only slightly less grand than the robes worn by the priests themselves. She quickly donned both as her mother's hands came up to tuck her hair into it's braid in the dozen or so spots it had escaped. Miriam had never had a single ounce of vanity, but she also would not leave her tent without being certain her appearance was clean and complete. She had told Datya, that it was her own consecration of sorts. She had always imagined that she would follow Miriam's conduct, but it seemed strange to finally go through the motions. She felt as though she were copying the real Prophetess, as though she were a pretender.

Shaking free of her webby thoughts, Datya hastened once more through the opening of the family tent. Cohen, who had been impatiently pacing the gap between their tent and the neighboring one looked at her approvingly. Was he proud that his daughter went to meet with Moses? Or was he proud that he himself would escort the Chief Prophetess to Moses' meeting? For the hundredth time in the nearly four weeks she had been home, Datya marveled uncomfortably at how different she felt. She was no longer Datya, Daughter of Cohen and Lisbet of the Levites. Now she was Datya, Chief Prophetess. Would she ever adjust? Her soul tugged towards girlhood, longing for the simple days of lessons, but her love for Yahweh pushed her forward. His work and his will were good and she refused to dread his calling.

Striding alongside her father, Datya longed to question him about the men and the meeting that were awaiting her. As the days since her return had tallied, she had wondered often about what tasks she should commit to. If only there was a messenger with a convenient list, but Miriam had not worked that way, and she suspected, neither would she. "Father, what does Moses summon me for?"

Expecting the question to be ignored in her father's hurry, she was startled when he stopped mid-stride. "Surely, Miriam told you, daughter, that the Prophetess learns about all decisions and changes facing the tribes before the populace does?"

At Datya's nod, Cohen smiled and resumed his pace as though he had fully satisfied her question. Dumbfounded, she followed, no closer to understanding the urgency. It would take them an hour, maybe even two, even with rapid footsteps to reach Moses' camp at the foremost of the tribes.

Beyond the vast queues of leather dwellings, the breeze could almost always be felt, slight but steady, swirling through the low grasses and shrubs, but here amidst the tents, little air penetrated. If necessity wasn't pushing them forward, Datya would have taken the time to walk to the edges of the dwellings to skirt the camp entirely. Passing between families, servants, wives, widows, children, and her people set to every task imaginable, she felt the collective stares that landed on her. It was peculiar enough seeing a Levitical man, clearly in his consecrated robes, wandering through the camp, but to see Israel's new Chief Prophetess hurrying through the masses, caught every single eye. In a twist almost humorous, she realized they were likely thinking the same thing she was: where on earth was she headed in such a hurry? And, more maddeningly, why?

Her breath was committed entirely to the pace set by her anxious father, and could not be spared in greetings to the hundreds of people they passed. Could she have spoken, what would she say? How did the Chief Prophetess greet the strangers around her that shared her blood? Without voicing it, she sent a harried prayer up to Yahweh's heavens. *Lord, grant my feet steady ground; fill in the separation I feel from my own people. Though you have set me apart, let me be close in heart to my brothers and sisters.* A sweet memory filled Datya. Her teacher had so often said that prayer took her through her days as much as the air she breathed did. In this moment, with her feet flying, prayers darting from her spirit, she felt a kindred understanding of just what Miriam had meant.

Prodded by her father's gentle nudge, Datya glanced up.

The discomfort she had felt from the curious stares had sent her eyes downward for the last leg of their journey. Now, she could see the tents were not so thick here. In fact, they were only steps away from passing the last of the tents of Judah's people. Datya knew the marching order well enough to know that very soon she would be spotting her own distant cousins, the Levite men who carried and protected the Ark of the Covenant. In their midst she would see Moses, and Aaron's sons. How strange it would be to be in this holy company without seeing the man who had been High Priest all her life. She had heard little talk of the ceremonies held for Aaron who had fallen forever asleep so soon after Miriam. She knew only that Moses mourned deeply for his sister and his brother; she had been told that much.

Having spent almost every day of the last four weeks in the confines of her own family tent, tending her brother or working on projects with Ziva, Datya had seen that life was much unchanged for the Israelites. Though she still cried most evenings from the ache of longing she felt for Miriam, she had seen few others spill tears for the former Prophetess or even for the High Priest. If anything, the people seemed to worry more over their own futures, than any loss. Grieving her even deeper still was that no one, not one person grieved the slow, painful death that Abel, Son of Palti had so recently endured. Would she have the courage to ever share what she had done? Would Moses be furious that she had offered a blessing on behalf of the Israelites for the cursed man? Hastening another brief prayer, Datya besieged Heaven that someday she would have the influence to spare someone, just one person, the type of pain and ostracism that Abel had unjustly endured his entire life. The curse on his head, brought on through the sin of his father, spoke poorly on Israel herself. Mercy was important to Yahweh's kingdom, and yet the Israelite's rarely offered the gift.

As Datya's eyes searched out the tent where Moses would hold his meeting, she thought ruefully of the first Abel. Miriam had told her the story when she was very young. It had frightened her terribly, to hear of the way that the brothers, Cain and Abel, had fought even from a young age. Abel who had fought with words and manipulated his brother's feelings and Cain who would often use his fists to pummel his own brother. Had Eve known how rocky the relationship between her sons was? Had she tried to intervene or was she complicit in some way? How long had Abel lain dead before Adam and Eve found out about their loss? She could not help but wonder if the name Abel would disappear from Israel. Little good had ever come to the men who had borne it, at least, that she knew of.

~ ~ ~

Spotting Moses seated in the midst of several elders, Datya turned to offer a farewell to her father, but saw that he had already retreated many paces. She knew that a prophetess would be ridiculed if she couldn't attend a counsel without the shoulder of her father, but she felt a tearing at his absence nonetheless.

"Greetings, Prophetess. We have been waiting for your counsel." Moses welcomed her, waving slowly toward a large cushion not far from himself and Joshua.

Waiting for me? What wisdom does he think I can offer? Datya lowered herself as gently as she could, begging the muscles in her arms and legs to cease trembling. She had spoken with Moses before! She had even sat on the edges of gatherings with the elders before. In fact, none of the faces around her were unknown to her. Why could she not quiet the tremors? Datya's confusion heightened as the discussion around her bubbled of things like herd disputes, Levitical supplies, trade caravans that had been spotted, and even marriage covenants that had been made amongst the most revered families. At times the voices were low, matter-of-fact. At others, the voices were raised, the priests and elders disagreeing over one point or another. But at no point was Datya's opinion asked, not that she could offer one, if they had. What did she know of the needs of the herds? What could she say about one marriage match or another? Datya left her head downturned but her eyelids raised as she watched and listened, entirely bereft at her summoning.

Finally, she saw Moses lean slightly towards Joshua. He spoke in his usual quiet way, and though Datya was close by, she couldn't make out his words. In the next instant, the whisper was made clear as Joshua stood with outstretched arms, "You are each dispatched to your own tasks and families; Moses' full confidence goes with you that all will be accomplished in good faith, just as it should be, and thanks you for your service." The dismissal was polite but firm. Joshua's low half-bows to each of the elders showed all due respect, even though he was near in age, if not older than, the majority of them. Bewildered though she was, she couldn't very well question Moses or Joshua about the bizarre way she was brought here. The dismissal was clear; it was time to go. Rising to her feet, she bowed her head toward the two great leaders, even though they were not looking at her and commanded her feet homeward.

"Datya!" Joshua, warrior commander that he was, had the unique ability to shout in a whisper, and she was thankful to hear her own name from his lips after a morning of being addressed as Prophetess. Just as quickly the formal title resurfaced, "I am sorry, Prophetess, but your presence is still required. If you could take your seat once more." As she turned, she saw that the circle of cushions had been amended by servants who clearly knew more than she how the morning would progress. Instead of a dozen cushions, only three remained. Joshua stood above his, his arms open in a beckoning gesture to her, Moses sat upon his, a slight smile revealing he found her predicament humorous, though she knew he would not mock her lack of knowledge. The third cushion, the one she had vacated only a moment ago, sat across from the two great leaders of her people.

Datya's heart raced. *Yahweh, help me overcome my fear! I've known these men all my life. They are kind and good, and yet panic grips me as I walk into their confidence. Strengthen me, Lord.*

As she sat, Moses' voice seemed to answer for the Lord, "Welcome, Prophetess. You will have many such meetings with the leaders of Israel from now on. I cannot speak for them, but for my own part, I am thankful for Yahweh's choice." This announcement surprised and pleased Datya. She could not know how Moses knew enough of her character to put such swift faith in her, but she was honored by the generous statement. "In ceremonies and before the people, I will always address you as Prophetess, but Joshua and I would like to call you by your name in our daily talks, if that is well with you?"

Datya's body, which had renewed its trembles, could only nod her ascent. *Daily talks? Had Miriam met with Moses daily?* How could she have? Datya was always at Miriam's tent within minutes of dawnshine. Surely Miriam had not walked all this way and back every morning without her realizing it.

Once more, as though her thoughts were audible Moses commanded clarity to her thoughts. "Of course, once you are more established and comfortable in your work, you will see less of this camp, of Joshua and the other Israelites, but it is vital you make your way forward each day through the next several Sabbaths."

Moses paused, looking at Joshua first, and then to her, as though giving them a chance to speak. When neither did, he continued, "For much of that time, you will speak with Joshua and myself, and you will be introduced to many of the elders, priests, and fellow prophets who serve the camp, both spiritually and physically, but after a time, you will no longer meet with me, but Joshua and his chosen workers. You see, Datya, the camp will begin to move. In but a few days time, we will approach a mountain that has been seen by Joshua's scouts. By the time the people pass by the mountain, I will be gone, as Miriam and Aaron are. From then on, you will work with Joshua to meet Israel's needs. Do you understand?" Moses startled them both by meeting their stricken faces with a chuckle. Its cadence was the perfect, masculine match of Miriam's beloved laugh. The man rarely laughed, and the current subject was far from humorous, but, nonetheless, he gave in to his humor heartily. "I can see neither of you are surprised by my statement, though it would surely alarm the rest of our people. How do you both come by such knowledge?"

Joshua, who recovered first, glanced briefly at her, before answering, "A dreamer in the camp, who is connected to my family, saw the mountain, and your long sleep in a dream. You, yourself, have hinted often enough as of late. Of course, with the countdown so close to its final days..." Joshua's words stopped short. The humor in Moses' eyes, a blessed change from their usual serious nature, suggested he well knew how Joshua had discerned that Moses was to die soon.

As both eyes turned to her, Datya released a prayer that her voice would manage to speak though she felt dry and weak in their presence. "A dreamer also made this known to me, M-M-Moses." As though a shake could silence the stutter that had never before been a problem for her, Datya bracketed her answer with a firm wag of her head. "Even before Miriam's death, a vision was told to me that foretold the loss of Miriam, Aaron, and you. The dreamer also saw the mountain and Miriam herself spoke to me that the wilderness days were coming to an end." The vehement refusal she had tried to offer Miriam following that revelation would, once again, do little good. Moses seemed to glow with joy over what was coming, just as Miriam had. How could the people doubt Yahweh when his presence radiated from men like Moses and women like Miriam?

Moses' eyes softened with the mention of his brother and sister, the last of the generation that had walked with him ahead of Pharaoh's thundering chariots. Datya could well understand why Moses felt a belonging with that generation, more than a tug to live and thrive in the Promised Land. Nevertheless, she wondered what chaos would erupt when all of Israel learned of this. They barely survived when Moses was away with Yahweh for a handful of weeks. How would they move forward, collectively and safely, knowing that Moses was never coming back? Moses' voice broke into her thoughts, "I can see worry hangs on you, Datya. You may be surprised to hear that once, Miriam was plagued with worry too. Many boast of her braveness, her clever courage, but she knew seasons of angst, just as we all do." After a pause, he entoned simply: "Yahweh will deliver you from it, if you ask it of him." Moses lifted his hands to a height just above his shoulders as though he was showing her how to raise her burden to heaven. It was the first time he had moved, other than his head. Listening to him was so unlike sitting under Miriam's tutelage. She had rarely presented a lesson sitting down, but rather she would pace, lunge, and even dance her way through the telling. Certainly her arms and hands would be flying and weaving the story as much as her words did.

Moses, whose agility still matched that of his youngest apprentices, was on his feet in the next moment. "Walk with me, friends." Datya was taken aback once more at the intimate address, darting a quick look to Joshua, somehow hoping to soak up understanding from him. Moses was a bafflement to her today. Often enough, she had seen his temper, and heard hundreds of other such stories to confirm it. Sometimes, she had witnessed his tender ministrations, mostly in times of mourning, or during one of the feasts. Frequently, the entire camp witnessed the intensity with which he worshiped Yahweh. But today, she and Joshua were being treated as and spoken to as beloved children, or indeed, friends. She longed to ask Joshua if this was private Moses' character all along, or was it a generosity born in his final days?

She could ask Joshua nothing, for he and Moses would quickly outpace her if she didn't spur her feet onward in the direction Moses was heading in. They walked silently for several moments, the tents of Moses' household and the tents of the Levites who carried and protected the Ark faded one by one behind them. Datya enjoyed the peace of the walk, for at this distance the noise of the people was a hushed hum, and the breeze of the desert could once more tease the hem of her tunic and lift the final length of her braid. She even had the pleasure of spotting a medium sized hen in the bushes to their left. "A sand partridge," Joshua had hurriedly whispered when he caught her enjoying the sight.

Birds were occasionally seen near the herds, and had been a slightly more frequent sight in the purification camp, but they were a rarity for most of her people. She supposed the naturally skittish creatures disliked the masses of people invading their homes and hunting grounds. Still, this little partridge seemed unbothered by the threesome who silently passed her by. The feathers of her dusty plumage ruffled only slightly at the intrusion. *I wonder if she has chicks?* Her maternal thoughts were cut short as Moses and Joshua came to a stop in unison. Had she missed some signal?

Covering her confusion by lowering her eyes swiftly to the ground, she waited. *What has he brought us here for?* Cautiously, Datya lifted her eyes to observe her leader. What thoughts coursed through the man? Was he praying?

Suddenly, Moses raised his hand, pointing straight ahead of him. "Friends," a kind but needless address since he had both Joshua and Datya's exhaustive attention. "The mountain lies only days ahead of us. It is there in the distance, though you cannot see it yet." At this, Joshua gave a light, firm nod. He likely knew the exact location, since the men under his own command had been the ones to find and report the looming landscape. Though his arm was still outstretched, Moses turned to face his companions. Datya marveled at the sheen in Moses' deep-set eyes. His joy did not seem diminished, and yet he was clearly moved to tears by the unseen mountain.

Looking at her long enough to capture her eyes, Moses spoke a commendation she never expected to hear: "I am thankful to witness your time of service, Datya. That Yahweh's mercy would allow me the honor of serving with two kind, faithful prophetess is an honor that humbles me. Your ministry will extend many days beyond that mountain, Datya, but I suspect it is the songs you sing there that will endear you to the people, forever." With those words, which seemed to steal the breath from her lungs, Moses stepped between his two companions as though headed back to camp. He paused in their midst, placing his right hand firmly on Joshua's mighty shoulder and resting his left hand on her own. "Rest well tonight, Joshua, Datya."

Their leader set a rapid stride toward camp, clearly releasing Joshua and Datya to their own duties. "Come, Datya, I will walk you home. You need no escort as Chief Prophetess. None will question your coming and going, though I suspect you have a handful of questions for me. You will likely find no other spare moment for such in the coming weeks." Joshua's friendly smile stopped short of his eyes. He meant to ease her nervousness, but Datya knew that he was feeling the same agonizing dread that she had felt in the days before Miriam's death. Would that she could comfort him, but if anything at all had made a difference in her wounded spirit in those days, it was lost in the hazy memories of loss.

CHAPTER SIXTEEN

Datya's first thoughts as she sought the early morning air were of Uncle Joshua. Yesterday he'd revealed little of Moses' character, as she had hoped, but conversed at length about the Promised Land. Although she felt he had been dismissive towards her questions - the very ones he had offered to answer! - she had enjoyed the walk with him. Having grown up in his shadow, it was easier to imagine working side by side with him for Israel than it would be if her main partner was unknown to her. His voice, deeper even than her own father's, had lovingly drawn the Promised Land out of his memory to be painted afresh before her very eyes. He had shared reverently of the abundance of creatures, and of the lush way the land supported the current inhabitants. Longingly, he spoke of the cool rushing rivers whose shorelines were a bespoke wonder from the Creator's hands. His tone had been ripe with disgust of the idols that marred the beautiful cities. Nevertheless, he also talked with compassion towards the people who would very soon find that Yahweh would not tolerate their wickedness.

Joshua had surprised her when he told her that by the time he and the other spies had entered the Promised Land, the stories of what had occurred in Egypt had already made it there. The people knew well the power of the God that was headed their way, but not a repentant knee could be found in the vast territory. Datya had felt grieved at this, but Joshua had continued bringing the details of the Promised Land to life for her. She had realized somewhere along the way that although he was mournful about the delay that the spies had cost Israel, he didn't seem to have the bitterness that was so typical of her people. Had he been freed in forgiveness just as she had so recently? Despite a nervous reluctance, she had shared with him Abel's story.

When she nervously finished the tale by revealing how she had offered redemption for the dying son of the wretched Benjaminite spy, she had looked to Joshua with trepidation. Would he shout with all the authority of the law at what she had done? Would he accuse her of abusing her authority? Datya's throat had been nearly too tight to breathe wondering if she had damaged their chance of serving Israel with a smooth transition. Smiling, Datya nearly chuckled, her silly fears had been in vain.

Joshua's face had shone with compassion, and he had quickly allayed her concerns. "You honor Yahweh as a vessel of his mercy, Datya. Few in Israel will ever know of your redemptive words for Abel, Son of Palti. Still, all in Israel will be blessed by your willingness to break the curse on Palti's line." The commendation from Joshua had cheered Datya immeasurably; how she longed to share the whole tale with Miriam, whose face would have surely brightened at the story. Palti's line, of course, had ended with Abel, and there would be no more men who lived and died under that stain, but she was thankful nonetheless to be an instrument of Yahweh.

Between Issachar's vast people and Zebulun's, Joshua had stopped at the tent of a pair of widowed sisters who had made a living for themselves collecting, crafting and selling various little treasures. He had selected a small wooden flute for Idan. "The boy is a Levite, he should have his own instrument by now!" He'd affirmed with an affectionate grin. For Ziva, he had selected a thin, airy scarf. Datya had assured him it was a good choice, knowing that Ziva would lovingly braid it into her dark curls. Though she'd expected none, Joshua had tucked a trinket away in his mantle for her as well, carefully shielding it from her view.

"Why the gifts, Uncle Joshua?" Datya had questioned him when she could stand the curiosity no longer?

Expecting the type of kind and playful answer he'd always offered in the past, she was overcome by his response. "It is proper to bring gifts to the family of the Chief Prophetess, Datya. Surely you witnessed the gifts people approached Miriam with?" Wondering if Joshua had meant the words that seemed to lengthen the distance between her old life and her new one, Datya had been unsure if his words were in teasing or not. He was right that Miriam had been approached with gifts more often than not, though hers had not been toys and scarves.

Often, the gifts given to her teacher had been of a spiritual nature, or a true rarity. Miriam had once laughed with delight when a young family had thanked her by offering an ownership share of their small sheep herd. "I thank you, friends," Miriam had answered gracefully, "but I already own enough shares of mother sheep that I could surely provide the sacrifices for an entire tribe! Perhaps, even Judah itself." Miriam's humor had been infectious, and the young family left gracefully, also clearly amused at the thought of Miriam offering sacrifices on the behalf of the largest tribe of Jacob's sons.

Datya had spent the remainder of their long walk lost in memories of Miriam, and more recent memories of the morning with Moses. She had gotten a few answers from Joshua, but much less than she hoped and the reason was slowly dawning on her. Joshua had been guided by Moses. She had been taught at Miriam's knee. But the teaching only went so far. Much of her ministry would be learned through each experience Yahweh led her into, including walking with Moses toward that unseen mountain.

Upon arriving at their family tent, she had called Ziva and Idan who quickly clambered for Joshua's attention. The gifts had been passed out and Joshua had whispered to Lisbet that he had ordered one of his sheep killed, prepared, and brought to them in honor of their daughter's new role. Her mother had answered with grace and swept her youngest two back inside. Before departing, Joshua had given Datya the gift that had been purchased for her. It was a small satchel, crafted of finest leather meant to hang at her side by means of a sash that would cross her body. The leather, stripped and tanned to a shining, smooth surface, had been etched with a lovely scene. A young woman in a simple tunic and mantle appeared to be singing to a small crowd of people. What captured Datya the most about the delicate image was the way the people's faces seemed alive with peace and joy, as though the young woman herself had soothed away all cares.

"Miriam often carried a timbrel in a pouch such as this, Datya," Joshua's consideration brought tears to her eyes. "I felt you would like to have something similar as you begin your own service." With that he had dropped a simple kiss on the top of her head, just as her father would, were he here, and departed. She had watched after him, tears brimming, until she could see his warrior shoulders no longer. How had she never realized before that Yahweh had put the kindest teachers in her life, since her birth, more than just her beloved Miriam?

Now, this morning, her thoughts dwelt on the man who gave her the satchel yesterday. With it strapped to her and filled out with Miriam's timbrel, she wondered about Uncle Joshua and the man he served. She would gather manna quickly for her mother and siblings, a task she knew would very soon, have to pass to Ziva, and then head for the camp far in the distance where she was expected.

~ ~ ~

Moses and Joshua were waiting for Datya when she arrived at the foremost tents. It was strange for her to walk into this place, alone. Yesterday, she had drawn resolve from her father as he escorted her in and Joshua, as he had led her out. Being so close to the Tent of Presence and the clear view of the Pillar of Cloud in the near distance set Datya's skin alight with a nervous excitement she had never felt before. Would she ever feel as though she belonged amongst these great leaders? To her knowledge, none of them had questioned the selection of Chief Prophetess, neither years ago when she was brought under Miriam's guidance, nor in recent weeks when Miriam's death elevated Datya to this new role. The transition had indeed been smoother than she had hoped for, though she still felt uncertain, as though she were on quaking ground.

Datya offered a slight bow, even as she knelt to take her place on the cushion across from Moses and Joshua. It had been barely grey light when she had delivered an abundance of manna to her mother's waiting hands, now the sky was advancing with the fiery colors of true dawn. Moses' face, of course, seemed to shed its own light as well. She had heard of and even seen the glory casting off of him many times before, but never from so close a position as today, and yesterday. When he appeared in camp proper, for a message, or even simply to visit Miriam, he had nearly always worn the veil that shielded the people's eyes from the glory that had baked onto his skin. Here, face to face with a man whose humility should be the real legend, Datya realized that the glory shine was not quite the fearful facade the elders had made it out to be. Or perhaps, Yahweh soothed her mind somehow? For there were many leaders, elders, priests, and Levites scurrying around them, and none seemed overly affected by the slight glow that lit Moses' face.

Realizing she had been lost to her thoughts even as Moses and Joshua had already entered into discussion, Datya's head dipped in shame. She must master her curiosity and devote her thoughts to this good work! Moses' words broke through her inner speech, "Come, Datya, for there is something I must do for you and Joshua." On their feet again, Datya followed as they headed beyond camp once more, this time angling a bit more northerly compared to their last excursion. Before the tents dropped behind them, a group of twelve young stewards approached Moses. Each of the twelve had a silver trumpet slung across their backs, and they wore not only the pure Levitical tunics, but also simple, sleeveless robes. She could see the *tzittzit* dangling from the corners of the garments were in the soft, sandy color Moses' own household was known for, and, of course, she could see the single blue chord that was carefully woven through each. None of Moses' household ever went about their work without flawless garments and the Yahweh-commanded *tzittzit*.

Moses was giving the young men final instructions, but she had discerned upon seeing them what it meant. They would likely be blowing the signal, for each tribe, that meant "tomorrow we journey." Moses' own words, just before sending them on their way confirmed this. She would need to hurry at once to help her mother after receiving her own instructions from Moses. Would there be a specific assignment for her today? Or was she here simply to glean wisdom?

Walking on, the three formed a silent triangle moving as one across the open land. Moses walked briskly ahead of them, she was beginning to realize what the people said about Moses' pace was true, for his strides hurried her. She walked as swiftly as she could at his back and a little to his left, while Joshua kept up easily to Moses' right. Joshua looked surprisingly joyful, despite the cloud that seemed to hover above him yesterday evening. He was a warrior and she doubted he would be prone to the same outward grief that she had displayed in the week leading up to Miriam's death. Still, she was bewildered that he could seem so overjoyed when uncertainty lay before them.

Joshua's keen senses, sharpened by years of leading and

protecting Israel, quickly took note of her observations. "Your face is riddled with a puzzle, Datya." His smile was lifted to his eyes as he teased, but his offering was genuine.

"What is your source of joy this morning, Joshua?" Then, lowering her voice, "When I faced the loss of my own teacher, I could find no such pleasure." Moses' feet stopped in front of them, and Datya's hand flew to her neck. Dread flowed over her. Had she misspoken? Would he rebuke her curiosity?

Turning just slightly over his right shoulder, Moses' voice questioned Joshua instead: "Have you not apprised the Prophetess of the coming weeks, Joshua?" With that, Moses continued on his way leaving his companions - one flustered, one amused - to surge after him.

"Forgive me, Datya. In my rapt reminiscing yesterday, I should have questioned how much you knew of what lies ahead of us. Here is the truth: A fleet-footed runner leaving this camp at dawn could be in the Promised Land before the evening meal. We are that close, and while the camp can not proceed with such speed, my heart sings once more to be so near to the homeland where my children and grandchildren will live out their days." As though his thoughts were distracted, Joshua's eyes skimmed the horizon before continuing. "I will mourn Moses when he joins Miriam, but my spirit cannot quiet it's gratitude for Yahweh's goodness. The joy is loud within me, Datya, as it should be in all who dwell under the covering of the Most High."

Watching him speak, Datya was once again caught by the difference between the countenance of one who had seen the Promised Land himself, stepped into its borders, and the ones who could scarcely believe it existed. Before she could form a reply, she realized a new sound had met her ears, a gentle, almost windy sound, like distant music. Looking about, she wondered if it was the guarding Pillar that caused the sound. Did the Pillar even make a sound? Datya did not know. She supposed typical clouds were silent, excepting the days and nights when the heavens rolled with clashing storms, but the Pillar was a supernatural cloud. Perhaps it did indeed emit the peaceful tone. Wanting to ask Joshua about it, and yet, not wanting to cover up the beautiful music with her voice, Datya longed to know the source.

She realized now that the earth mounded gently beneath their sandals. It was not unusual for hills and dunes to be spotted around the camp, but Moses nearly always led the people along the flattest plains possible. To be walking up an elevation, even one so slight as this was a peculiar feeling for her. Then she spotted the source she had been looking for. Just as swiftly as the little hill had begun mounding, it stopped. The land continued in much the flat way she was used to, but there was a narrow gully right below their feet, and in it, a little stream rippled along. If she retraced her steps even twenty footprints, she would never know that the little stream was there. The drop was so sudden and so narrow, it seemed tucked in the earth itself, like a tear filling out a wrinkle in one's face.

"The people will march directly east, and will not see this stream." Moses' voice flowed gently, as though the water itself carried it to her. "Beyond this place, the stream flows into a crack in the earth and disappears into its depths. The shepherds will pass by this way and likely enjoy the waters for a few moments before the herds muddle the water, but the main body of camp will not know of its existence." She knew that Moses was not keeping the people from the wilderness treasure. It was simply that there was so little water to be had, that should the people rush upon it, it would be desecrated beyond use. Her people had to depend upon the deep wells they dug and the careful storage they made when rainy seasons opened above them. "When I came upon this stream in my wanderings, days ago, Yahweh whispered to me, 'this is holy ground, Moses.' I have heard such a decree many times before in my life and I knew what to do."

With his eyes bearing witness to the event, Moses shared the experience. "Immediately I left my sandals in the sun, and walked to the shoreline." At these words, he reached down and pulled each sandal off, Joshua and Datya quickly followed the directive. "I cried out to Yahweh to let me enter into the stream, the living water rushing before me. Upon hearing his consent, I stepped into the water, and lifted up my hands. I knew in these waters, Yahweh meant to bless me, so I waited upon him. A sacred sensation met my feet. I looked down once more. The water had begun to swirl around my feet and legs, and was rising in just the spot where I stood, and nowhere else as far as I could see. I lifted the hem of my robe, my *tzittzit* having already been touched by the water. Yahweh's voice spoke over me, "Look and see, Moses. I am pouring living water over you. At your feet, this water obeys me, as you have obeyed me. Today, I wash the wilderness from your feet. With this cleansing, I consecrate you unto myself for the last time." Tears flooded Moses' eyes and fell onto the blue lines of his robe. Immediately, upon testifying, he fell to his knees and began to worship. Joshua and Datya, both stunned at the beautiful, intimate moment with Yahweh, dropped to the ground as well, arms stretched up towards heaven.

Though Datya longed to silence the stirring within, she knew that Yahweh was prompting her to sing, to match, in worship, the tune of the living water flowing beside them. Doubts in her calling, in her ability were carried away by the little stream, a mercy in and of itself. Throat warmed from the walk, Datya released a hum into the air as she began to dwell on all she knew of her King: God of Covenant. God of Life. God of All Power. God Who Sees Me. And more personally: God Who Called Datya. God Who Adopted Datya. God Who Created Datya to Sing. God Who Gives Her Purpose.

My soul reaches up to the heights of heavenly love

My face turns to see the One who covers me.
My all in all dwells in Life itself.
The Giver's presence washes over me.

Sweet river flow!
Sweet waters come!
Lord, I open up my soul anew!
Sweet river flow!
Sweet waters come!
I wait once again for You!

His servant washed, in water from his hand
Life forevermore, the precious gift for me
My all in all, safe in Yahweh's care
Heaven's goodness has transformed me

Sweet river flow!
Sweet waters come!
Lord, I open up my soul anew!
Sweet river flow!
Sweet waters come!
I wait once again for You!

Though she had not drawn out the timbel for her song, since it was paired with the water music, Datya realized that she had drawn the timbrel within her satchel close to her as she sang. It was no surprise that her hands found their way to the beautiful, old relic. Miriam's own love and talents poured into Datya had been a blessed gift, and she longed to share today's song with her teacher. Keeping the timbrel close was the best she could do. Moses and Joshua, each of their mouths still moving in prayer, began to rise and walk toward the stream. Datya wondered if they had heard her song at all? Had the presence of Yahweh overpowered her voice? The answer did not matter, as she followed the men to the edge of the water; the song had been from and for Yahweh, an offering for the Creator.

Moses caught her eye and then Joshua's. "Step in, please, friends." Laying his robe along the shoreline, Moses knelt in the water before Joshua and began to cup his hands in the cool water. Gently, he splashed water over the bottom third of Joshua's legs and over his feet. Aged, flat and well calloused, Joshua's feet began to look almost young once more as Moses carefully cleaned each one. Looking up, Moses spoke to the man who had served him for so many years, "You too are cleansed by Yahweh's living waters, Joshua. The dust of the wilderness has been washed away and he has prepared you to go before the Israelites into the Promised Land." With no power to resist Moses' tender service, Datya stood in shock as he moved towards her.

Kneeling in the rocky waters, Moses poured the same ministrations over her. The bottom several inches of her tunic had soaked up plenty of water, but it mattered not as she watched Moses swirl the cupfulls of water about her feet. She had not exactly felt dirtied by life in the wilderness, though its dust was incomparable, but she certainly had felt burdened by it.

Standing on holy ground, being washed by the servant of the Lord, she felt the burden departing from her and realized for the first time just how heavy the load she had been born under truly was. Moses spoke a similar blessing over her, "Datya, in these waters Yahweh consecrates you unto the high office of Chief Prophetess. It will be his own words and his own power that flow through you to fulfill this role. To prepare you, he has washed you in the stream provided by and created by his own hand. He has washed away the stains of the wilderness, and the residue of idols."

Standing, Moses put a hand to each of their shoulders once more. Though Datya felt the drops of the stream soaking through to her skin, she felt even more the anointing of heaven as Moses smiled at them through tears. "I can rest with permanent peace now, Joshua, for I have consecrated the ones who will lead my people into their homeland." Turning, Moses stepped on his own mantle and began to dry his feet. He could just reach the place where his sandals lay, and quickly strapped them on once more. Her breath caught as he gestured for her to also step out of the river, onto his mantle. Her own father would be furious if anyone ever dared to tread on one of his garments! But here, Moses used one to dry feet! "Do not worry, Datya. It will come clean, as fabric does. It is only a mantle, just as the water you stand in is only a stream. Such gifts are important, sacred to our people, but they are only objects nonetheless. Come," he reached further to help her from the brook, and then bent himself to pat dry the skin of her ankles and feet. After fetching her sandals and supporting her weight while she tied them on, Moses offered the same service to Joshua.

Datya was humbled in every way as they began their trek back towards camp. In all her years with Miriam, she had never heard a tale even remotely similar to this one. The closest she could recall was when Miriam had explained the meaning of Moses' name to her. "Moses, named 'To Draw Out,' was so named, not only because he was drawn out of the river, but also because, by him, Israel would be drawn out of Egypt." Thinking back to the story, Datya saw it with a new light. Perhaps all those years ago, when Moses had been a babe in a basket, he had indeed gone through a consecration of sorts in the water.

Even upon this realization, Datya's shock remained. She knew not if she would ever speak again, the astonishment ran so deep. Just as deep was the comforting conviction, that as the waters had washed away her doubts and insecurities only a short time ago, they were gone for good. Even before she had stepped into the water, Yahweh had made a provision of deliverance for her. Tears sprang up once more as she realized the holy gift. She had been too overcome by the washing ceremony to recognize it at the time, but Yahweh had reached down and gracefully removed the last stumbling block between her and her ministry.

The tents of Moses' household and the Levites that camped near him came into view as they walked. She could see that preparations for the camp to travel had begun while they were gone. When she found her way home later this morning, she would see the same work being undertaken all around her. Tomorrow, her people would trek towards the Promised Land and towards a monolith, far in the distance, where Moses' life would become completed. The people would be thrust into the warring emotions that Joshua now endured, the joy of the Promised Land coupled with the sorrow of loss. As her footfalls traced the mighty man of Israel, she gave thanks to God, who had prepared her heart to know that it must be this way. The joy and the sorrow could not be separated, but now she knew, undoubtedly, that she and Johsua could lead the people through it.

EPILOGUE

Datya smiled at Ziva, as the young girl rose to head home from their daily prayer time. Ziva had sought out her sister so often over the last few months in her new home, that she had decided to make their new relationship official. Though Ziva was not called by God to train as a prophetess, Datya had discovered that the young girl shared her heart for families like those at the tannery camp. The tannery camp had split into a few factions upon entering the Promised Land, heading out to a handful of cities to work their trade, in the same way the Levites had begun to disperse. The largest portion of people, both true descendants of Jacob and their fellow travelers, still resided here in Gilgal, until more territory could be conquered. Datya would remain in this city or in another Levitical city all of her days, serving Yahweh in whatever ways he directed.

Thankfully, he had stirred her sister's young heart to reach out to and love on the families who still considered themselves foreign. Ziva had begun to overcome her own doubts in the past few months, to trust Yahweh for herself, but she still had a wildness about her. Datya no longer chafed at the differences in her sister-student. She saw now how Ziva's fire and courage were gifts, tools that Yahweh would use to display his heart for the people around them. Still, Ziva needed training, and to that end, she poured into her sister each morning, as Miriam had so lovingly done for her.

During their first few days journeying to this lush city, so close to the River Jordan, Datya had been able to look back and see the mountain that had become the tomb for Moses. It had towered above the people as a stone guardian. The mountain itself, bare on one side and heavily forested on the other reminded her much of Moses himself. The forest, filled with mysteries and provision was crafted by Yahweh's heaven, filled with resources for his people, while the stone cliffs of the opposite face sharply reminded her of Moses' Great Stones and the mysterious work his household had been set to.

She had been taken aback when, on the day following their ceremonial cleansing, Moses had given her and Joshua a complete tour of the stones that had been completed. The number was more vast than she could have imagined. Dozens of wagons were loaded and ordered carefully carrying what Moses called the "History of the World." Though she could not determine what the carvings actually said, she was stunned by the undertaking. Moses had told them both that his scribes had worked tirelessly to record the history according to his word, and that they had nearly caught up to the current day. He revealed too, that nothing was written down without having first been passed through the Tent of the Presence. Moses himself received the history from the very lips of God to be recorded. The stones had left Datya with a sense of marvel that had stayed with her for several days.

Shortly before ascending the mountain, Moses had gathered the people. He spoke every word of Yahweh's law over them once more, commanding their faithfulness from atop the stone outcropping he was perched on. Sometimes thundering with impatience and other times imploring with desperation, he commended the people to trust and obey the Sovereign God - to heed, forever, the covenant. Finally, he had told them of the great mystery, of the stones that had traveled, unknown to many, all the way from Egypt. Mumblings had erupted instantly, though they were so blended together that Datya had not been able to determine if they were pleased or furious.

Regardless, Moses had not lived long enough to be troubled by the people any longer. With peace dripping from him, he had ascended the mountain alone. He had not looked back, nor spoken again, but the message of his life had reverberated through the people. Chiseling had sounded in the distance, even as she and Joshua watched their leader climb. She'd known what the tools were carving into the stone. Moses' final day.

As their leader's footsteps carried him further away, Datya had lifted her voice in song, just as Moses had said she would. Her mind recalled the words, but it was her heart that had ushered out the melodies honoring Israel's savior. The camp had moved around her for many hours, finally settling in a sprawling formation beyond the mountain, but Datya had remained still. The songs for Moses had lasted until the sun was sinking; Yahweh alone had sustained her voice. She had met many of her fellow sojourners since arriving here in Gilgal who told her that they had heard her voice through all the long hours of the day, no matter how many steps they took. Those closeby and those distant had heard the reverent psalms, carried only by the mysterious power of God to the people who needed her words.

Since settling into this new city with many of her fellow Levites, as well as, thankfully, her own family, she had begun to feel at home. It was a feeling she hadn't known she was missing. A tent had been her home all of her days, and even though she knew the Promised Land would come one day, she truly had always pictured herself living out her life in the walls of Miriam's tent, serving the people from within the humble goat hides. A Levite elder and his wife, their one surviving son and his wife and their children had been given one of the standing abandoned homes within the city. Datya had been gracefully invited into the household and given her own private chamber which was separated from the rest of the family by a lovely courtyard. Miriam's tent had been erected in a corner of the courtyard, which was open on one side to the street, and Datya served the people under the safety and protection of one of the most trusted Levite elders. The walk to her own family's tent was not far, and she hoped that soon they would be given one of the remaining abandoned houses which were being given to Levite families in birth order, as quickly as they could be repaired.

Datya knew that far to the north and all around them, battles raged with the mighty men of Israel cleansing this land of its pagan desecration. She prayed day and night that the land might be won and that her people would enter the long awaited peace and prosperity.

Often, her thoughts wandered to Egypt. Little news had come to them over the years of Egypt's condition. Miriam had assured her that the Plagues of the Creator had surely issued many years of devastation upon the land. Of course, losing their Pharoah and several members of their royal line would have made circumstances grave as well. She wondered if they had recovered yet? Did they know of the beautiful, blooming land that had been given to their former slaves? Did they care? Even the Egyptians made it into Datya's prayers as she asked Yahweh to send more signs to them, that they would choose Yahweh and let the River Nile wash away the evil of the false gods who reigned there now. Afterall, many of Egyptian descent had indeed left with her people that long ago day, choosing to follow Yahweh instead of a prideful man. They had made sacrifices, become circumcised, and now shared in Israel's inheritance. She would not forget about the land that had birthed them.

Some in Israel would say that Datya invested her time foolishly in such prayers; but her heart was for all people, not only the Israelites, and she believed it was Yahweh himself who stirred her heart to pray for the men and women of kingdoms far and wide.

Datya's duties in Gilgal had gone far beyond praying and

teaching her sister. Many days she had been called to public squares to recite tales of Yahweh's glory to give the people courage, understanding, and fresh hope. Often she had been sought out to witness the words of a dream or a vision that had been given to one of her fellow worshipers. Many times, families would fetch her to minister to new brides, new mothers, and widows, or anyone who was entering a new season, who needed the words of Yahweh to bring them peace. Ravit had joined her on many such missions and now often worked side by side with her in Miriam's tent to minister to the people in her own way. Her favorite duty, by far, had been singing the songs of Yahweh through each Sabbath, and walking the city's paths with Miriam's timbrel as she sang songs of victory over Israel. All these things, she had been trained for and she delighted in each opportunity to serve the God of Abraham, Isaac, and Jacob with them.

Though Datya had stolen away to her chamber for a few minutes, knowing that a small platter of bread, cheese and fruit would be left there for her needs, she saw a movement in the courtyard from the corner of her eye. Her tutor had arrived. Before leaving Gilgal to supervise the battles, Joshua had appointed a Levitical tutor for her from Moses' apprentices. He had been chosen to work with her to teach her the carved language of the stones, their own words in written form. The generous act had moved her to tears, for she knew well, that few women in Israel would have such an opportunity. Returning to the tent, Datya's hand rested tenderly on the embroidered patch that would forever stir the memory of the one who told the desert stories. She had no idea how long the shelter would last, though she took good care of it. With a humor that resembled her former teacher's, she wondered if she would always sit within this tent learning one thing or another. She hoped so. For hadn't Miriam promised that Yahweh himself would become a mentor over her for all her days? Smiling, she went in to study the stone primer that her tutor had brought today.

THE END

WITH THANKS,

I find it impossible to contain my joy as The One Who Told The Desert Stories finds its way into the hands of readers. This story, begun before my first book, Messiah Resounding, published, had to wait more than its fair share to see the light of day. I am thrilled to know that my debut novel is finally being read on e-readers, finding its way into libraries, and being enjoyed over cups of tea, coffee, and the odd chocolate cake.

In addition to celebrating, I must also thank the people who stood in the thick of my dream with me, encouraging, editing, and brainstorming to make this book happen. My husband, Paul Robinson, and my mom, Joann Garman were my chief editors and, believe me, I needed their help! My sister, Julie Garman, deserves a golden set of pom poms for the consistent cheerleading she threw my way. The remainder of my friends and family, as well as my sweet church family filled in the blanks with plenty of prayer and support. Finally, as a mama first, I am so proud of my two sweet kiddos who encouraged me in their own way.

While this story is largely fictional, it demanded a heavy amount of research. Those who are curious for the history of the people of the Bible will find the following note and resources to be an excellent starting point for their own trek through the days of the Exodus.

Thank you, reader, for traveling with Datya and I through this story. I hope to see you in the pages of my future books! In the meantime, I pray that you will be blessed in life, and especially that you will pursue the Father, just as Datya did.

Shirley

HISTORICAL NOTE

When the seed was planted within me, many years ago, to write beautiful stories, I had no idea that Miriam and Datya would take the stage for my first novel. However, whenever these characters began to weave a story in my imagination, I knew I wanted to harvest deeply from the well of historical knowledge to present their world to you. After combing through museum databases, Biblical commentaries, and scholarly resources, I crafted their story upon three equally important pedestals: accuracy, creativity, and relatability. Above all, I sought to honor the word of God which is the original source of our beloved Miriam. The Bible, as a source for this book, reigned above all other sources, and yet, as you know, the Bible can be maddeningly sparse of the details we long for. In an effort to draw out the distant past for our viewing, I pieced together what is known historically, what is scholarly agreed upon, and the words of the precious Bible to bring Miriam and her people to life for you.

Within this informal index, you will find an answer to questions that may have arisen for you as you read The One Who Told the Desert Stories. I will also point out to you the places where Biblical scholars disagree with one another; it was at such junctures where I made a judgement call for what to include and why. In addition, I will leave you with a valuable "jumping in" list for anyone who would care to dig into what is known, historically, about the ancient Israelites and the region of the world that hosted the legendary Exodus. This is by no means an exhaustive, nor endorsed, list, but if you love Biblical history, as I do, you will find it educational. Finally, within my thoughts below, I have attempted to follow The One Who Told the Desert Stories chronologically, for your benefit. If you find that your questions regarding the story remain unanswered, I welcome your questions, and comments via Instagram (@srobinsonauthor) or on GoodReads (https://www.goodreads.com/shirleyrobinson)

Perhaps I will start with some general observations. Keen history observers will want to know that while modern Bible translations speak of the Israelites traveling for forty years in the desert, the people weren't traveling through what we would think of as a desert. The land which hosted them for forty years was likely arid and dry much of the year, but not the endless sand and cacti of a typical desert. Desert is more accurately applied in a metaphorical sense. Additionally, the Israelites may have felt negative about their surroundings, because it lacked civilization. They likely saw a good bit of vegetation, but it was not in neat, cultivated rows, as they were used to along the Nile and in Goshen. A lack of houses, and towns, and walls, and farms gave the Israelites an isolated feeling, much as one would have in the desert. Describing the land they traveled in as a wilderness is much closer to the mark. It was, at that point, uncultivated and mostly uninhabited. Now, this does not mean that they were traveling through lush vegetation either. It is likely that they had times of plenty for their herds, and times when some of the herds died off for lack. I have often wondered, though the Bible doesn't say, if the manna provision included Israel's herds. Perhaps, I can ask God when I see Heaven, on some faraway day. One inconclusive detail I found in my research still puzzles me. Some scholars suggest that there was, in fact, very little traveling during the forty years. Rather, it is believed, by some, that the Israelites largely stayed put, but traveled much further distances when they did move. Scholars who take this view seem to be influenced largely by the works of ancient Hebrew scholar, Flavius Josephus. While I read certain accounts from Josephus' works for this story, I avoided allowing it to become a primary source. My main reasoning for this decision is that some of his details seem to contradict the Bible, and if I have to pick a history book to win at accuracy, I'm going with the Bible. (For this story, I chose to imagine Miriam and Datya's life with the traditional belief that the Hebrew camps moved frequently during their forty years.)

Another general observation I wish to draw your attention to regards the characters of the book. Miriam, Moses, Aaron, and Joshua are all real people who lived many years ago - as most of the readers of this story will already know. Aaron's sons, Moses' sons, Moses' wife Zipporah, and Miriam's parents are all true to life characters mentioned briefly in the Bible. The pharaoh of the Exodus period as well as his daughter who adopted Moses are also true accounts. Characters like Datya, Ravit, Lisbet, Cohen, Ziva, Idan, Abel, and Miriam's son-in-law, and grandsons, were all created in my imagination as a method of showing you what life in Ancient Israel during the days of the Exodus may have been like.

Within this story I refer to God as either "God," "Father," "Abba," or "Yahweh," with Yahweh making the most frequent appearances. When deciding how to address our Lord within this story, I had my work cut out for me. While many of God's biblical names are well known, I felt it best to stick to one or the other for this story. I've included a resource that is a primer on the names of God in the index below, but the short answer is that Yahweh, is a heavily used Name of God common in the Old Testament, that is less specific than other well known names (like Elohim and Adonai). This means it can be applied to every circumstance, and so Yahweh is the name of choice for The One Who Told the Desert Stories.

Let me tell you a little more about Datya's family. Cohen and Lisbet are both descendants of Levi who lived and died more than four hundred years before our story takes place. This means they were distant relatives, which would be fairly common for the Israelites (to marry within their own tribe). The story suggests that Cohen and Lisbet were born in the earliest days of the Exodus, perhaps their mothers were carrying them already as they left Egypt. I wonder what joy an expectant mother who had been born into slavery would feel for her unborn child who would now be born free, but with a murky future? Cohen and Lisbet would have married as teenagers, within a year or two of the onset of Lisbet's menstrual cycle. Although a Jewish couple, in reality, would have consisted of an older male (who had gone through the necessary training, particularly among the Levite tribe, and outside of the Levites, a man who had provided his required military service, or perhaps an apprenticeship of some sort.). Likely, this would have meant a marriage between a young woman between the ages of 14 and 17 and a young man who was at least in his late twenties, or older.

Before Chapter One concludes, Datya shows us a glimpse of her prayer time. A couple of questions spring to mind: Did the Israelites pray as individuals? Or only through priests? And, Datya addresses the Lord as "Father." Would the ancient Israelites have done this? The Bible doesn't answer the first question in a direct way, but we do have evidence of ancient Israelites praying in an individual way. Jacob himself had conversations (prayer) with the Lord. Hannah, the mother of Samuel, was a beautiful example of individual prayer. Of course, King David, and several other kings and prophets also prayed to God, without the oversight of a priest. Yes, Datya's character, had she truly existed, would have prayed, likely on a daily basis. Secondly, would an ancient Israelite have addressed the Lord as "Father?" No, this is unlikely. Although a picture of fatherly care is occasionally associated with God in the Old Testament, (particularly in the Davidic Psalms where David talks about an inheritance in God,) the concept of God as Father, for use in prayer, was initiated through the most famous Rabbi of history - Jesus.

Datya and her mother offer us an opportunity to take a closer look at the dress that would have adorned the people of the Bible's Exodus. Did they look as they are portrayed in Biblical movies every few years? Or were their styles of dress unlike anything seen today? More often than not, movies set in a Biblical time, show the people dressed in a primitive version of what Bedouin, or middle-eastern nomadic families, wear today. A long shapeless veil, or head covering for women; long, shapeless robes for men and women, and a simple belt around the middle. Often, sandals are shown on their feet and the layers of fabric are so generous, that it's hard to tell where one seem ends and another begins. Is this depiction accurate? It is unlikely. While written records from this time period are in short supply (we'll talk about this in a minute!) pictorial records show some distinct differences. Men and women of this region and time period are both depicted most frequently with short (think, tea-length, or mid-calf length) tunics, not ankle length. Men and women of a slave-class would often wear even shorter skirts, and unfortunately, nothing at all on the torso. Another mode of dress that would be common, especially among people who could not afford linen, would be animal hide clothing. This could be animal hides with the hair intact or without. The Israelite people are also known for having the historic "mantle" which would have been similar to an open front robe. Mantles were most commonly made of wool, which was an inexpensive fabric in that time, or sometimes of linen which was a costlier choice. It could have sleeves, or not, but would be edged with tassels and increasingly decorated as the years went by. This garment makes an appearance in the Bible multiple times, which means it is confirmed by the historical, written record. It would have been a pillow when one was in a hard place, a blanket when one was in a cold place, and a symbol of status, depending on the finery of the handiwork. An important note: it is notoriously hard to determine whether or not historic peoples from any era wore anything that we would consider an undergarment, since it would be shocking to make a pictorial record of this. However, it is generally thought that there would be no undergarment. Since a mantle was optional during this time period, the linen or hide tunic would be the singular piece of clothing. Lastly, shoes. Did the ancient Egyptians and Israelites have shoes or just sandals or nothing at all? I was surprised to learn, within the scope of my research, that historians have definitive proof that a full shoe would have been commonplace in ancient Egypt - in the time leading up to the Exodus! It would have been made from either animal hide or, more commonly, plant fibers, much like a basket. In fact, ancient Egypt had workers, similar to a cobbler, whose job it was to create these shoes. Sandals that tied about the feet were also common. It stands to reason, that the Israelites took this shoe technology with them when they left Egypt. (Please see the included Index, for resources that will help you learn all about Biblical dress, for those interested.)

Briefly, let's talk about the *tzittzit*. This sacred tassel, commanded in God's law, is mentioned several times within the story. It is connected with several male characters, but it's worth pointing out that the *tzittzit* is not regulated to men alone. All Israelites were told to wear them. All of said tassels were required to have a single blue cord running through them, but other colors could be included by choice. I interpreted this, for the purpose of this story, to be a tribal tradition, much like the patterns and designs of kilts dictate the Scottish tribe of the wearer. So, even though they are not specifically mentioned on the garments of the women in this story, today, and in history, they would have been worn by men and women alike.

So we come to the first aspect of The One Who Told the Desert Stories that may be controversial. Did Moses have one wife or two? Was the woman Zipporah a Midianite or was she Ethiopian? Well, Biblical scholars are divided on this issue. For centuries, Biblical scholars concluded that Moses had one wife, Zipporah, and that she was a Midiantie and that the text used the term Cushite (Ethiopian) later on to describe her, even though it wouldn't have been strictly accurate. (For reference, you can read Exodus 2 to view the first instance of Zipporah in the Bible, and Numbers 12 to see where the Bible describes Moses being married to a Cushite.) In more recent years, scholars have been able to decipher the history of the region a little more accurately. This, combined with the works of ancient Hebrew scholar, Josephus, have formed a new school of thought among scholars. It is now widely believed that Moses married Zipporah, a daughter of the Midianites (who were distant relatives of the Israelites. See Genesis 25 for the family line descended from Abraham and his final wife Keturah,) shortly after his expulsion from Egypt. She must have died at some point during the forty years of wilderness wandering at which point, Moses then married an Ethiopian woman. Some accounts suggest this woman was a fellow sojourner whose family joined up with the Israelites in the wilderness, while other accounts (notably, Josephus') tell a tale of her being the daughter of Ethiopian royalty given to Moses after a skirmish. For the purposes of this story, I read extensively in scholarly works new and old, like Josephus' famed accounts, however I did not give these sources the same weight as the Bible. The Bible reigned as the supreme source, and the only completely accurate source. I worked to create a story for you that would be enjoyable and historically accurate without compromising what we know to be true from the Word of God. That said, I decided to lean towards the camp of scholars who believe that Moses had two different wives and this is the view represented in The One Who Told the Desert Stories. I would encourage you to read through the entire Pentateuch for understanding of Moses and the ancient Hebrew tribes. If, after that, you are still curious, perhaps you will enjoy reading the works of Josephus or modern Biblical scholars. For this story, I chose to suggest that Moses' second wife had been traveling with them, likely born into the camp and that her ancestors had been slaves in Egypt for some time, just like Moses' had.

On the heels of discussion regarding Moses' wife, I must address the work of the Great Stones, which plays such a critical part in this story. The work which consisted of creating a **written** Hebrew language, gathering history from the carriers (history would have been an oral tradition prior to this), and then inscribing all of that onto stones. This is a complicated issue, so allow me to break it down.

1. Was this task mentioned in the Bible? A: No. Not exactly. We do know and believe that Moses wrote the first five books of the Bible, even though he could not have possibly have witnessed the many years that passed before his birth. It stands to reason that he gathered this knowledge in some way, since we have numerous evidences that the Bible is true in its entirety.
2. Is there any historical evidence that the Pentateuch may have been written this way? A: The origins of language are like many things in history: murky. Scholars and historians often give their best educated guess based on the evidence available to them. Evidence that is favorable to the story of the Great Stones is that written language is believed to have derived very close to this time, perhaps in Egypt itself. However, very recently, historians have made discoveries that are leading many people to wonder if Moses' commission to write the Pentateuch was, in fact, a key propellant of the rise of the written word! This is fascinating to me! (Links for relative research are included in the Index.) With this wonderful insight in mind, I chose to use my own written words to propose a likely scenario for the birth of the Pentateuch and the birth of the written Hebrew language.
3. Would he have used stones? A: Great question! I am sure you can imagine that it would have taken a mind-boggling amount of stones to carve the entire first five books of the Bible. While pa-

pyrus type "paper" was coming into use in and around this period, it was not a ready resource. It was also difficult to preserve, and easily damaged. Reasoning suggests that Moses would have used stone for it's longevity, though I suspect that once the Pentateuch was written "copies" were made without ceasing. Since this time period falls before any modern metals or alloys were invented, any carving would have to have been done with a hard stone as the chisel and a slightly softer stone as the "paper."

4. When I talk about the pictorial record from this time, I do mean paintings, cave drawings, and archeological finds that have been photographed since, but I also mean the stone edifices and monoliths that were the most common ways for kings and kingdoms to record their history, pictorially, in this time period.

I highly recommend using a study Bible if you'd like to understand more about the timeline of the book of Exodus. (Genesis, Numbers and the book of Joshua would also be helpful for understanding the nuances of this story.) In addition, many timelines are available from scholarly resources that will make the events of ancient Israel a little more clear. (I have included one below.)

In The One Who Told the Desert Stories, we witness Israel's fierce fight with the Amalekites. This is in the Biblical record, although there are imagined details that I included. Miriam's vision is imagined, although she may well have had a similar experience. The Bible confirms that the Lord does in fact say that he will wipe the memory of Amalek from the earth. The retelling of Moses' altar and his proclamation of Yahweh-Nissi or "The Lord is My Banner" is also in the Biblical record.

It's time to address some details about Miriam. This book was conceived, researched, and created to help bring some insight into what the Bible means when it calls Miriam a "prophetess." While we can't infer every duty that may have fallen under that title, or even if it was an official role, we can use Biblical context clues and historical cultural clues to piece together a resume of sorts for her. Hopefully, after reading The One Who Told the Desert Stories, you have some inkling of what Miriam and any possible understudies would have spent their time doing. The Bible also confirms that Miriam did contract leprosy and spend time outside of the camp proper. One divergent aspect from the story that keen observers will have noticed is the timeline of her death. In all likelihood, considering that Miriam was older than both Aaron and Moses, she probably died within a handful of years into the wilderness journey, rather than toward the end. When reading the Bible, discerning an accurate timeline can be difficult because the information is not always presented in a linear way. While simple math can be helpful for determining who lived when and for how long, we simply don't know if Miriam died two years after the Exodus or twenty. For the sake of the story, I decided to place her death towards the very end of the timeline. I hope my fellow historians will gently accept that decision.

Shortly after the death of Miriam, the story shows Datya praying over the tribes. You will be interested to know that these prayers are modeled after the blessings spoken over each of the twelve sons as Jacob lay dying in Goshen. The Biblical account of this story can be read in Genesis chapter 49.

Finally, I will briefly address the epilogue. Datya's story closes as she settles into life in the city of Gilgal. I chose to place Datya here because it is the city where the Ark of the Covenant resided, for a time, while the rest of the Promised Land was being conquered and divided up. I imagine many Levites, and people from every tribe, ended up in this city, at least for a time.

Below you will find a plethora of resources to further study the amazing period of history that hosted the Exodus, the plagues, the Promised Land, and a wise and wonderful woman named Miriam. Enjoy your studies.

THE ONE WHO TOLD THE DESERT STORIES - INDEX

Links to historical articles pertaining to the story:

Tassel and Tzittzit on Messianic Jews .com :
http://messianicjews.com.au/articles/details/3/Tassels-and-Tzitzit-
A-Research-Study-Paper
Miriam by Nissan Mindel on Chabad.org :
https://www.chabad.org/library/article_cdo/aid/112396/jewish/
Miriam.htm
The Death of Miriam by Ismar Schorsch on JTS.edu
http://www.jtsa.edu/the-death-of-miriam
Aaron and Miriam by Nissan Mindel on Chabad.org
https://www.chabad.org/library/article_cdo/aid/112070/jewish/
Aaron-and-Miriam.htm
Was Hebrew the First Alphabet on Patterns of Evidence.com
https://patternsofevidence.com/2019/03/09/hebrew-first-alphabet/
Who Was Moses' Wife on NotJustAnotherBook.com
https://www.notjustanotherbook.com/moseswife.htm
The Amalekites Are Alive and Well Today by Natan Lawrence on
Hoshanarabbah.org
https://hoshanarabbah.org/blog/2020/08/29/the-amalekites-are-
alive-and-well-on-planet-earth-today/
The Defeat of Amalek by Jacob Isaacs on chabad.org
https://www.chabad.org/library/article_cdo/aid/246634/jewish/
Amaleks-Attack.htm
Names of God on Got Questions?.com
https://www.gotquestions.org/names-of-God.html
The Tabernacle's History After Crossing Over Into the Promised Land
on bcooper.wordpress.com
https://bcooper.wordpress.com/2017/07/13/the-tabernacles-his-
tory-after-crossing-over-into-the-promised-land/
Marching Order of the Israelites from Bible Charts.org
http://biblecharts.org/oldtestament/theorderofisraelsmarchingin-
thewilderness.pdf

Articles explaining the location:

Pharoah's Mudbrick Palace on the Torah.com
https://www.thetorah.com/article/pharaohs-mudbrick-palace
Did the Ancient Egyptions Practice Human Sacrifice on History of the Ancient World.com
https://www.historyoftheancientworld.com/2014/08/did-the-ancient-egyptians-practice-human-sacrifice/

Map of Levitical Cities
https://biblicalgeographicdotcom.files.wordpress.com/2012/06/levitical-cities-map.pdf
The Unknown Yet Known Place of Moses' Burial on theTorah.com
https://www.thetorah.com/article/the-unknown-yet-known-place-of-moses-burial
Ethiopians / Cushites from Encyclopedia.com
https://www.encyclopedia.com/religion/encyclopedias-almanacs-transcripts-and-maps/ethiopians-cushites

Study Bible and Resources:

Cultural Backgrounds Study Bible (NIV)
The Complete WordStudy Dictionary: Old Testament
Exodus: God, Slavery, and Freedom By Dennis Prager
Christ-Centered Exposition: Exalting Jesus in Exodus

Historical Time Period Resources:

Costume of the Old Testament Peoples By Philip J. Watson

HEBREW WORDS & CUSTOMS:

Nechadim - grandsons
Ma-yim - water
Sabbatou hodus - Sabbath Day's Journey
Emma/Immi - mother
Achai - sibling
Racham - mercy

ABOUT THE AUTHOR

Shirley Robinson is a Christian creative who works to bring the light of God's goodness to the online mission field. Writing, storytelling, and designing Bible quotes for Instagram are some of the ways you'll see her tinkering around the Jesus fandom. Shirley, her husband Paul, and their two kids are East Coast natives. Together they enjoy amassing troves of books and board games. To connect with Shirley, follow along on Instagram @srobinsonauthor or on GoodReads https://www.goodreads.com/shirleyrobinson

BEFORE YOU GO

If you enjoyed The One Who Told The Desert Stories, please leave a 5-star review on Amazon (& GoodReads). Your review is a word-of-mouth compliment that helps other readers find this story.